Praise for
END'S BEGINNING: THE GATHERING

"A tale of intrigue, suspense, and sacrifice, *The Gathering* will also speak to your heart. You'll be flipping pages to find out what happens next, all the while rejoicing with the Saints of God. A fantastic addition to the LDS genre."
—ELANA JOHNSON, author of *Possession*

"All I can say is WOW! *End's Beginning: The Gathering* is a riveting and timely story. . . . Randy Lindsay does an incredible job portraying the condition of the world in the season immediately preceding the Lord's arrival and, at the same time, shares a touching story with characters you can't help but love and understand. A powerful story. There should be a copy of this book in every Latter-day Saint home. Five stars on all accounts."
—CHAS HATHAWAY, author of *Scripture Study Made Awesome*

"*The Gathering* is an intriguing tale about faith, fortitude, and endurance in the face of even the most difficult of circumstances. With well-developed characters, a driving narrative, and even a dash of political intrigue, Lindsay has created a novel that will not only entertain but also leave you with something to think about long after the story is over."
—JENNY PROCTOR, author of *The House at Rose Creek*

"*The Gathering* addresses an emotional topic that has been prophesied for centuries: the upheaval leading up to the Second Coming of Christ. Lindsay's treatment of possible conflicts range from small town troubles up to a national defense danger that directly involves the President of the United States. If you are fascinated by portents of things that are surely to come, then Lindsay's fictional account of brotherly love interspersed with violent self-defense is sure to leave you satisfied, yet wanting more."

—SHIRLEY BAHLMANN, author of the popular "Odds" true pioneer story series

"Government tension at the highest levels. Spiritual tension on a personal level. A world on the brink of the end. Author Randy Lindsay's debut novel will keep you flipping pages until the very end—highly recommended."

—TRISTI PINKSTON, editor, and author of *Agent in Old Lace*

THE GATHERING
—END'S BEGINNING—

RANDY LINDSAY

BONNEVILLE
BOOKS

An Imprint of Cedar Fort, Inc
Springville, Utah

ISBN 13: 978-1-4621-1373-6

Published by Bonneville Books, an imprint of Cedar Fort, Inc.
2373 W. 700 S., Springville, UT 84663
Distributed by Cedar Fort, Inc., www.cedarfort.com

LIBRARY OF CONGRESS CATALOGING-IN-PUBLICATION DATA

Lindsay, Randy, 1959-
 End's beginning : the gathering / Randy Lindsay.
  pages cm. -- (End's Beginning)
 ISBN 978-1-4621-1373-6 (perfect bound)
 1. Missions--Fiction. I. Title. II. Title: Gathering.
 PS3612.I5353E53 2014
 813'.6--dc23
                         2013034886

Cover design by Kristen Reeves
Cover design © 2014 by Lyle Mortimer
Edited and typeset by Melissa J. Caldwell

Printed in the United States of America

10 9 8 7 6 5 4 3 2 1

The dedication of your first novel is a special event because it only happens once. How fitting that this dedication goes to people who are equally unique and wonderful. Thanks, Dad, for teaching me that it was all right to follow the beat of a different drummer. And thank you, Mom, for always being ready to pick me up when I fall.

I love you both.

1

Robert sat in the dimly lit cabin, stared out the dark window of the plane, and wondered why he'd been sent home early from his mission.

He had followed all of the rules. Each of his companions had been great. He'd had five baptisms in his eighteen months out and a family of four had just committed to taking the plunge. He was just hitting his stride.

Then yesterday morning, the mission president told him to pack it up.

Anguish flared in Robert's chest as he thought about it again. He reached up, placing the heels of his hands over his eyes, and tried to block the tears that threatened to form. A deep breath helped ease the trembling assault on his nerves. Helped. Not stopped.

"Are you okay?"

Robert jumped in his seat. He looked over to see a flight attendant with a concerned look on her face.

"Yes." Robert gulped. "I'm fine. Just couldn't sleep."

"Can I get anything for you?"

His first response stuck in his throat. Robert hadn't had anything to eat or drink since leaving Italy, declining the in-flight meal and offered juices and sodas; now his neglected insides protested—loudly.

"Some water would be great," he managed to croak.

The flight attendant gave him a nod and then headed toward the back of the plane. She returned seconds later and handed him bottled water and a plastic cup with ice. After a brief pause, she smiled and continued on, checking the other passengers on her way to the front of the cabin.

Robert stared at the bottle of water in his hands. His throat screamed for it. His grumbling belly seemed to tell him it would settle for that if not for something more substantial. He'd been too upset to worry about food earlier, but the real reason he hadn't eaten was he had decided to fast.

Well, that had been his intention anyway.

Fasting should be accompanied by thoughtful prayer. It should be focused and have a purpose. Instead, Robert's mind drifted over the events of the last two days, looking to make some sense of his early return.

The mission president had told him he had completed an honorable mission.

But that couldn't be true. An honorable mission would have been two years of service to the Lord, and Robert still had six months left. He wanted to be in Italy. He wanted to serve.

No explanation had been given for his early release. Several others had been sent home as well, all of them going home honorably. They had their release papers explaining the completion of their missions, despite the reduced time spent, to show their families, their friends, their bishops.

Regardless of what the mission president had told him, Robert still felt like a failure.

Outside, the combination of clouds and moonlight created an eerie glow on the wing of the plane. Beyond that he could see nothing. Just like his current situation, only a small portion of the events that had sent him home could be seen; the real reason for it lay beyond his vision.

Wasn't that the way of it, though? Wasn't everyone flying through the darkness?

Ice shifted in the cup. Robert still held it and the water bottle in his hands. Looking at them reminded him of his thirst and how he couldn't stay focused. What was the point of fasting if you were too distracted to receive an answer?

He wanted to serve a full mission. He wanted to baptize more people. He wanted to do the Lord's work. So why was he being sent home?

His hand was nearly numb from the ice. He lowered the tray table on the seat in front of him and placed the cup on it. Then he covered the back of his neck with his hand and let the coolness sink into his weary muscles.

He closed his eyes and enjoyed the short relief from the cabin's heat. The plane had little vents that supposedly blew a cool breeze on the passengers, but from his experiences so far, the air coming out of them smelled like moldy plastic.

When the coolness faded, Robert opened his eyes. They didn't want to open. They ached from his having stayed awake all night. He'd tried to sleep last night but had given up when his mind had refused to yield to the blessed refuge of slumber. Instead, he had sat up in his bed and tried to come to terms with being sent home.

Obviously, trading sleep for deep contemplation hadn't worked; otherwise, he wouldn't still be thinking about it and hoping that if he fasted for just a little bit longer, the Lord would include him in the current game plan. If there even was one.

This wasn't how things were supposed to go. Robert, like all good LDS boys, had planned from his earliest recollection to serve a mission. Then he would go to college and become an engineer. After that, he and his wife would raise a family and serve in a long line of callings. That was the life he'd planned. That was the life he wanted.

Now what? How did this affect everything else?

How did this affect his faith?

Two days ago he had told people that he knew the Church was

true and that the Spirit would guide them in their choices. He thought he had a solid testimony, but now he had to wonder how real it was. Could that be the reason he was being sent home? Had the mission president seen that Robert's testimony was too weak to serve the Lord?

Up ahead, one of the passengers clicked on the small overhead light. Seconds before, he hadn't even known the woman was there, and now she stood out in the dark cabin. A tiny bulb cast its light on the area around her, and it was enough to allow the woman to conduct whatever business she had.

The still small voice was supposed to work like that tiny cabin light to hold back the darkness. Robert gave the water bottle in his hand another look and then set it down next to the ice-filled cup. He reached under his seat, unzipped his backpack, and pulled out his quad.

He ran his hand over the leather book cover protecting his copy of the standard works and remembered when his parents had given it to him just before leaving on his mission. How different he had felt back then.

Boy, what he wouldn't give to feel that way again.

2

Robert stopped at the bottom of the ramp. He shrugged his backpack into place, making sure that his hands and arms were free. A few stretches helped relieve the stiffness in his back and legs. He took one last deep breath and headed toward the security checkpoint.

Passing through the gate into the reception area, he failed to spot anyone he knew. Hopes for a happy reunion dimmed. Then he heard Sara.

"Maybe he missed his flight."

Robert followed her voice through the small crowd gathered around the gate. It only took a matter of seconds to get through the unfamiliar faces and locate his family. His mother noticed him at the same time.

"Oh, John, there he is." She clutched her husband's arm and pointed to Robert.

The family, what there was of it here, turned to greet Robert. Mom, Dad, Lucas, and Sara represented the entirety of his welcoming committee.

His family rushed forward. He surged toward them with equal enthusiasm. Hugs, smiles, and backslaps formed a whirlwind of activity with Robert at its center.

After the second round of hugs, Robert stood back to take a good look at his family. A year and a half was a long time. So much could have changed. When he looked at his mother and father, he knew that it hadn't. They appeared the same as they always had.

Tears rolled down his mother's cheeks. That was nothing new. Send-offs, homecomings, and even "landmark" birthdays caused her to cry. She held a pink tissue in her hand and dabbed her eyes with it. The blue dress was the same one she'd worn when Robert left for his mission. It wasn't that she didn't have other clothes, but she always picked this one for special occasions. She called it her gala gown.

Then, of course, his father had on the same charcoal gray suit that he wore to any event that required him to dress up. He'd had it for years now and it fit a little snugly. Dad may have put on a little weight over the years, but he still was in pretty good shape and far from what anyone would consider heavy.

Lucas and Sara, though, had changed. Both were taller. In addition, Lucas's face had thinned and his short hair had darkened from dirty blond to a medium brown. He sported the typical jeans and T-shirt ensemble that he'd always worn. For Sara, the changes were cosmetic rather than physical. She wore more makeup, the pony-tails had been replaced with a short bob cut, and she had on a bright red blouse that was less modest than their parents were probably comfortable with.

Yet for all that they had changed, they looked surprisingly the same.

Robert had expected a few more people than this. At least, he had hoped that a few more would have been here. Having all of his siblings present would have doubled the number of welcome-homers. Maybe his parents had thought it too late for the younger children to be out. Then again, maybe they weren't sure this was really an event to celebrate.

"You're home early," John said when the clamor died down.

"Dad," Robert said, sighing. "I didn't do anything wrong."

"I didn't say that you did." John stumbled over the words as if unsure what to say.

"I received an honorable release from my mission."

"That's what the mission president told us when he called yesterday," said Becky. She laid a hand on John's chest, a sign that she was worried about the direction the conversation was headed.

"There were a lot of us released early. All of us were notified yesterday."

Tension fled from John's face only to be replaced with worry. It was the same expression he'd had when he lost his job a few years back.

"Really? How many?"

"Five or six, besides me."

"That's weird," said Lucas. "A couple of the guys at the dance were talking about their brothers coming home early. Maybe World War III is about to start."

"I doubt it," said John. "Still, it's curious."

"You think something's wrong?"

His father smiled. Not the smile he used when he was happy; the smile he slapped on his face when he didn't want anyone to worry. "Nothing's wrong. Our oldest son is home again. That's good. And that's all I want to think about right now."

He clapped Robert on the shoulder and gave him a gentle nudge toward the baggage claim area across the room.

"Sorry about the turnout," Becky said. "It was such a short notice and your flight was coming in so late. We just weren't able to get a bigger welcoming committee arranged."

"And you weren't sure if I'd be coming home with honor."

His mother stopped and stared Robert straight in the eye, her hands latched onto his arms. "That is not true. I know that you served the Lord with all your heart. I knew that you would come back and make us proud. And you have."

Her expression said more than mere words. This was Robert's mother, the person who believed in him without reservation. This was the woman who saw the good in her son—even when he didn't.

Robert embraced his mother and couldn't prevent himself from crying. He tried to wipe away the tears forming in his eyes before anyone could see them.

"We plan to have everyone come over tomorrow night and welcome you back then," Becky said, her smile bigger than ever. More comforting than ever.

"Yeah," said Sara. "I wanted to invite everyone to it. Dad says we have to limit it to the number of people that can fit into our house."

"You think that many people will show up?" Robert asked.

"Sure. I have a lot of friends. And besides, Mom's cooking."

Robert chuckled. The great LDS motivator: free food.

"What about you?" Robert looked at Lucas. "Who are you inviting to the party?"

His younger brother shrugged. "No one. I'm just glad you're back."

Lucas grabbed Robert's bag when it rolled off the conveyor belt and onto the luggage carousel. Sara chatted endlessly about who was dating whom and which of the single girls would be right for Robert. Mom put an arm around Robert's waist on one side, and Dad had his shoulder covered on the other.

They were almost to the door leading to the parking garage when a commotion sounded from the lounge area. People gathered around the television that was mounted on the wall. The voices were loud and animated. A few tried to shout the others into silence.

"I wonder what's going on," said Sara.

John dismissed the event with a wave of his hand. "Probably a football game."

Sara had already gone, though. She jumped up several times to peer over the crowd. Eventually, she squeezed between a couple of women who stood there with shocked looks on their faces.

John tapped his foot as he waited for his daughter to return. That stopped when she poked her head back through the wall of people. Her face held the same shocked expression as the rest of the crowd, except she was crying.

By the time the rest of the family raced over, someone had managed to quiet the crowd so they could hear the television.

". . . government officials are refusing to comment at this time, but with the video footage we've just seen, it would be irresponsible for us not confirm to the public at large that Houston has just been the target of a terrorist attack."

3

WASHINGTON, DC

Calvin McCord wended his way through a sea of tuxedos, fine suits, and elegant evening gowns, worn by people much less attractive in person than on film. On every side of him, people toasted the man of the hour, hooted, and cheered. Until they saw Calvin. When they did, their smiles faded.

He pushed forward, ignoring the disapproving looks. Passing from the outer rooms to the central banquet hall, the noise grew to a tremendous roar, reminding him of the sound of jets heading off to war.

Here the crowd was thicker, forcing him to push his way through the tightly packed bodies. He resisted the urge to nudge those in his way a little more forcefully than necessary to pave his way to the center.

Eventually he broke through the hard press and walked into the sparsely populated area around the podium. Secret Service responded to him at once. Three of them had reacted and moved to intercept, but two returned to their posts when they recognized him. The third blocked his path.

"Mr. McCord, can I help you?"

In political talk this meant, "You're not welcome here."

"Are you stopping me because I'm a security threat?"

"No, sir!" The agent's voice was steady and forceful, but his manner gave subtle clues that Calvin's question had made him take a mental step backward.

"Then step aside."

Calvin could have told the man his reason for being here and made the approach that much easier, but he wasn't particularly in the mood to explain himself to the staff.

The Secret Service agent glared at McCord as he pushed his way past. Sunglasses may have hidden the man's eyes, but Calvin had been playing the game long enough to know what was going on behind those dark windows.

Ms. Wilks, the President's personal secretary, spotted Calvin and tried to head him off.

Calvin pulled the social equivalent of a head fake to draw her to the back side of Senator Robbins, while at the same time squeezing between the robust politician and his wife. The only way Ms. Wilks would be able to stop him now was to throw a headlock on him from behind. A feat he wasn't going to necessarily rule out.

The already announced members of the Cabinet and those hopeful of being announced formed the last ring of protection around the man of the hour.

Their tight-lipped smiles warned Calvin not to make a scene. He ignored the warning just as he ignored the people giving them. Looking directly at the Vice President, he invoked a powerful phrase of summoning.

"You might want to hear about this before it goes to the press."

Vice President Phillips looked confused and McCord repeated the message. Phillip's smile dropped as he waited for confirmation that this was not a ploy. No more than a few heartbeats passed before he leaned over to the president and whispered in his ear.

President Nelson Boggs didn't miss a beat. Smiling and waving, he looked over at Calvin. Then he extracted himself from the adoring fans, political leeches, and yes-men that surrounded him and strode over to where Calvin stood.

"Come to congratulate me, Calvin?" Boggs's voice held more than a little smugness.

"Congratulations, Mr. President," Calvin offered without emotion. "A matter has come up that I think requires your immediate attention."

"This isn't funny, Calvin." Boggs shook hands and continued to mug for the cameras.

"No. It's not, Mr. President."

"Then what is it?"

Calvin leaned in close and spoke just loud enough to be heard above the sounds of celebration. "There's been another terrorist attack on American soil."

Calvin had to hand it to Boggs; he kept his cool. He continued to shake hands and swap small talk with his people, flashing smiles to the camera before he graciously excused himself with a minimum of disruption. He was smooth, all right; slick as a Teflon blade.

With a few barely perceptible nods, Boggs collected his key people on the way out. They too practiced a stealthy withdrawal from the celebration. Those who remained rallied around the Vice President and continued the shouting, cheering, and mutual backslapping.

The small procession moved well out of range of the party, assembling in a secluded conference room. No doubt President Boggs wanted to keep this meeting off the radar until he could determine the extent of the disaster.

"How bad is it?" Boggs asked before anyone had the chance to be seated and the meeting formally started.

"A bomb was detonated in downtown Houston. The early estimate of casualties is thirty to forty dead and a larger number wounded."

Boggs nodded his head in acknowledgment. The rest of the room exploded into outbursts of shock and denial. Rather than query Calvin further, they engaged one another in bouts of speculation.

The President cleared his throat. Twice. The room quieted to a low murmuring of hushed conversations.

"What was the target?" Boggs asked.

"Governor Ross's party headquarters," said Calvin. "They were celebrating his reelection."

Calvin scanned the table, studying the reactions to his statement. The vast majority seemed to be reeling from the news of the attack, but among Boggs's cabinet there were a few who appeared lightened by the announcement that the opposing party had been targeted.

"Ross and his family are safe," Calvin added finally. "They were attending the celebratory events at the state capitol when the attack happened."

"That's good news," Keegan Roscoe spoke up. "Arnold Ross is a good man. Texas will need his strong leadership in the aftermath of this tragedy. Political opponent or not, we should all count ourselves fortunate that he was spared."

"Nicely stated, Keegan." The President allowed a moment for the rest of the assembly to applaud or otherwise give their affirmation, and then he continued. "Has anyone stepped up to claim responsibility for this action?"

"Not yet," said Calvin. "I brought this to your attention as soon as I heard it."

"Okay, people," Boggs said loudly. "Opinions! Options!"

"How big of a concern is this?" asked one of the President's new cabinet members. Calvin didn't recognize the man as anyone of significance.

"You mean besides the loss of human life? Or beyond the fact that terrorists have struck against us once again at home?" Calvin swallowed hard and tried to reign in his temper. It took all of his will to hold back from acting on the instinct to leap across the table and throttle those idiots who minimized the loss of life and the suffering of their fellow countrymen.

"I agree with Calvin," said Keegan. "Just because this has happened to our political opponents does not make it any less of a tragedy. Please, let us set aside our partisan tendencies for the moment and look to what needs to be done."

The President raised his hands, preventing any responses. "I suspect that what Ken meant to ask was what level of impact is this going to have on us."

"We're not going to know that until we find out who conducted the attack," said Marion Salazar, the new Secretary of Homeland Security. "For all we know, this could've been done by a group of Texans who are protesting Ross's commitment to look into repealing the death penalty."

"It's fruitless to make any unfounded speculations," said Keegan. "We need to act quickly."

"Right," said Boggs. "The news networks will be covering the event even as we speak, and we need to reach out to the public."

"Reaching out to America," said the new head of the Department of the Interior. "This is definitely an opportunity to reinforce your campaign slogan."

"This isn't about campaign slogans or boosting the polls to ensure your reelection in four years!" Calvin shouted. "This is about people. American lives have been lost and the citizens of this country will look to us to protect them from more of the same."

"That is exactly the point we want to make." The President motioned to his personal speech writer, Richard Donnelli. "I need you to get working on something that I can go to the public with in fifteen minutes. In addition to what Calvin just said, let them know that 'Reaching Out' was not just a campaign slogan; it's how this new administration is going to do business."

"They're going to want to know what you plan to do next," said Calvin.

"Very good," said the President. "I'll let them know that we're looking into the situation right now and will report on what we find as soon as we know ourselves. Anything else, Calvin?"

"No." Boggs had said all the right things, but Calvin still felt uneasy. Did this president have the country's interest at heart, or was he just concerned with putting out effective sound bites?

"I think we might want to consider the possibility of a much different reaction from the public," said James Crouse, the returning Secretary of Commerce.

"And what might that be?" asked the President.

"That it's an omen."

Quiet filled the room for several moments. Boggs steepled his hands in front of him. Calvin noticed that Crouse's suggestion hadn't slid off the President's sleek hide like everything else tonight.

"The timing is suspicious," Crouse resumed.

"Suspicious?" The Department of Defense leaned in as he tried to tackle the concept. "You make it sound like the President could be held responsible."

"No, not the President," said Crouse. "Look at the circumstances. The explosion happened during the inauguration ceremony. Religious zealots might take that as a sign from God."

"That's ridiculous," said the Department of Interior.

"Yes, it is," said Crouse. "But that's how some of the public thinks. They'll associate the tragedy with President Boggs taking office, even though the two events are not related."

"So far as we know," said Calvin.

"What?" Boggs asked.

"We don't know who's responsible for the attack at this time."

"Are you suggesting that the President ordered this done?" asked the Department of the Interior.

"I'm not suggesting anything. What I am stating is that at this point we can't be sure the attack is unrelated to the President being elected to office. Instead of jumping to conclusions, we need to investigate the attack and see where that takes us."

Boggs looked directly at Calvin for the first time. "I'm curious why the Secretary of State is bringing me this information. It doesn't fall within your realm of responsibility, does it?"

Calvin took a deep breath. "All your people are here celebrating, so the message came to one of my associates. He thought I would have the best chance, under the circumstances, of getting through to you."

"In other words," said Crouse. "They wanted to make sure the fallout for this disaster fell fully in our laps."

The others at the table muttered their support for the idea. Except for the President; he watched Calvin.

"No," Boggs said. "That is reasonable. You are still the Secretary of State. No one is going to prevent you from seeing me if you tell them it's important." Boggs took a dramatic pause. "The effort on your part wouldn't be an attempt to sway me to keep you on in your current position, would it?"

"My first concern is for the safety of the American people. More lives may be at stake. This may be the first step of a much larger terrorist campaign."

"Of course," the President said in his smoothest voice.

"Although," Calvin was quick to add, "I hope you will consider my request to remain as Secretary of State. We are in the middle of several important negotiations that I feel depend upon the relationships I've built with Russian officials over the last eight years."

"Of course," Boggs said in the same smooth voice.

Calvin burned at the smug, placating response. He attempted to keep his face neutral, but doubted that he succeeded.

"I think it is time to show the people what we meant by reaching out to them," the President said. "What's our next step?"

"The usual," said Marion Salazar. "We get Homeland Security and the FBI to determine exactly what happened and who is responsible for it while you give a speech stating that you share the grief over the loss of American lives. We can have the speech ready in an hour."

"Why wait?" Calvin asked.

"In case it escaped your attention, there is an inaugural ball going on." Crouse's voice was filled with incredulity.

"I believe Mr. McCord has a point," said Keegan. "We shouldn't wait. They deserve immediate action from their elected officials. And if that doesn't convince you, please consider how acting decisively will improve the mood of the people. Isn't that what you want?"

Boggs turned to Calvin. "Excellent suggestion . . . Mr. Secretary of State."

The President stood and prepared to leave the room. "Donnelli, whip together a five-minute speech as fast as you can."

The President continued issuing instructions as he walked out the door. The rest of his inner circle followed in his wake, leaving Calvin alone in the room.

Long after the others had left, Calvin remained seated. His hands clasped together, he stared blankly at the tabletop. He looked nothing like someone who had gained a concession from the most powerful person in the United States.

4

obert checked the time. His alarm clock still read 3:07.
For the last hour he'd worked to fall asleep. The bright
red numbers of the clock marched along at a pace slower than he
thought possible. If it weren't for the steady sound of his father's
snoring across the hall, he might have considered the possibility that
he'd entered some *Twilight Zone*–style time warp.

With a heavy sigh of resignation, he sat up and turned off his
alarm. Almost a week at home and he still operated on Italy time.

Italy. Robert did a quick calculation in his head and figured that
about now he and his companion would be stopping by the Bianchi's to eat lunch and do their laundry. On Mondays, Sister Bianchi
made mas-cio al late and Bishop Bianchi usually tried to organize a
soccer game late in the afternoon.

A vigorous shake of his head whipped the memories away.
Robert launched himself out of bed, grabbed his scriptures, and
went out to the kitchen.

He finished reading Second Nephi before he poured a bowl of
cereal and doused it with milk. At least he wasn't looking around
for his companion anymore when it came time to bless the food.

While the rest of the family continued to sleep, Robert sat at the table and ate. It felt strange to be alone after spending so much time with his mission companions. One of the things he'd looked forward to after his mission was being left by himself once in a while. Except now it didn't feel that great.

Life hadn't instantly returned to normal when he got back home. He had changed. The situation at home had changed. He wanted to feel the same way he had before he'd left, but now he realized that would never happen.

Before he left on his mission, his goals had been to get a job, go to school, and eventually obtain a career as an engineer. Somewhere along the way he expected a wife would show up.

He still planned to get a job. At least that much of his previous goals remained the same. Even though his mother and father had said nothing about it, Robert knew they were struggling financially. Lucas had let slip that Dad had taken a cut in salary in order to keep his job. Not having to support a missionary in the field would help, but he didn't think that alone would be enough.

They were having trouble with Sara too. She no longer attended seminary and often missed church altogether. Robert noticed that she had a new set of friends with different standards. Maybe all she needed was a little fellowshipping. Now that he was home, he could make sure to spend some time with her.

That would have to go on his to-do list. Today he needed to find a job.

If he rode his bike down to his old job, he could arrive just as they were getting started for the day. With any luck, he could start tomorrow. Robert threw on some clothes and scribbled a note to his mother.

Chill air flowed across his bare forearms as he flew down the silent streets. He passed Jenny Johnson's home, Mr. Hough's corner hardware store, and other landmarks that brought back memories of pre-mission life, memories that seemed out of place with the dark, motionless scenes that surrounded him now.

Were these only images from a dream while he slept still in Italy?

The front tire of Robert's bike caught in a pothole and sent him sprawling along the street. His bike tumbled after him.

Wincing in pain, he lay on the hard asphalt. He checked for injuries and found only a couple of minor scrapes. The bike appeared equally unharmed. Then he smiled.

Nope! It wasn't a dream.

The rest of the trip to Golden Construction went without further pondering or another accident. Robert leaned his bike against the trailer that served as the company's office and waited for Howard Jenkins to arrive. He stood in the cold for thirty minutes and tried to ignore the stinging from the road rash on his palms.

At six fifteen he switched to sitting on the steps leading up to the trailer. It was odd; Brother Jenkins arrived before anyone else, usually before six.

Right at seven, a white Ford pickup pulled into the gravel parking lot. The crunching of tires as the truck approached jolted Robert out of his thoughts, and he jumped up, ready to greet his former employer.

"Hi, Brother Jenkins."

"What are you doing here?"

"You said when I got back from my mission, I could have my job back."

The smile that had been forming on Howard's face vanished.

"I did, didn't I?" Howard took a deep breath and then continued. "Robert, I would love to put you back to work, but—"

Why did there have to be a *but*?

"I finished my mission," Robert interrupted.

"Good. I hope it went great for you. I . . . just . . . don't have a job for you anymore."

"Why?"

Howard shrugged. "Because there isn't any work."

Robert looked around at the nearly empty parking lot. The lack of vehicles and workers gave eerie support for Howard's announcement.

"I'm down to a single crew," Howard continued. "And I don't

know how much longer I'll be able to keep them busy. The economy is down right now."

"One crew," Robert mumbled.

"That's it. I kept Ben and Chris on to work with me and Steve. My daughter, Kelly, works in the office part-time, mostly afternoons after I'm gone. If things don't pick up soon, we may have to cut back even more."

"Business was booming when I left for my mission."

"It sure was." Howard nodded. "Then the housing market crashed. Several of the banks stopped evicting people out of foreclosed homes as long as they agree to keep the house in good repair. They already have more empty houses than they know what to do with."

Robert stared at the dark trailer while he considered Howard's words. His parents hadn't written to him about this while he was gone. Then again, it wasn't exactly the sort of thing that went into missionary letters.

Howard slid his hands into his jeans pockets and waited.

"I'm sorry business is slow for you," Robert offered.

"If the economy picks back up, go ahead and swing by here, and I'll see what I can do about hiring you then."

"Thanks."

Robert shook Howard's hand, climbed on his bike, and headed home. Navigating the streets on autopilot, his thoughts were on the unexpected loss of his old job. He stopped when his mother called his name—for the second time. Without realizing it, he had made it back home and now stood in the kitchen.

"How'd your job hunting go?" His mother slipped in a quick hug as she passed him on her way to the stove.

"Not as good as I'd hoped."

"What'd you expect?" asked Lucas. "No one wants to hire some crazy person who rides his bike around in the middle of the night."

"Lucas," Mom said, emphasizing his name. "That's not true. Employers respect a person with ambition. Robert, you just sit down and I'll fix you some breakfast."

At the mention of food, Robert noticed the smell of bacon as it popped and sizzled on the stove. He washed his hands in the sink, gingerly cleaning his scraped palms, and then sat down next to Lucas.

"Hey, bro." Robert draped an arm around his brother's shoulder and smiled.

Lucas returned the smile. "You're not getting my bacon."

"I see you wised up to that one while I was gone."

"It never worked on me."

"That's right—it didn't." Robert removed his arm and straightened up. "What I really wanted was to find out if you knew about any jobs that are available."

"Bob's Burger Barn is hiring. They're always hiring."

"I think I'll pass. I was hoping for something that required a little more skill."

"And one that pays better than minimum wage," his dad added as he walked into the kitchen.

"That too," said Robert.

John took a small detour to kiss his wife before sitting down at the table across from Robert. "I guess that means you'll be job hunting today."

"Looks like it," said Robert. "I just hadn't thought I'd need to."

"There's a lot of that going around," said John. "We didn't think we'd have to cancel our vacation last year, either."

"I didn't know you had to do that. What happened?"

"It was no big deal." Becky carried over two plates loaded with bacon, eggs, and toast and placed them on the table. "We had a campout in the backyard. With all the time and money we saved by not driving around, we were able to fix up the house."

"True." John nodded. "It was the most productive vacation we've ever had."

"It stunk," said Lucas. "There wasn't enough money to take a vacation *and* support a missionary, so we had a family meeting and decided to do the whole 'staycation' thing. It was lame."

Guilt hacked away at Robert. His family had gone without so he could serve a mission. Then he'd been sent home early from it.

"But," Lucas added, finally, "I'm glad we did it. It felt like I helped you do something important."

Becky reached over and patted Lucas on the back. "That was nice of you to say."

Lucas shrugged and then let Robert catch him rolling his eyes when Becky walked away.

"Besides Bob's Burger Barn, what's out there for jobs?" Robert asked.

"Not much," said John.

Lucas nodded.

The rest of the family trickled into the kitchen and sat down to breakfast. John read the morning paper. Lucas vanquished the meal in quick order, then excused himself from the table. The rest of the children chatted about school between bites. And once everyone else had been served, Becky joined the family with a plate of almost still-warm food.

Robert bused his dishes, kissed his mother on the cheek, and then headed out to the garage. His parents had agreed to lend him the car. Despite what Lucas and his father had said, if he looked hard enough, he was sure he could find a job.

Six hours and fourteen construction companies later, Robert had lost most of that confidence. He'd stopped by every construction site on the west side of town and most of the ones on the east side too.

Nothing.

Maybe he'd be flipping burgers at Bob's Burger Barn after all.

Robert wanted to work construction. That's what he'd been doing before his mission. It paid reasonably well, and he enjoyed the physical exertion it required. When he finished a day's work, it felt as if he'd accomplished something. He didn't want to find employment in a different field.

As he pulled into the driveway, Robert noticed Mrs. Evans working in her yard. The elderly neighbor held a weeding hoe in both hands and was leaning on it. She looked as if she were trying to catch her breath.

If no one was willing to pay him to work, then he'd just have to volunteer. Robert gave the keys for the van to his mother, changed into his work clothes, and then headed across the street to where Mrs. Evans still stood.

Her flushed face brightened as she spotted Robert. She brushed her gloved hands against the faded, blue coveralls she wore and stood a little straighter.

"Robert, it's so nice to see you again. Did you move back home?"

"I guess you could say that." Robert motioned toward the yard. "Do you think I could help out with the weeding? It's been a while since I've had a really good battle against the green hordes of doom."

Her eyes held a hopeful expression for a moment and then she forced a smile. "That isn't necessary. I need to do this on my own. Besides, I can't afford to hire you."

"Are you sure about that? I work cheap. If you have some of that lemon pie around and a glass of lemonade to go with it, I think we have a deal."

Mrs. Evan's wrinkled face crinkled even more as she smiled. She reached over and gave Robert's arm a light squeeze.

"In that case, I think I could let you wield that hoe for a while. I'll go inside and get you a down payment on that work—a tall, icy glass of lemonade."

Robert attacked the weeds with an enthusiasm that surprised him. Within an hour he'd cleared the entire yard of the unwanted plants. He stood up straight and took a deep breath. When he did, he noticed that a sizeable amount of fall leaves still littered the ground and the sidewalk leading up to the house needed to be swept. This yard was simply too large for Mrs. Evans to take care of herself.

With her family living out of town, she must not have wanted to burden her friends and neighbors with the task of taking care of her. How sad that people could think that way. It was Mrs. Evans who had watched Robert after school while his mom had been working. And it was Mrs. Evans who had come to his baptism, even though she wasn't a member of the Church, because she knew how much it had meant to him.

After all of the things she had done for her neighbors, how could she think she was a burden? How could she think that raking a few leaves was an imposition?

Maybe the rest of the world thought that way, but not Robert.

He walked around the back of the house to the gardening shack and exchanged the hoe for a rake, a broom, and some garbage bags. It took a couple of hours to rake and bag the leaves, but when he'd finished, the yard looked much improved.

It took Robert five minutes to sweep the walk. When he turned around, he found Mrs. Evans standing behind him. Her eyes glistened with tears. She slowly scanned the yard, her hands covering her gaping mouth, and then turned her focus on Robert.

"It looks wonderful. I've been trying to clean up those leaves for the last two months." Mrs. Evans paused; whatever she was trying to say seemed to catch in her throat. "I don't have enough pie and lemonade for all this extra work. Please, come inside. I made a roast for dinner. It's not much, but I'd like to share it with you."

"You don't have to do that," Robert protested.

"Oh, yes, I do." Mrs. Evans's tone was firm. "You're not afraid of my cooking, are you?"

"Not at all."

"Then I insist that you let me feed you dinner. And afterward we'll have that pie."

Robert nodded and followed Mrs. Evans into her home. He called his mother to let her know he wouldn't be there for dinner. Mrs. Evans set the table while Robert washed up, and then the two of them had dinner and talked about many of the events that happened in the neighborhood when he'd been growing up.

For the first time since his return, Robert felt content. This is how he felt whenever he had the opportunity to serve others. It was the driving force in his life. It was the reason he wanted to be an engineer.

How strange. As much as this reminded him of serving on his mission, it struck Robert that sitting here with Mrs. Evans was his real homecoming party.

5

Becky navigated the battlefield of morning ritual and took a running head count of the family members. When she came up one short, she instinctively routed herself to Sara's room and knocked on the door.

"Time to get up," Becky announced through the door.

A faint, muffled reply signaled a successful wake-up call. With everyone finally accounted for, she headed to the kitchen to start cooking breakfast.

All right, she knew she was wildly off the mark. Her family had never marched on an enemy position—in the traditional sense. None of them were members of the armed forces. The truth be known, Becky didn't even like military movies.

What her musings represented was Becky's creative flair. Ever since she had watched *Saturday's Warrior* as a teen, she'd pictured herself as a latter-day soldier of God. While she hadn't faced any angry mobs in defense of her religion or marched across a thousand miles of wilderness to test her faith and establish Zion, she did see the activities of everyday life as mission critical.

How many times had she heard lessons about how everyone formed the troops in the fight against evil? The mundane, unspectacular acts of service that seemed so minor to most people were in reality the actions of a true hero. Anyone might have a single shining moment with spectacular effect and be called a hero by many. However, the true test of a person's mettle came in the form of small acts of kindness known only to those for whom it was performed. Or even more, those acts that went completely unnoticed.

Making dinner every night, giving the neighbor a ride to the grocery store, and taking a moment to comment on how nice a person's hair looked were not the elements that filled the pages of heroic novels, but they were among the endless number of little things that made life better for everyone around Becky.

Robert bounded out of the kitchen. He wore a grungy pair of sweats and had a basketball tucked under his arm. A piece of toast was clamped between his teeth as he tried to zip up his jacket.

"Good morning." Becky walked over to her son and wrapped her arms around him. He might be fully grown and capable of taking care of himself, but she had missed him every day he'd been gone. She held the embrace until Robert mumbled a protest past the toast.

"I was going to make breakfast for you." Becky stepped back and let Robert reclaim his morning snack before it fell on the floor.

"Sorry, Mom. I have plans to play ball with Kevin. If that's all right with you."

"Of course." Becky patted his arms.

The doorbell rang.

Robert raced across the room and opened the door.

"Ready to go?" Kevin asked. He too wore sweats, but his were cleaner and tighter fitting.

"Hello, Kevin." Becky joined Robert at the door.

Kevin shoved his hands in his pockets and nodded to Becky.

"We have to get there before the courts fill up." Robert leaned over and gave Becky a kiss on the cheek and then darted for Kevin's car. Then the two boys got into the sleek red Mustang convertible and drove away.

Becky hadn't seen Kevin at church for several months. Now that she thought about it, he hadn't been there for nearly a year. He only lived a couple blocks away, so she'd seen him occasionally at the store, and the park, or driving along the street, but not at church.

With Robert home, maybe that would change.

Shouts burst from out of the hallway. Jesse and Elizabeth called for Becky.

"Mom!" the twins hollered in unison. "Cody won't get out of the bathroom."

With a sigh, she followed the din of battle to its source. Jesse and Elizabeth stood outside the bathroom door in their pajamas with their arms crossed.

"He is such a brat," Elizabeth said to Becky. "We've been waiting for twenty minutes, and I need to meet with Tabitha and Ashley so we can practice our parts for the play."

"Yeah," said Jesse. "I got stuff to do today."

"Cody." Becky raised her voice so she could be heard over the running water. "Please hurry up; other people are waiting."

"Aw, Mom," came the impatient reply from her youngest child.

Becky turned to the twins. "Both of you aren't going to be able to use the bathroom when he's done. So, Jesse, if the stuff you have to get done is video games, I think you can let Elizabeth go first."

"I guess." Jesse dramatically exhaled and then trudged down the hall. "Geez, you'd think being ten minutes older would earn me an advantage once in a while."

Elizabeth gave a triumphant nod toward Jesse's retreating form.

"It wouldn't hurt you to appreciate his gentlemanly offer to let you go first," said Becky. "And Cody has only been in there ten minutes, not twenty. Let's give him the time he needs to get ready."

"Okaaaay," Elizabeth said as she propped herself against the wall.

Mission accomplished, Becky marched on to the next objective.

After dropping Cody off at school, Becky drove over to the grocery store on Northern Avenue. She'd just pulled into the parking lot when her cell phone played Beethoven's Fifth. She suspected that others might find her default ringtone a bit dramatic, but the heroic notes reminded her of the daily battle being waged to make this world a better place. It worked. Instead of wondering who was pestering her now, that bit of music readied her for another challenge.

Becky flipped open her phone. "Hello."

"Sister Williams, are you busy?"

"No more than usual," said Becky. She recognized the voice as Camile Ramsden. "Is there something I can help you with?"

"Our washer is broken and I don't have any way to get the kids' school clothes cleaned for next week."

"You're welcome to come over to my house this afternoon and use the washer and dryer."

Camile didn't respond immediately.

"Was there something else you needed?" Becky asked.

"I don't have a way to get over there," Camile hinted.

"That shouldn't be a problem. I'm at the grocery store right now. When I'm done, I can pick you up on my way home."

"That'd be great. See you then."

Becky put her phone away and then grabbed a shopping cart. She stopped just inside the doors to look at the sign to see what was on sale. A notice was posted along with the daily specials; it apologized to the customers for the number of items that were out of stock and made suggestions for alternate choices.

The store was short of a surprising number of items. Most of them Becky could do without altogether, and the others were easy enough to draw from the family's year supply to meet their needs until those particular food items were available again. Still, it seemed odd for the store to have run out of so many different items.

She made a few mental adjustments to her shopping list and wheeled the cart toward the dairy aisle. Milk happened to be available on a limited basis; two gallons per customer. Her family went through three times that much in a week.

Well, that just meant that she'd have to come back Tuesday, or probably Monday, and get some more. It seemed like a waste of gas to come back here for a couple gallons of milk. Fortunately, the store was pretty close to the house.

Da-da-da—duuuuuh.

Becky pulled her phone back out of her person and answered it. "Sister Williams."

It was Anita Bethel.

"Yes, Anita. What can I do for you?"

"I'm worried about my mother."

"What's wrong with her?" Becky asked.

"Nothing that she'll tell me. When I talked to her this morning, she sounded evasive. She claims everything is fine, but I don't know. I think she may need some help."

Anita lived in the northern part of the state. Her mother lived in the same ward as Becky. Calls like this were almost a weekly matter and most of the time there was little, or nothing, wrong with her mother.

"Maybe I could stop by and check on her," Becky said with as much cheerfulness as she could infuse into her words.

"Oh, would you? I hate to put you to so much trouble. If I didn't live two hours away, I'd do it myself."

"No problem; I enjoy visiting Martha. I'll see if I can stop by her place later on and then call you when I'm done."

"Thank you, Becky. You're a gem."

Becky disconnected the call and pushed her cart over to the butcher counter. The price of beef had skyrocketed in the last month. She looked at some fatty, low-grade hamburger for five dollars a pound and decided against it. Then a red tag sign caught her eye. It looked as though they had roast beef for sale at a reasonable cost, but only had one left.

As she pushed forward to take a closer look at the roast, another cart rammed into hers.

"Excuse me," a woman said. She didn't sound very apologetic. After giving Becky a contemptuous glance, the woman called out to the butcher. "I'll take this roast."

Becky took a deep breath and let it flow out slowly. No need to get upset. Definitely no need to start an argument over a roast. How silly would that be? Plenty of food existed for all of them to feed their families.

She rolled her cart over in front of a line of pork chops. The price was good. In fact, a much better price than the roast that was on sale. Getting a half dozen of the chops would let her try out the "Pull Your Pork—Stretch Your Dollar" recipe she had seen on her favorite cooking show.

The butcher wrapped up the chops she selected and handed them to her.

Becky steered toward the lady with the roast to tell her about the golden potatoes that were on sale that would go well with her roast, when—

Da-da-da—duuuuuh.

"Hello," Becky answered the phone.

Someone cried on the other end of the connection. Becky noticed that the caller ID showed Pam Tice.

"What's wrong?" Becky asked. Her *Saturday's Warrior* predilection kicked in. "Are you okay?"

The crying continued.

"Take it easy. Situations usually look worse than they really are. If you let me know what the problem is, we can work on fixing it."

The caller sniffled. "Oh, Becky! I don't know what we're going to do."

"You're not in this alone," said Becky. "What do you need?"

"With Greg out of work, we can't afford diapers for the baby." Pam burst out crying again.

"I can get diapers for you. Is there anything else?"

After a long pause, Pam added, "And maybe a few jars of baby food."

"Consider it en route. If you want, we can talk about the situation when I get there."

A single sniff sounded. "That would be great."

Becky closed the phone and snagged the rest of the weekly

shopping on the fly. Then she strolled through the baby aisle and grabbed what Pam requested. On her way to the checkout stand she passed by a chocolate cake.

Chocolate made everything better.

Dessert wasn't on her grocery list. With money as tight as it had been, she'd cut back on snacks. Besides, Becky was trying to lose weight and she couldn't be tempted by sweets if there were none in the house.

But this was chocolate. No, it was more than chocolate. It was deluxe chocolate cake with thick layers of cream cheese icing.

She didn't have time to debate with herself over whether she and her family deserved a treat this week. They did. And Pam was waiting. She put the cake in the cart and wheeled it toward the cashier.

Five minutes later, she pulled up to the Tices' house.

Pam opened the door before Becky even knocked. "Bruhb ga frent moblick."

Barbara's crying made it difficult to make out exactly what she was saying. It didn't help that she had little Desirae in her arms—screaming.

Becky motioned for Pam to hand over the baby and then walked into the house.

A change of diapers and half a jar of baby food were enough to put Desirae in the mood for a bottle and bed. By then Pam had calmed down enough to be understood.

"We used the last of the money in our checking account to pay the utilities for the month," said Pam between sobs. "The bank has already started foreclosure proceedings. We don't have any family in town that we can move in with. We're in big trouble."

Becky moved over to sit next to Pam and put an arm around her shoulder.

"Have you told the bishop about any of this?

"No," said Pam. "We didn't want to be a burden on our friends. We wanted to take care of the problem ourselves."

"That's silly to think that you're a burden. All of us have

problems. And at one time or another we need help. That's what friends are for."

Pam shrugged her shoulders.

"Listen." Becky took Pam's hand. "There's no disgrace in needing help. It's a part of our earthly experience. You're used to being on the giving end of charity. Now you have a chance to learn from receiving it."

Pam squeezed Becky's hand and nodded.

A sudden thought hit Becky. She went into the kitchen and checked the fridge.

It looked sparse. Besides a pitcher of water and the usual collection of condiments, it held only a couple small plastic containers in the back. Probably leftovers. She wondered how long they'd been in there.

An inspection of the cupboards revealed some scattered bits of food: bullion cubes, a half dozen cans of green beans, a box of saltines, and two cans of cranberry sauce. If they used all of it and ate sparingly, the Tices might be able to feed themselves for another couple of days.

Becky walked out to her Chevy Tracker and started splitting up the groceries. She left most of it for her family, brought the rest inside, and stocked the refrigerator and shelves. Since she had shown some restraint at the store, this didn't leave a lot of food for the Tice family, but it would be enough for another couple of days. It took several trips from the street back into the house, and on the last one she spotted the cake.

Chocolate made everything better.

Becky walked back into the house with the cake.

"Call the bishop this afternoon and make an appointment to see him."

"I will," Pam said in a voice almost too soft to hear.

"I'll have John check with the rest of the men in the ward and see if anyone has some work for Greg. If nothing else, they can probably arrange for some odd jobs until something permanent comes along."

Pam forced a smile.

"And I'll ask around to see who's been hitting the sales at the grocery store and are overstocked on a few items. I can guarantee that some of the sisters have bought more food than they can eat just because they got a bargain on it. That should tide you over until the bishop can make other arrangements for your family."

Becky handed the cake to Pam. "Things will get better."

Pam started to say thank you, and tears welled up once again. Becky gave her a hug carefully, so as not to crush the cake, and then left.

Two men stood next to her Tracker. They had the doors open and the groceries that had been inside it were now gone. As she approached, they turned and faced her. Both wore grungy clothing and looked like they hadn't bathed in a few days. They looked Becky up and down and then one reached into his jacket pocket and pulled out a knife.

"Give me your purse!"

6

The cabinet meeting starts in five minutes, Gwen," Calvin said as he walked into his office. "Give me the streamlined version of whatever messages you have for me."

His assistant scooted her chair back from her desk and stood up. She sorted through the top layer of papers on her desk and retrieved the notepad lying next to the phone. She scattered most of the papers on the floor but retained hold of the notepad.

"I'll pick up the papers," said Calvin. "You just give me my messages."

"Keegan Roscoe called to congratulate you on—"

"Gwen," Calvin interrupted, "only what I need to know before I go into the cabinet meeting. Did Keegan say anything about the bombing?"

"No," Gwen said quietly.

"Then move on."

"Tommy Grayson has intel reports on troop movements for eastern Russia. He's going to courier them over this afternoon."

"Good." Calvin finished putting the scattered papers on top of Gwen's desk. "What else?"

"Barbara Warner wants to set up a meeting with you to cover this year's party strategy."

Calvin sighed. "She only wants to make sure I'm still toeing the party line. Put her off as long as possible; I have enough on my plate trying to keep my job without having to hold her hand and tell her everything will be all right."

"Harry Lipinski wants a lunch meeting with you tomorrow to look over—"

"Come on, Gwen, only the important stuff."

Gwen opened her mouth, then obviously changed her mind and shut it along with the notepad. "That'd be it, sir."

"I'll get the rest of it from you after the meeting."

Calvin grabbed his briefcase and headed out of the office. Assistants and junior staff members scrambled out of his way as he marched through the halls. That changed the closer he came to the central halls of power. The middle and upper members of the staff he encountered did not move for him. Those lacking significant political juice merely stood in his way, but several of the senior staff members actually moved to make his passage more difficult. They feigned their actions as accidental and apologized, smirking to make it clear that he was not welcome.

Ken Farr and Dennis de la Pena blocked the door to the meeting chamber. Calvin nearly had to push them out of the way to get inside.

Farr leaned in close enough not to be heard by anyone except Calvin. "You may have sold Boggs a bill of goods about your worth as Secretary of State, but the rest of us aren't fooled. You'll be out of here as soon as we can get him to listen to reason."

Calvin squeezed past and took his seat at the conference table. His new seat. Place cards had been put on the table for this first meeting of the new cabinet. Calvin had been situated at the far end of the table from the President, off to one side. Whoever had made the arrangements had been careful to isolate Calvin from the President as much as possible.

Boggs arrived twenty minutes late. Without apology, he flashed a big politician's smile to signal the meeting had begun. Then he went to the cabinet members closest to him and worked his way down the table.

So far, little had been discovered about the bombing in Texas. Whatever the rest of the cabinet had found out was being kept from Calvin. The rumors from his own side of the political divide indicated that radical members of the opposing party had been behind it. Boggs's party.

The thought sent a chilled trail of goose bumps down his back. A terrorist attack on American soil was frightening enough. To have such a heinous act originate from his fellow Americans was unthinkable.

The few bits of information that were presented at the meeting Calvin had already heard on the cable news shows: the number of dead, the names of the victims, and the type of explosive that had been used.

Most of the meeting dealt with the *other* important issues of the day.

It came as no surprise to Calvin that he was dead last on the agenda. By the time the President actually recognized him, they had taken a dinner break and several key members of the cabinet had excused themselves for matters that needed their immediate attention.

"Mr. McCord," Boggs called. "Let me first congratulate you on the success you've had in getting the Russians to the table, so to speak."

"Thank you, Mr. President," Calvin stood. "I have a good relationship with them."

"Apparently," said the President with less enthusiasm, "they seemed inclined to forgo diplomatic dialogue unless you are involved. Quite the accomplishment. Some day I hope you will fill me in on how you managed it."

"Yes, sir." Calvin waited for Boggs's go-ahead to start his report.

"Very well, Calvin," the President said after a lengthy stretch of silence. "What can you tell us?"

"Of primary importance is the Russian troop buildup on the Ukrainian border. I have these handouts of their position as of two weeks ago."

"Mr. McCord"—Ken Farr's voice was clipped and condescending—"two-week-old information. Surely the President and this cabinet need to be kept up to date with the most current data available. I spoke with General Scalise just yesterday, and his sources are less than twenty-four hours old. Perhaps we should have him take over that particular responsibility if it is beyond you."

Calvin cursed the political tomfoolery that kept vital information out of his hands because he represented the other half of the political system. He was swimming with sharks here, and coming in without those reports was like chumming the water.

"No, Senator." Calvin tried to swallow his anger. "That won't be necessary. Just an oversight on my part; be assured that I am constantly monitoring the situation there."

The President waved Farr off, preventing any further needling. "What do you think they are up to, Calvin?"

"It could be a precursor to an invasion. Taking control of the oil pipeline would allow them to put significant political and economic pressure on the European Union, especially if it's combined with support of the current Iranian regime."

"That could be problematic," said Boggs, his tone reflective.

"While that is the most pressing situation in front of us, it's not the only one. The rice blight in China is causing civil unrest. My sources indicate that they have reinforced their police agencies with military units in anticipation of this getting ugly."

"Is this really a concern for the Secretary of State?" Martin Posey asked. The question sounded theatrical, doubly so because of his Southern drawl. "Matters of foreign aid are surely outside the boundaries of your assigned duties."

"The security of this country is everyone's responsibility." Calvin rose as he spoke, his temper rising with him. "I work with foreign countries to make sure their problems don't become our problems.

This situation in China—and India—can very easily become our problem."

Calvin's voice grew louder the longer he talked. "We're talking about starving people; over two billion of them between China and India combined. When they get hungry enough, the shooting will start, and we don't want it to spill over into our front yard when that happens."

"Now, Mr. McCord," the President said calmly. "No one doubts you. Please return to your seat."

"Right," Ken Farr spoke up. "It isn't a matter of doubting the situation; it's a matter of wondering why we need you to deal with it. If the situation with Russia is any indication, we may have the wrong man in place. We're told that you are indispensable to the negotiations with them, but the truth is they are amassing for an attack against Ukraine. How effective is the kind of diplomacy you are practicing? Exactly why is it that we need you?"

Calvin slammed his briefcase down on his desk. Thinking better of his actions, he shut the door to silence any further outburst that might be loosed.

How could those idiots play political games at a time like this? For an old soldier like him, only one thing mattered: Americans had died and someone was going to pay.

Calvin sat down at his desk and pulled out the fifth of bourbon he kept locked in the bottom drawer. He downed a shot and poured himself another as he considered his next move.

The phone rang. It was his private line.

"McCord here."

"I need to meet with you," said Mike Costa. "Discreetly."

"When?"

"Now."

Calvin looked at his watch. It was well past twenty-two hundred hours. Too late for this to be anything minor.

"All right. See you at the usual place in about thirty minutes."
Mike disconnected from the phone.

Calvin put on his jacket, grabbed his briefcase, and left. He and
Mike went way back. If they were meeting for a drink, then Mike
had something for him he didn't want to talk about over an unsecured line.

Calvin walked through the pouring rain and hailed a cab. It took
ten minutes to get the cab and five minutes to drive to the Patriot's
Corner bar. Calvin tossed the driver a twenty and went inside.

Mike hadn't arrived, so Calvin ordered a couple of beers and
then situated himself in a corner booth.

A couple of minutes after the drinks were set down, Mike
walked in. He was a man of average height, athletic build, and looks
that didn't stand out in a crowd. All were attributes that helped the
FBI agent in his intelligence-gathering duties. Mike looked straight
ahead as he sauntered across the room, but Calvin knew that he was
scanning the bar to see who was there. Even though Mike didn't do
a lot of fieldwork anymore, old habits died hard.

Mike grabbed the waiting beer and downed a good quarter of
the bottle as he sat. He let out an *ahhhh* of appreciation. "Just how I
like it—cold and free."

Calvin chuckled. Here he sat, facing what was probably the most
critical event in his career, and Mike was able to break the tension.
"Good to see you again. How's Elaine?"

Mike took another swig. "Same as always. Kids too. Let's drop
the small talk and get to business. We can swap niceties when you
have more time."

"Okay," Calvin said. "What have you got for me?"

"We've uncovered some interesting leads on the bombing in
Texas. I figured that you're being kept out of the loop, and this is
too big for one side to be controlling. There's going to be trouble."

"I'm sure there's any number of ways this can turn worse,"
Calvin said. "What have you found out?"

"Keep in mind that we're talking about Texas."

"Got it. Whenever they find out who did this, I don't expect them to sit idly by and wait for justice to take its normal glacial course."

"Exactly."

Mike took another long pull on his beer and continued.

"Witnesses saw someone dressed like one of the Political Anarchists, who support Boggs, enter the building about an hour before the bomb exploded. Then as soon as response teams started sifting through the rubble, they found a hat with the Anarchists' insignia on it. I don't buy it, though. It's too easy. They're being set up. Someone wants the Texans to think that Boggs's party attacked them"

"If this gets out of hand," said Calvin, "the whole country could be ripped apart."

"Exactly." Mike finished his beer and signaled the bartender for another.

Calvin mulled the new information over until Mike's second drink arrived. He waited for the bartender to retreat back to the bar. "If the Anarchists didn't do it, then who did?"

"We don't know yet. Whoever is responsible went to a lot of trouble to make it look like it came out of the Middle East."

"Who's your source?"

"You know better than to ask me that."

Calvin took a drink and let out a low whistle. "Setting up the Arabs to look like they set up Boggs. Whoever did it has to have a lot of juice to pull off something this big. That only leaves us a couple of possibilities."

"Russians," Mike suggested.

"Or the Chinese."

"I don't envy you, Cal. I can imagine how Boggs is going to take it when you let him know that you uncovered a secret plot by an undisclosed foreign power to throw the United States into a bloody civil war."

7

Robert put his shoulder down and tried to sprint around Kevin. Midway through the maneuver, his feet tangled and he collided with his friend. Both of them crashed to the concrete court.

"You really stink at this." Kevin raised himself to a sitting position. "Didn't you play any hoops while you were in Italy?"

"Not really," said Robert. "Just a lot of soccer."

Kevin grabbed the basketball and walked over to the sideline, near the net. He tossed the ball to Robert. "That's a charge. I'll bring it in here."

Robert checked the ball and readied himself to block Kevin's drive to the basket.

"How's your mom doing?" Kevin asked as he dribbled toward the free throw line.

"She's fine. The men didn't hurt her. She's just scared."

Kevin stopped, still dribbling, and gave Robert a "duh" look. "Yeah. Getting robbed by men with weapons is scary. She's lucky that's all that happened."

When Robert paused to respond, Kevin sped past him for a layup.

"You've lost your edge, boy." Kevin chuckled. "Did you give up thinking too while you were on your mission?"

"So we're going to play that way?" Robert nodded and rubbed his hands together.

"We always play that way!"

"All right. Bring it." Robert tossed the ball out to Kevin at half-court.

"Three, zero," Kevin said as he dribbled toward the basket.

"You make it sound like I'm the one that changed over the last eighteen months." Robert reached out, snagged the ball between dribbles, and ran to half-court with it.

Kevin gave Robert the evil eye but moved to block him from scoring. "You did."

"True. It's not just me, though." Robert made a move to the right, again, and then dribbled back to half-court when Kevin out-maneuvered him. "The country's changed, my family's changed . . . you've changed."

"I haven't changed."

"Okay. You haven't changed. That still leaves everything else."

Robert led to his right and then blitzed left when Kevin moved to cut him off. Four quick steps and he popped a short jumper to score.

"If you're going to whine about the country being in such bad shape, I'm going home and you can walk."

"You think I'm whining?" Robert carried the ball out to the half-court line and started dribbling.

"Only because you are. Things change! Big deal! Move on!"

"I want to, but since the housing market crash, there aren't any jobs."

"Wrong." Kevin lunged for the ball and missed. "There aren't any *construction* jobs right now. But change creates new areas of opportunity. If you want a job, find out which industries have responded to recent events. They'll have jobs."

Robert missed an under-the-basket layup and Kevin hauled in the rebound.

"Great. All I have to do is figure out which industry thrives on chaos and destruction, and I'll be all set to start work."

"Lawyers." Kevin drove straight at the basket, catching Robert flat-footed once again. The ball rebounded hard off the backboard and nearly fell into Robert's hands.

"What do you mean?"

"Lawyers thrive on chaos and destruction. You don't hear any of them complaining about the economy, except when it's part of a lawsuit they're pursuing."

Robert held the faded leather basketball on his hip and thought about it. He remembered hearing that even during the Depression many people had made fortunes while others went without. Those who adapted survived, or even thrived, while those who didn't lost everything they owned.

"That makes sense. It must be why the Church has been implementing so many new programs lately."

Kevin waved a dismissive hand toward Robert. "Don't get me started about *your* church."

"You mean *our* church. And what are you talking about?"

"Whatever. Just play ball." Kevin motioned to continue playing.

Robert dribbled to the left and took an ugly shot that circled the rim twice and then finally fell in.

"Two to three."

Kevin went into a hard press at the half-court line and forced Robert out of bounds. He grabbed the ball out of Robert's hands and waited for his friend to get back into position.

"I suppose all these changes in the Church are in preparation for the Second Coming," Kevin sneered.

"Members are always saying that. Even if it were true, it doesn't do us any good to speculate about it."

"That's what scares me."

"What? That members are always seeing signs of the Second Coming?"

"No. That it doesn't do any good to speculate about it. People should question what's going on, especially what the Church is doing."

Kevin charged the basket. He blew past Robert and scored.

"I don't see the Church doing anything questionable," Robert said as he watched Kevin return to the half-court line. "What are you talking about?"

"The Church tells the members to hoard food."

"It isn't hoarding. At least it wasn't when we were told to start a year's supply. Our buying extra supplies didn't prevent anyone from getting the food they needed. They could have done the same."

"All right, I agree. What about the gathering of the Saints?"

"Like I was doing on my mission? The Church has always done missionary work. All churches do that. How can you object to that?"

"No." Kevin shook his head emphatically. "I mean a literal gathering. To physically separate the members of the Church from the rest of the world. A decision to turn their backs on what's happening to everyone else."

"I wasn't aware they called for that." Robert followed Kevin downcourt and got his hand on the ball to block the shot. He grabbed the rebound and brought it around for a shot of his own, high, smooth, arcing. Nothing but net.

"Look around, will you? There was another terrorist attack last Tuesday; this time they missed their target, but that makes the third one against us at home. The grocery stores are starting to ration select food items. There've been six school shootings so far this year. And the media is worried there'll be more before summer."

"Does that mean you believe the Second Coming is here?"

"No. I'm only passing on what *your* church has to say about all of this."

"*Our* church."

"Maybe."

Robert brought the ball downcourt and tried a tricky dribble between his legs, which set up a fake that sent Kevin turning the wrong direction. An easy layup tied the score.

"Game point," said Robert.

"If the Second Coming is about to happen, then there is going to be change. Drastic change and a lot of it. I don't know if I like what the Church might be planning."

"Like what? Planting gardens. Buying solar ovens. How can you dislike that?"

Robert brought the ball into play and tried another trick dribble, but this time he bounced it off his foot and it rolled out of bounds.

"Have you bothered to read about it?" asked Kevin. "Church leaders have talked for years about the Constitution hanging by a thread and how it will be up to the members to hold it together. Do you think they expect to accomplish that by sitting back and singing hymns? That requires action and you need to be wondering just what it is they plan to do."

Kevin retrieved the ball and took it to half-court. "Not to mention that if there're horrible disasters and war raging across the continents, the true believers aren't going to be bypassed by all of it. If civil war breaks out, then you and your family can expect to be part of it. Everyone will. Better start learning how to fight now."

Kevin drove to the basket—uncontested. The ball bounced lightly off the backboard and into the net. Jumping into the air, Kevin pumped his fist and shouted, "That's game!"

Robert hadn't moved, hadn't tried to stop his friend's drive on the basket. He snapped his fingers and turned to face Kevin. "I know where to look for a job."

8

"You need to be careful." Kyle Dalton's eyes rapidly scanned the musty-smelling, second-chance bookstore and then slipped into the history aisle in back.

"Sounds as if this has you spooked." Calvin studied his longtime friend and CIA contact. He knew about several of the covert missions Kyle had participated in before they put him behind a desk at the Pentagon. That kind of experience put steel in a person's blood. Kyle exhibited grace under pressure and his instincts were good.

Calvin had hoped Kyle's information would contradict what Mike Costa had said. Or even that Kyle would disagree with the conclusion that some foreign power had gone to great lengths to set the two political parties in America to fighting one another and then to blame it on the radicals in the Middle East. What Calvin absolutely didn't want was for Kyle to agree with him.

"I am." Kyle dragged his hand through the dark strands of his hair. "This is one scary scenario. If al-Qaeda blows up a building—and I sure don't want to see that happen again—people die, Americans set aside their differences, and we go after the bad guys. But if one half of the country sees the other half as the enemy. . ." Kyle shrugged his shoulders and shook his head.

"All right, we both agree. This is bad. What intel do you have on the situation?"

"Like I said before, you need to be careful." Kyle punctuated his statement with a quick glance around the bookstore. Other than a bored cashier up front, no one else was inside. "I'm willing to tell you whatever you want to know, but word at the office is that you're persona non grata. If they catch you talking with me and this thing blows up, you'll be the first suspect Boggs's cronies go after."

Treason. That's what Ken Farr and Dennis de la Pena would call it during their witch hunt. Calvin's efforts to find out who really orchestrated the bombing could be twisted into an attack against him that would distract everyone from the evidence pointing to the fringe elements of Boggs's own party.

"I can't sit back and let this happen," Calvin said. "Neither can you."

"Yeah." Kyle exhaled loudly. "That's what I thought you'd say."

"Then let's stop wasting time."

"At this point, there's nothing to connect the bombing with either Russia or China. The threads we're tracing right now lead to Iraq. It's not an obvious trail either. Iraq has plausible deniability. We can claim that al-Qaeda has moved operations into the country, and Iraq can claim that we're blaming them to cover up an internal problem. Plenty of opportunity exists to fan the flames at home and abroad.

"If you hadn't filled me in on your suspicions, I wouldn't think any different."

"But since I did . . ." Calvin prompted him to continue.

"It looks like we have a new player in the game. We picked up a lot of chatter just before the attack that couldn't be traced back to any of the known intelligence or terrorist organizations. That alone got my interest. Now, I'm thinking they're connected to the situation here.

"So far, we found a couple of cells in Afghanistan. Well-funded from what we can tell. On the surface they look like a new terrorist network."

"What makes you think they aren't?"

"There's no such thing as a *new* terrorist network. Usually, the core of any new organization is spun off from another group. Happens all the time. Leaders disagree on some minor point and they part ways. We have tabs on anyone with enough influence to pull off an attack like this and none of them seem to be involved. There's also none of the normal indications of a fallout between the known terrorist leaders."

"I hope you have more to go on than that."

"The methodology isn't Middle Eastern. I spent enough time in Afghanistan to know the activities of this new group have a subtle Russian flavor."

Calvin knew it even before Kyle had said it. The best way for Russia to keep America from interfering in the Ukrainian conflict was to give her problems of her own to worry about.

"Keep me posted about anything new that turns up," said Calvin.

"And you watch your back." Kyle picked up a couple of tattered books from the discount bin and headed to the counter. He paid for the books and left without a second look in Calvin's direction.

Calvin spent a few minutes looking at covers and finally found a book on Hannibal's campaign against Scipio that he'd plausibly be interested in buying. He purchased the book and then headed back to his office.

The cabbie had his radio tuned to a news talk station. Calvin listened to the scratchy, static-filled coverage of the bombing. Boggs's press secretary assured the audience of the President's commitment to restoring the security of the United States and bringing those in the Middle East responsible for the attack to justice. No mention was made of the Political Anarchists or any evidence linking them to the event.

He didn't blame Boggs for wanting to bury that part of the story. Eventually, though, the truth would come out. It always did.

Calvin exited the cab, passed through the security checkpoint, and was almost to his office when he heard his name. He looked behind him and saw Barbara Warner, the Minority Leader, and

Harry Lipinski. Even though Harry and he were in the same party, they'd never been allies.

Barbara, a matronly looking woman who dressed on the flashy side, took her time traversing the hallway. Harry skulked along beside her, his thin frame and thinning, slicked-back hair making him look like a host for late-night horror movies.

"I'm afraid I was only stopping in to get a few files from my office before I left for the day," Calvin said when they got close enough that he didn't have to yell.

"That will be fine," said Barbara. "I'll be brief."

"Here or in my office?"

"I think your office would be better. More friendly, don't you think?"

As they walked, Lipinski prattled on about a bill he was trying to push through Congress that supposedly meant higher standards for military equipment procurement. Calvin knew the legislation was filled with enough pork to feed Harry's district for a year.

Calvin threw in a "tell me more" whenever Harry paused, a little trick he had learned in dealing with senators and congressmen who were too obtuse to understand that they weren't the center of the universe.

They breezed past Gwen, who stood with her mouth open and any messages for Calvin frozen in her throat, and closed the door.

"How are the talks with Korshanenko going?" Barbara asked. She didn't bother to take the seat offered to her by Calvin.

"Victor supports our position that their troops should be moved off the Ukrainian border. Together, by the end of the week, we hope to get an agreement for them to at least reduce the number of forces in the area."

"Good," said Barbara. "Your efforts in the matter are certainly appreciated."

"Especially since *that* is what you're supposed to be doing." Harry's tone sounded critical.

"Care to explain that, Harry?" Calvin asked.

"He meant," Barbara interceded, "that you are presently involved in a key political situation. The President needs you. It looks good for our party to have you playing such a critical role at this time. We want you to keep your focus on resolving this matter."

"Right," said Harry. "Keep busy with the Russians and let Homeland Security handle the bombing."

Barbara winced at the comment. But she didn't correct Harry.

"That's what this is about," Calvin said, more statement than question. "You want me to forget about our enemies attacking us here at home and score as many political points as I can while I'm still valuable."

"Be reasonable, Calvin." Barbara laid a hand softly on his shoulder. "You won't be able to help anyone if they remove you from office. Not us. Not yourself. Not the American people. Besides, I've heard you tell the President that if the situation in Ukraine isn't diffused, it could lead to war."

"Right." Harry pointed a finger at Calvin. "That's important."

"I'm working on it," said Calvin. "I think they'll back down when they see we're united with the European Union on the issue."

"Good." Barbara smiled. "I'm glad we're on the same page now."

"Aren't you interested in finding out who set off the bomb in Houston?" Calvin asked.

"Of course we are," said Barbara. "And we want to see justice done. We just don't need you helping President Boggs get the credit for it."

"Try remembering which political party you belong to," said Harry.

"It's been a while since we got together and chatted," said Barbara in a tone that indicated the meeting was over. "Let's meet for dinner later this week."

Calvin escorted them to the outer door of his office. Barbara shook his hand, Harry barely gave him another glance, and the two of them glided out the door.

Moments like this made him miss being a soldier. You had allies, you had enemies, and you didn't have any problem telling them apart. The goals were simple: locate your opponent and take him out.

Now he was here. All because a friend had convinced him he could do more good in politics than leading a bunch of wet-behind-the-ears marines into battle.

Calvin gathered up what papers he wanted to take home to work on and put them in his briefcase. He told Gwen he would be out for the rest of the day and left the office.

At the opposite end of the hallway, two men marched in his direction. Black suits, pitch-black sunglasses, and the tell-tale sign of earbuds. Even if he didn't personally know these two men, he'd be able to identify them as Secret Service agents.

"Mr. McCord," Agent Jones said when he got closer. "The President would like to see you. Please, come with us."

It may have sounded like a request, but it wasn't. To hammer home the point, the agents took up flanking positions on either side of Calvin, and each put a hand on his arm to guide him along.

Jones and Hebner had reputations for using more force than necessary when dealing with threats to the President's security. Calvin suspected that Boggs had specifically sent them to fetch him.

The trip to Boggs's private office was quick and silent. Jones and Hebner waited outside while Calvin met with the President.

"Calvin." The President smiled. "Thanks for meeting with me on such short notice."

"Did I have a choice?" Calvin's voice betrayed his mood, but he didn't care.

"No."

Boggs didn't offer one of his normal disarming smiles. Here. Alone. He leaned forward on his desk, his eyes fixed on Calvin.

"Stop your inquiries into the Houston bombing."

"Sir, my focus has been on Russia."

"Calvin." The lines around Boggs's eyes softened, now more glint than glare. "You have your sources. I have mine. Mine are more extensive. Leave this alone."

For a brief moment, Calvin resolved to tell the President what he knew about the situation. There was no reason they couldn't work together on it.

Then an alarm flared inside Calvin, the same sort of inner warning that had saved his life in combat. Something didn't add up.

It had to be obvious, even to the idiots that worked for Boggs, that the troop movement along the Ukrainian border gave the Russians an obvious motive for the terrorist activities in Houston. If Calvin knew about all of this, then so did the President.

But that didn't mean Calvin knew everything the President knew.

What was it that Boggs didn't want him to find out? And to what length was he willing to go to prevent it?

9

Becky jumped at the sound of a crash.

She turned around. A can of peaches rolled away from her. It must have fallen as she rearranged the shelves in the pantry. Her heart thudded heavily against her chest. Short, panicked breaths eventually gave way to normal breathing.

A can of peaches!

She wanted to be brave and put the memory of the robbery to rest, but for all her talk of being a latter-day warrior, the first time she'd encountered a real hardship, she'd fallen apart. The pioneers faced daily hardship and the threat of death from the elements, disease, starvation, and hostile bands of Indians.

All Becky had to deal with was a couple of desperate men who may have only been trying to feed their families. She hadn't been hurt. The loss of food and money was minor. And if she bothered to think about it, there was probably a story she could harvest from the encounter about how the Lord protects His faithful servants.

That wasn't where her mind kept going. People didn't get mugged in her neighborhood. *She* didn't get mugged. Things like this—just—didn't—happen.

At least she had John around the house today. Her husband may not be a hulking brute or a martial arts expert, but she felt safe with him nearby. She felt safe in her home.

Two passes through the canned goods and still no sign of mandarin orange segments for her fruit salad. A quick trip to the grocery store would solve the problem. She was pretty sure the paper had a coupon for them; buy one, get two free. You couldn't buy them any cheaper than that. Once Lucas got home from school, she could take him along with her, and, between them, they could buy the maximum number of cans allowed. Then she'd be set for a while.

Or she could stay home. The fruit salad didn't have to have orange segments. For that matter, the family didn't have to have fruit salad.

"Hey, Mom," Lucas called from the kitchen.

Becky jumped. Again. Her hands knocked cans of kidney beans and packets of noodles to the floor.

"What are you doing home?" Becky asked.

"Not just me." Lucas aimed a thumb over his shoulder as Jesse and Elizabeth walked into the kitchen.

"Is today an early-release day?"

"Nope," said Lucas. "They shut down the cafeteria. We came home for lunch."

"You should've seen it, Mom," said Jesse. "There was a huge fight at school. A bunch of the kids that got transferred over from Jefferson at the beginning of the year had it out with some of the jocks. I bet twenty of them were fighting."

"Learn how to count." Elizabeth rolled her eyes. "Five of the Jefferson kids and four of the football players went at it."

"It was epic." Jesse seemed amped.

"It was pretty exciting," Lucas agreed. "No one really got hurt, though. Teddy Warton had a bloody nose, and one of the Jefferson guys had a fat lip. Nothing major."

"A brawl." Becky was having difficulty processing the news.

"Yeah," said Lucas. "Good word choice, Mom. Now I can say that I've seen a real-life brawl."

"Sweet," said Jesse.

"Whatever." Elizabeth gave her brothers a "talk-to-the-hand" gesture and headed for the fridge. "It was a stupid fight. Can we just eat and go back to school?"

"What do you mean 'go back'?" Becky asked.

"They didn't shut down the school because of the fight," said Lucas. "Just the cafeteria. We still have our afternoon classes."

"Unless you want to call and excuse us," said Jesse.

Kids had fights all the time. It couldn't be too bad; otherwise, they would've shut down the school altogether. And her children had perfect attendance for the year so far.

"All right," she heard herself say. "I'll call the school."

"Sweet." Jesse pumped a fist in the air. "I'm going to go play *Castle Deathenstein* in my room."

"I have homework to do. You should do the same," Elizabeth told Jesse as she grabbed a spoon and a container of low-fat banana yogurt and headed to the table.

"I think I'll head over to the courts after lunch and see if anyone's playing basketball," Lucas said. He pulled out a couple of mini pizzas and put them in the microwave.

"How about helping me instead?" Becky asked Lucas. With a teenage son present, her earlier indecision about going to the store had vanished. "I need to go shopping and could use the company."

Lucas sighed. He seemed to think about it for a moment and then nodded.

"You two stay at home." Becky pointed to Jesse and Elizabeth. "I'm not excusing you from school so you can go out and play."

"No." Elizabeth looked pointedly at Jesse. "You're just excusing us so he can stay *inside* and play his games."

"That's enough, dear." Becky gave Elizabeth a maternal pat on the shoulder on her way to the phone.

It took almost fifteen minutes to excuse the children for the afternoon. The line for the school kept ringing busy. She finally put the call on speakerphone and made out a shopping list while she waited.

Becky drove past the school on the way to the store. A couple of police cars were parked in the lot, and a large number of adults had gathered around the office door. It didn't look like a place of learning right now.

When she pulled into the store, she looped through the parking lanes until she found a spot close to the entrance. She assigned Lucas to cart duty and made sure he stayed nearby.

They avoided the butcher counter and swooped through the dairy section long enough to grab the daily limit of milk—times two. Together, they stocked up on orange segments, canned asparagus, toaster pancakes, and a dozen other unbelievably discounted items. By primarily using the food in their year's supply, they avoided having to buy what the store happened to have in stock on any given day in order to eat. While the other customers waited in long lines to buy extremely overpriced meat, her family could pick and choose from the bargains that were still available.

On their way home, Becky's mind was still reviewing the scene at the school when Lucas pointed off to the side of the road.

"That's weird," he said.

A man in a dark gray business suit stood on the corner. He held a sign that said:

I HAVE A FAMILY.
WILL CONSULT FOR FOOD!

"It's sad," Becky said. "We're lucky your father has a good, steady job."

"I guess so." Lucas shrugged and scanned through the stations on the radio.

Becky continued to watch the man in her rearview mirror. A nice suit. Clean-shaven. He wore his hair respectably short. The man stood straight, almost like a soldier at attention. If he'd looked arrogant, or shifty, Becky wouldn't have spared him a second glance.

He didn't. He looked humbled.

Briefly, she considered turning around and giving the man some of the food she'd just purchased, but she decided he'd have no use for canned yams and bags of frozen okra.

During dinner, Becky kept throwing out ideas for family activities that night. Which happened to be Friday night. Offerings of home-baked cookies and a friendly rivalry around a Monopoly board might be tempting for younger children, but it had no chance of keeping teenagers at home.

She didn't even know why she tried keeping them there.

Something niggled away inside her. It wasn't the robbery. It wasn't the fight. This felt different. It felt like something big was about to happen.

Then the house phone rang.

John answered it.

After a brief discussion, he hung up and called out for her. "Becky, the stake president wants to meet with us. Can you be ready in fifteen minutes?"

This was it. Whatever the stake president wanted had to be tied to the nagging feeling she'd had for the last couple of hours. She could always sense a big event before it happened.

"I'm ready to go now."

"No need to leave right away," John said calmly. "I want to change into my church clothes. It wouldn't hurt me to take a quick shower either. We can go when I'm done."

Becky fixed her hair, checked her makeup in the mirror, and looked in on Jesse and Cody as they played video games in the living room.

Surprisingly, she and John didn't have to wait to see the stake president. Joseph Banks waited for them at the front entrance of the stake building. He exchanged small talk with them as they walked back to his office.

President Banks asked John to offer a prayer, and then he opened up his scriptures and read Doctrine and Covenants 133:10–15.

> Yea, let the cry go forth among all people: Awake and arise

and go forth to meet the Bridegroom; behold and lo, the Bridegroom cometh; go ye out to meet him. Prepare yourselves for the great day of the Lord.

Watch, therefore, for ye know neither the day nor the hour.

Let them, therefore, who are among the Gentiles flee unto Zion.

And let them who be of Judah flee unto Jerusalem, unto the mountains of the Lord's house.

Go ye out from among the nations, even from Babylon, from the midst of wickedness, which is spiritual Babylon.

But verily, thus saith the Lord, let not your flight be in haste, but let all things be prepared before you; and he that goeth, let him not look back lest sudden destruction shall come upon him.

"Brother and Sister Williams," President Banks said with great solemnity, "it's time to start gathering the Saints."

10

Robert's parents had called for an emergency family meeting. He didn't know what it was about, but Mom and Dad had been stressed all weekend. It had to be something major.

Whatever it was, he'd find out tonight. Until then, he still needed to find a job, and today he had a few new ideas about where to look.

Chaos.

An hour and a half of Internet searches had given Robert a promising list of companies that may have benefited from the troubled events that plagued the country. His first stop would be Handy Hal's Security Doors and Shutters. Not only had Hal opened another location last month, but Robert had seen a "help wanted" sign out front when he drove by on Saturday.

The security industry seemed to thrive on chaos. Robert had noticed that as conditions in the country worsened, there was a greater need for measures to protect people and their property. He planned to take advantage of that to find a job.

He pulled into Handy Hal's and parked. As soon as he walked through the doors, he stopped dead in his tracks. A cute brunette sat at the front desk. She had freckles, stunning blue eyes, and a smile that struck Robert dumb.

"Can I help you?" asked the girl.

"Oh. Yeah." Robert snapped out of his daze. "I'm here to apply for the job."

"You look fit enough." The girl grinned. She took a handful of papers and placed them on a clipboard, then handed it to Robert. "Fill these out and give them back to me when you're done."

"Thanks," Robert said as he took the clipboard and walked to one of the chairs in the reception area.

Thanks?

A good-looking girl flirted with him, and all he could come up with was *thanks*. At least, Robert thought she'd been flirting with him.

He started work on the stack of forms. It took far longer than it should have. His eyes kept drifting over to where the girl sat. A nameplate on the desk read "Sierra Wientraub."

Sierra glanced over at Robert and caught him watching her. "Stuck on one of the answers?"

Robert shook his head and looked down. After that he kept his head down—for the most part.

"Here you go, Sierra," he said when he finished.

"I guess that means you can read my nameplate," she said, giving Robert a mischievous look. "You must be a college boy."

"No. Not yet."

"I'll have to knock off a few points for that."

"Really?" Robert asked.

"No." Sierra laughed. "Wait here and I'll take this back to Mr. Roth."

She had barely passed through the door when she reemerged and beckoned Robert forward.

They walked into the warehouse area, and Sierra introduced him to Mr. Roth, a heavyset man with a full, bushy beard and a completely bald head.

"Ever work in a warehouse before?" Roth's tone was loud but businesslike.

"No," Robert said.

"Can you drive a forklift?"

"No."

"Do you have an operator's license?"

Robert sighed. "No."

"Sorry, kid, can't use you right now."

Roth went back to his work, and Robert shuffled toward the front door. He waved to Sierra on his way past her desk.

"No luck today?" Sierra asked.

"'Fraid not." Robert stopped next to her desk, glad for the opportunity to talk to her again.

"You can try back in a few weeks. Usually we need some general help that just requires bulging muscles. But we might be able to use you anyway." Sierra covered her mouth with the papers she had in her hands. The laugh lines along her eyes gave away her smile.

"I will." Robert returned the smile and left.

He was still smiling when he walked into Camden Security. A middle-aged receptionist wearing a crisply ironed white blouse sat at the front desk and gave him a careful once-over. The initial interview consisted of, "Did you finish high school?"

Then the receptionist, Mrs. Landing, walked him back to a conference room that looked like it housed more break room chats than company planning sessions. A TV and VCR both occupied the room.

Mrs. Landing pulled a series of tapes out of a cabinet and set them next to the VCR. Then she handed Robert some papers that were stapled together.

"I'm going to have you take a test," said Mrs. Landing. "I'll start the video and you can fill in the answers whenever you hear them. When you are done with this tape, just rewind it and go on to the next one. There are four of them altogether. You can take a break whenever you need to, but you have to finish all the tests within six hours."

"That sounds simple enough," Robert said, hoping for more detailed instructions.

Mrs. Landing gave Robert a "thank you—bye-bye" smile and left the room.

Robert glanced at the question on the first test as the introduction played on the video. Half were true or false; common sense alone seemed enough to provide the answers. The rest were multiple choice.

Training videos made him snicker and this one was no exception. They portrayed life in such an unnatural way. Robert had never seen anyone act the way they did in these videos. He was so busy being amused that he nearly missed the first answer. The narrator repeated, word for word, what was on the test.

It couldn't be that easy. He was about to rewind the tape and listen again when the second answer came up. Again, it matched the exact phrase that the test used. Better yet, it was even the next question in line. The five questions after that were all given in order, one right after the other.

Robert listened to the tape for another five minutes without hearing anything he recognized from the test. That seemed a long time without saying anything important enough to be quizzed about. Then another six answers rattled along in quick succession.

The rest of the morning and part of the afternoon went by in similar fashion. Robert spent five minutes looking over the test to find out what it asked, and then he just listened for key phrases to find the answers.

When he turned in the test pages, he worried that it couldn't be that simple. He tapped his feet nervously while he waited for the results and tried to avoid looking over to where Mrs. Landing was grading the qualifying exam.

Over two hundred agonizing seconds passed before Mrs. Landing brought the test results to the counter. She smiled at Robert and said, "You did good—98 percent. Can you start tomorrow?"

"Ninety-eight?" Robert asked.

"Yes," said Mrs. Landing. "That's a very good score. Can you start tomorrow?"

"Tomorrow? Work?"

"Yes. Can you start then?"

Robert nodded.

"We just need you to take a drug test today. Here's the paperwork."

Another test. At least Robert wouldn't have to study for that one.

The testing facility was busy. Fortunately, they moved the people in the lobby through the process pretty quickly. Fifteen minutes after he arrived, Robert left. Unbelievable. He had a job. He could go home now.

On the way he passed Handy Hal's. Without thinking, he turned around and pulled into the parking lot. Taking a deep breath, he walked into the building and up to Sierra's desk.

She looked up, surprised, but she recovered quickly.

"There haven't been any more job openings since last time," she said with a smirk.

"Do you want to go out?" The question burst out of Robert's mouth.

Sierra sat, momentarily silenced.

"You know," Robert continued. "On a date."

"I sort of gathered that all by myself."

"How about Friday?"

"I don't know," she said, turning back to the paperwork on her desk. "I have a rule against dating anyone without a job."

"No problem. Someone in this town finally saw my potential. I am now officially employed."

"Then I guess I'll have to say yes."

11

She missed John.

How ridiculous. He'd only left for work half an hour ago. She'd see him again tonight when he returned. In the meantime, Becky had a house filled with children fighting for access to the bathroom, all except Sara, who still hadn't surfaced from her room.

Other than arranging for Tina Nelson to take the children to school because Robert had the Tracker, today was like any other Monday. Which meant it was like all the rest of the days of the week—just less organized.

She wandered through the house. There was plenty to do. The children needed a few motherly urgings to move them through their morning ritual. Breakfast still needed to be prepared. She half remembered offering to help someone tie a quilt this week.

Becky needed to get busy. But every time she thought of a task, it made her think of how much tougher things would be without John. Every time she entered a room, it prompted memories of her and John's life together. Seeing the children reminded her that families, especially marriages, were a team effort.

How could she do all of this alone?

She stifled a sob and closed her eyes, offering a micro prayer.

When she opened her eyes, she still wanted to cry, but she moved to the refrigerator instead and took out the ingredients for pancakes. Chocolate pancakes, she decided. Not the healthiest breakfast she could serve her family. But she was okay with that this morning.

Cody was the last to leave. Once he walked out the door, silence enveloped the house. Sure, the old clock in the living room ticked away and the heat pump hummed as it cycled air throughout the house. But they were mechanical sounds. Not the sounds of life. They did nothing to ease the sense of being alone.

Becky turned on the radio and buried herself in chores. That worked until lunchtime. She pulled out a head of fresh romaine lettuce and separated it for a salad. Tomatoes, cucumbers, a hard-boiled egg, and homemade bacon-ranch dressing went into completing it. When she flipped the switch on the disposal to grind up the scraps, nothing happened.

Immediately, she thought to tell John about it when he came home. He worked on the disposal every couple of months. She wanted to buy a new unit, but he argued that they could get by with the old one for now.

That was going to change. She needed to learn how to fix things around the house herself. Or hope that Robert and Lucas knew how.

Becky sat down to eat and started crying. She didn't know if she could do it. When the stake president had extended the calling to John, they had accepted. Church leaders had always counseled the members to accept callings. The tougher the task, the greater the reward.

Maybe they could call the stake president back and tell him they'd changed their minds. That too much was being asked of the family. Becky knew that she wasn't strong enough to do what they had asked.

She cried until the phone rang.

Carol Spence wanted to come over and finish the quilt she had started last week. She planned to send it to her niece as a wedding gift and needed to mail it by tomorrow.

Becky agreed and then went into the bathroom, washed her face, and brushed her hair. She put on a little makeup to cover any signs that she'd been crying. The doorbell rang as she finished checking herself in mirror. On the outside, she looked like her normal self. But on the inside she was a total wreck.

Having another person in the house helped. Becky and Carol talked about who had moved into the ward and who was planning to move out. They took a cookie break at about two o'clock and discussed the latest developments on their favorite television show, *Super Moms.* They had just put the last touches on the quilt when Robert returned home from job hunting.

"Great news, Mom," Robert announced as he walked through the door. "I start work tomorrow."

A sense of relief flowed through Becky as she heard the news, the power of the emotion disproportional to the actual importance of the event. Then again, maybe not. The family certainly could benefit from Robert having a job.

Becky rushed over and gave him a hug.

She was so proud of her tall, strong son. He'd left on his mission a promising youth and had come home a grown-up, wonderful man.

Then it hit her. This could be the reason so many of the missionaries had been coming home early. They were needed at home.

She didn't need to call the stake president.

Becky realized that her family would be up to the task set before them. Robert, Lucas, Elizabeth . . . all of the children had been raised in a good home that had taught them the value of faith and hard work. She wouldn't be doing this alone; she'd be doing this with her family.

Now all she had to do was explain that to the kids.

After dinner, Becky gathered everyone into the family room. She didn't know how to start the discussion. This was going to be a shocker. Eventually, she decided to start off with a hymn and a prayer. "Put Your Shoulder to the Wheel" struck her as an appropriate choice for a song. She hoped it would inspire her as to what to say.

"The stake president has asked us to prepare for the Second Coming," she blurted out when they finished singing.

The children all looked at her, apparently not sure what to make of her statement.

"This has to be kept just between us," John said. "The Church leadership wants to start gathering the Saints in preparation for the Second Coming."

"Are you sure?" asked Robert.

"That's intense," Lucas said.

"That's insane," said Sara.

Becky let the bedlam of responses ebb slightly before raising her hands to get their attention. "Let me finish and I'll answer your questions then."

Most of the children looked uneasy. Sara looked upset.

"The scriptures talk about a time of great unrest before the Savior returns," said John. "This may require us to physically remove ourselves from the rest of society."

"Like the weirdos who still practice polygamy?" Sara asked in a snide tone.

"No," said Becky. "Like Lehi and his family when they came to the Americas."

"And," said John, "like Lot when he left Sodom, before it was destroyed."

"Is the rest of the world going to be destroyed?" Cody asked. His voice trembled.

"We don't know what's going to happen," Becky replied quickly. "Right now, we're just being asked to get things ready in case that's necessary."

"Are we going to have to move?" asked Jesse.

"Not yet," Becky said. "Maybe not for a long time."

"We just don't know," John said. "I'm sure that at some point the prophet will make an announcement to all the members about the situation. Until then, I've been given a calling and asked to keep the matter within the family."

"They're keeping it secret?" Sara asked.

"I don't think it's that," John said. "They probably aren't ready to make a general announcement about it yet. It really isn't a secret if the bishoprics, the stake presidencies, and the families of everyone being asked to participate know about it."

"What are you being called to do?" Robert asked.

John placed his hands on the table and took a moment to look at each of the children. "I will be overseeing the construction of a self-sufficient, fenced community. A few buildings, a worker dorm, and an enormous farm."

"What about your job?" Sara asked.

"The General Authorities have been telling us for a year to be prepared," John said. "Having a year's supply includes stashing away enough money to pay your rent and utilities for a year; besides, I already took a salary cut, and they're talking about another round of layoffs."

"You have enough money saved for a year?" Lucas asked.

"More like six months," John said. "We should be fine."

"So everyone who will be working with you has a year's supply of money?" asked Lucas.

"I doubt it," said Becky. "There are a lot of people out of work. I'm sure there's a way to get them involved."

"How far will you have to drive every day to get there?" asked Cody.

Becky and John exchanged glances.

"I won't be driving," said John. "I'll be living there for the next six months. And while I'm gone, the rest of you will have work that needs to be done here."

12

'm still unable to reach Mr. Korshanenko," Gwen announced through the intercom.

The message broke Calvin's concentration on the files he'd gathered about the Houston bombing. He set the folder down and reached forward to activate the intercom button on his desk. "Keep trying. Let me know when you reach him."

"Mr. McCord, it's past midnight in Moscow. His office hasn't answered any of our calls all day. I don't think we'll be able to reach them until tomorrow morning."

That couldn't be good. Victor might be busy with other matters, but his assistant should be accepting calls and taking messages for him. Calvin considered the possibility that it was only a matter of a technical failure with the phone system.

He discarded it almost immediately. The upper echelon of Russian politics had a strong intolerance for mistakes, especially the type that left them looking weak to their Western counterparts.

Either Victor was avoiding his calls or his superiors were blocking them. In either case, it tipped Calvin off to their current frame of mind.

"Mr. McCord." Gwen's voice sounded through the intercom again.

"Go ahead and take off for the night, Gwen. I want to get an early start tomorrow. Can you be here by six?"

"I suppose so."

"See you then."

Calvin looked at his watch. Quarter till five. He had enough time to grab a quick bite before the "Washington After-Hours" show began. For years he'd despised the need for the backroom games that most of the Capitol crowd seemed to enjoy. Tonight he planned to take advantage of the city's addiction to secrecy.

He tossed the folders he had on the two terrorist attacks and Russian troop movements into his briefcase and locked it. No reservations would be necessary if he stopped in at one of his regular spots. They tended to be fast, greasy, and unpopular with the higher-ranked politicians.

By the time he reached the elevator, Calvin had settled on some Kentucky-style barbecue from the Rack Shack. Politics tended to kill his appetite, but if he planned to be working the bars, clubs, and popular hangouts most of the night, then he needed food in his stomach. It might as well be something he enjoyed.

He hailed a cab and instructed the driver to drop him off at the corner of Eighth Street. A short walk to the restaurant would give him time to plan out his tactical routing for the night and work up an appetite.

A young man dressed like a valet ran toward Calvin.

"Mr. McCord?"

Calvin nodded.

"Mr. Roscoe requests that you join him for dinner." The valet pointed to a fancy restaurant that Calvin had passed only moments ago. Keegan Roscoe stood on the front steps and waved.

Keegan had been the only person in Boggs's party to treat Calvin with respect. Most of Calvin's supposed allies in his own party didn't treat him nearly as well. That deserved some consideration in return.

"Tell Mr. Roscoe I accept."

The valet took off at a brisk pace and Calvin lifted his hand to signal Keegan he was on his way.

As Calvin walked, he considered how to best take advantage of this opportunity. In this new administration, he was essentially operating alone and behind enemy lines. He had to change tactics. To gain information about what was really happening with these terrorist attacks would require a stealthy approach.

The first step in a covert operation was to successfully insert yourself into the enemy ranks. From a hidden position he could gather intel until he was ready to strike and then launch a surprise attack. Dinner with Keegan fit the bill.

It seemed like sound military doctrine, but he wasn't taking on an army in the field; he was facing seasoned politicians on their home turf. Could the lessons of Sun Tzu be applied to this kind of a war?

For the sake of the country, he hoped so.

"Calvin." Keegan reached out and grasped hands. "Thank you so much for joining me. I hope I'm not disrupting any plans you had for the evening."

"Not at all." Calvin did his best to return the seeming warmth of the greeting. "You have saved me the trouble of deciding where to eat, and I appreciate the company."

Keegan escorted him through the restaurant to a large table where several people were already seated.

"I think you've met my wife, Eleanor." Keegan motioned toward an elegant-looking older lady. He went on to introduce Walter Hoff and his wife, Leslie, and Peter Fenton and his wife, Dora. Hoff and Fenton were both congressmen Calvin hadn't previously met. Handshakes were exchanged and Calvin sat down.

"I had started to think you were a myth," Hoff said.

"What do you mean?" Calvin asked.

"Considering the position that you hold in this administration, we don't see very much of you."

"Surely," said Keegan. "We can find a less confrontational

subject to discuss. Please keep in mind that I did ask Calvin here as my guest."

"Of course," said Hoff as he picked up a burgundy menu with antique-style bronze lettering and examined it.

Eleanor, Leslie, and Dora launched into a stream of banter about the freshness of the catch of the day, the correct wine pairing for the dishes they were ordering, and a smattering of news related to their pet charities. Polite. Safe. Banal. They fulfilled their roles as politicians' spouses with amazing proficiency.

The men ordered food, ordered drinks, and then talked about the stock market until the meal arrived. Calvin participated as much as his limited financial portfolio allowed.

"What is your take on the current economic situation?" Keegan asked Calvin midway through the main course.

Conversation had been carefully steered away from any topic ripe for dissension. Calvin scrambled to find a way to turn this into an exchange he could mine for information.

"I think it's a ticking bomb."

"That seems rather dramatic," Keegan said with a good-natured laugh.

"Yes," Hoff said dryly. "Want to explain yourself?"

"We are waist deep in the middle of a volatile situation," said Calvin. "If there is a continuation of recent events, I believe that we could see a second Civil War very soon."

"Is that a threat?" Fenton asked with a raised eyebrow.

"Mostly a prediction," said Calvin. "But it could stand as a warning about the consequences of our actions."

"Our party is not responsible for the botched attack in Charleston." Fenton sounded irritated. "That was an act of a lunatic. We could never condone violence against a women's support group."

"Oh, my." Keegan clasped his hands together, looking amused. "I guess the cat is out of the bag."

"What do you mean?" Hoff asked.

"Boggs is keeping me out of the loop on the terrorist investigation," said Calvin. "I only know what's been reported on the news channels. And they haven't said anything about identifying a suspect."

Fenton looked over at Keegan and Hoff, possibly hoping for them to help pull his foot out of his mouth.

"That's what I meant." Keegan grinned at Fenton. "Unless Calvin has a source inside our party, he was unaware of that information. Not to worry, Walter. It's only a matter of time before the investigating committee releases the details of the attempted attack to the press."

"The carefully selected details," said Calvin. "I imagine certain portions will be edited for the public."

"Why, Calvin," said Keegan. "You say that as if it's a bad thing."

"I have to admit that I'm not a big fan of censorship."

"And neither am I," said Keegan. "However, there are occasions when a full disclosure of an event can have catastrophic repercussions. I'm convinced that this may be one of those times when an exception must be made."

"All right." Calvin gave Keegan his full attention. "Convince me."

Keegan leaned over and placed his hand on his wife's arm. "Eleanor, would you and the rest of the ladies excuse us for a few minutes?"

"I have a better idea," said Eleanor. "Kendra Laney just arrived. You can excuse us so that we can talk to her about the upcoming Bethesda Literary Social."

The women made a gracious withdrawal from the table and the men sat back down.

"If the President wants Calvin kept in the dark about this," said Fenton, "I don't think we should discuss the matter any further."

"Nelson and I have been friends for a long time," Keegan said. "But we don't always agree on what needs to be done. Calvin is a resourceful individual. He will eventually uncover all of the details of this unfortunate event. Why not work with him instead of against him? These are troubling times that will require better cooperation between the two political parties if we are to prevail."

Hoff fidgeted with his suit jacket, giving an inordinate amount of attention to it.

Fenton grabbed his glass of wine and leaned back in his chair

Calvin thought they both looked a little nervous.

"Since there are no objections, I'll continue." Keegan shifted in his seat to face Calvin. "They have found the man who created the car bomb in Charleston. Unlike the suspects in the Houston bombing, this man is a United States citizen. He claims to be associated with the Political Anarchists group, but it is believed that he was recruited by a foreign power and merely used that as his cover."

"Is that what you're going to tell the public?"

"Actually, we're going to connect the dots for them. Since the Anarchists have no membership records to prove otherwise, we plan to advise the public that the suspect was recruited by a terrorist organization located in the Middle East."

"The fact that he posed as a member of a fringe element of your party will be left out," Calvin said.

"As you mentioned previously," Keegan said, "we're waist deep in the middle of a volatile situation. There is no need to escalate the already high levels of tension between our two parties. Don't you agree?"

Keegan made a good point, especially when one considered that Boggs's party was being framed for the attacks. As soon as any connection was made between the Political Anarchists and the terrorist attacks, a segment of the population would blame Boggs. It wouldn't matter that it had all been a setup; Boggs and his party would be considered accomplices and the blood would flow in the streets.

Which probably accounted for why Boggs had made no attempt to ferret out the real masterminds behind this plot. If the early leads pointed them in the direction of the Middle East, the public would willingly accept them as the culprits. Without knowing who was pulling all the strings, the trail of accusations could lead anywhere, including right back to Boggs.

"Is that why you asked me to have dinner with you?" Calvin asked.

"You give me too much credit." Keegan waved off the comment. "If I could manipulate a dinner conversation in the manner you suggest, why . . . I'd be the President."

The crafty old devil. Calvin had accepted Keegan's invitation in the hopes of mining the seasoned politician for information. Now he wondered if Keegan had planned this all along. Calvin suspected that he'd been played.

He lifted his glass of wine in the air. "Agreed."

Long after the wives returned and the conversation had moved on to matters less political, Calvin's mind remained on what Keegan had said. Keegan was, after all, a politician. What if this terrorist hadn't been recruited by agents in the Middle East? What if this terrorist hadn't been recruited by any foreign agency?

The dinner with Keegan lasted longer than Calvin had expected. It was nearly twenty-one hundred hours by the time they went their separate ways. Keegan picked up the tab and made Calvin promise to dine with him again next week.

For what Calvin had in mind, working the Washington hangouts at a later hour meant that his contacts in the military community had had plenty of time to drink themselves into a talkative mood. Not that they'd reveal anything that would get them into serious trouble.

It took three stops and twice that many rounds of drinks before he connected with the son of an old army buddy. The unit Tadd served with would be the most likely to be deployed in response to a Russian threat. They swapped war stories for a couple of hours, and in the process Calvin got a better picture of the current status of the active units and a feel for the kind of action they were expecting.

If the Russians were planning a military action, the United States was in no position to respond. Worse yet, based on the scuttlebutt

Tadd had picked up from his friends overseas, the Russians were on the move.

Maybe Boggs shouldn't be blamed for not wanting to keep a closer eye on the Siberian Bear. It'd been a long time since the nation had demonstrated any aggressive tendencies. It made no sense for them to start now.

The President expected Calvin to bring the Russians to the diplomatic table based solely on the strength of his relationship with Victor Korshanenko, but that wasn't going to be enough political clout to prevent the war that was brewing.

Calvin took a cab home. He went into the den and sat down at his desk. In the bottom drawer he kept a cell phone locked away. A single number had been programmed into it that would connect him to a private phone that only Victor answered. The two of them had arranged this hotline years ago.

Looking at his watch, Calvin calculated it to be 10:27 a.m. in Moscow.

He punched the number and let the phone ring.

And ring.

And ring.

"Do not speak." Victor's voice came through the phone. "Is sad day for me. For us. I can no longer work with you toward a mutual goal of peace, my friend. I am sorry.

"Do not contact me again."

The line disconnected.

13

It took two hours to reach Camp Valiant. John's Suburban, hauling a large generator on a trailer, and a pair of extended passenger vans with gear-packed roofs all stopped next to a construction trailer. Piles of wood, rolls of wire, and pallets of other building supplies occupied the ground nearby.

When the vehicles stopped, John stepped out of the Suburban, stretched his legs, and looked around. The land was mostly flat and full of grayish-green brush. A few cottonwood trees broke up the otherwise plain landscape. There were no signs of civilization within sight. The closest community was over twenty miles away along a thin path that didn't even qualify as a dirt road.

This would be his home for the next six months. Dull. Isolated. Primitive.

He suspected that this was just one of many parcels of Church-owned real estate being prepared for the literal gathering of the Saints. How many times was this same scene being played out across the country? Across the world?

Over the next few months the men gathered here would labor to transform this consecrated land into a budding town. They would clear the land, erect fences around the borders, and build the key structures that would be necessary for the town to grow to its full size. However big that might be.

They were on the eve of the great and terrible day. How truly great and wonderful it would be when this place reached its fullest potential; families working side-by-side in the spirit of true fellowship and brotherly love. And how terrible would be the destruction that had been prophesied to soon follow.

"I don't want to rush you," said one of the drivers. "But we'll need to be headed back home in a couple of hours. If we unload the vehicles right away, Rick and I can help you set up the tents before we take off with the vans."

"Good idea," said John. They had a little over six hours until dusk. An interim camp needed to be set up before dark.

He climbed on top of a bundled stack of preassembled rafters and called out. "Can everyone come on over here, please?"

John motioned for Bill Summers and Luis Garcia to stand with him. Bill was a tall, lanky man with an infectious grin. Luis had the swarthy skin of his Hispanic heritage and was built like a fort. The three of them represented the leaders who had been set apart for this venture.

He wasn't much for giving speeches, but it seemed like the appropriate time for some sort of motivational talk. John worried, briefly, that this might amount to an historic moment and that his unprepared comments would somehow be recorded and forever mark him as an inarticulate doofus. Fortunately, the handful of men who were gathered here weren't likely to remember much of what he said long enough to record it.

"While all of you are working out the kinks in your muscles, I wanted to take a minute to address everyone. As you know, I have been assigned to oversee the first stage of this project. Luis Garcia," John motioned to the man on his right, "will be directing the construction of the worker dorm, the warehouse, and the machine shop."

John pointed at Bill. "Farming operations will be led by Bill Summers. His group will have the responsibility of building fences and clearing the trees and bushes from areas where we will eventually be planting crops."

"Does anyone have a question about which group they belong to?" None of the men raised their hands.

"That's a good start," John continued. Then his mind jammed.

Here they were, on the brink of the next era of human history. Prophets had foretold of this time for thousands of years. Dozens of books had been printed on the topic. People frequently speculated about the end times. But all the things that John could say about their current endeavor and the events that soon would come to pass—nothing came to mind.

Except fear.

John hated public speaking. He feared standing in front of a crowd, however small, and drawing a blank on what to say. For long seconds he could only focus on how this was the moment he had so often dreaded.

"I—," John croaked. He took a deep breath. "I know how easily someone could be scared by this moment. We are moving from lives of comfort and routine toward the unknown. None of us knows what awaits us there. The next many years will be a journey that is sure to test our faith and our resolve."

The words flowed from him. Not his words. They passed through his mouth without conscious thought.

"If those are the thoughts that occupy your minds, then, brethren, you need to change your focus. You need to put your mind on a different path."

John paused to let the words sink in.

"The Lord is eternal. His work is eternal. And this is an important part of His work. All of us have participated in service projects where we have picked up a hammer or rake and worked together. Many of us served missions in foreign lands that seemed strange to us at first. This is not so different from what we have already done. Concentrate on the work and let the Lord take care of the rest."

That was it. The words stopped flowing. It was time to move on.

"All of that starts tomorrow. In the meantime, we need to set up camp. The first order of business is to unload the vehicles. If everyone is ready, let's get started."

John hopped down from his impromptu platform and consulted with Bill and Luis. He assigned Bill's group to set up the tents the men would be sleeping in until the dorm was finished. Luis and the men in his group were tasked with hooking up the generator to the construction trailer that would serve as their temporary kitchen/command center and then unloading the food and medical supplies from the vans.

By one o'clock both groups had accomplished their initial tasks, and John called for a late lunch break. All twenty-four men called to serve at Camp Valiant, and the two drivers, pulled out sack lunches and ate.

None of the men seemed interested in talking. A few of them knew each other, but for the most part this was a gathering of strangers.

"If I can get a couple of volunteers," John said to break the silence, "I'll work on making sure we have something hot to eat for dinner."

Several of the men raised their hands. John selected two that he didn't already know. They introduced themselves as Jeff King and Curtis Powell.

A conversation-free lunch was a quick lunch. The drivers finished eating and left. John put everyone else back to work. He had a reasonably long list of tasks that were necessary to make the camp habitable.

Jeff and Curtis were sent inside to take inventory of the food and see what could be whipped together to make a reasonably quick meal that night. John planned to hand out assignments to the rest of the men and then help the dinner crew set up the kitchen. That included devising a menu and kitchen-duty roster for the rest of the week. Afterward, he could make bunking assignments.

Midway through his list, a truck arrived with the two portable outhouses that they would be using in camp until permanent facilities had been built. He directed the driver where to unload the potties, signed for delivery, and then returned to handing out work assignments.

Tools were handed out to the crew tackling the first item on the list. John had almost finished explaining what needed to be done when a truck arrived with their water.

He excused himself from the men and directed the placement of the mobile water tank. That took longer than he expected. Jeff and Curtis were now waiting in line to see him.

It took another hour before everyone had been put to work. Trucks delivering a tractor, a compact track loader, and a mini-excavator delayed him even further. By the time they had the kitchen ready to cook the evening meal, it was already dark and the men were gathered around the trailer.

Fried Spam and canned pork & beans. Really, not a lot different than what John fixed the kids at home when Becky had a meeting. Everyone was hungry enough that they ate what was given them without too much complaining.

As the three of them were cleaning up after dinner, John remembered that he hadn't made a bunk chart. Did he really need one? These were grown men, not a bunch of teenagers on a campout. He decided to forgo any formalized sleeping arrangement and returned to cleaning the kitchen.

After he finished cleaning, he retrieved his sleeping bag and wandered over to the mismatched collection of tents. Jeff, Curtis, and two more men stood there, personal gear at their feet.

"The tents are full," said Curtis.

No way. John had done the calculations himself. Twenty-four men. They had six four-man tents. There should be plenty of room for everyone.

"We'll sort it out tomorrow," John said. "It might be a little snug, but two of us could fit in the back of the Suburban and the rest of us can either make room inside the trailer or sleep outside."

"It's pretty nice outside," said Jeff. "I think I'll just sleep on a tarp. I'll pick a spot away from the outhouses."

"Good idea," said one of the other men. "Maybe tomorrow we can look into getting them moved somewhere else."

John grabbed another tarp and followed Jeff. He unrolled his sleeping bag, kicked off his shoes, and crawled into bed. It took several tries to position himself so there were no rocks prodding him in the back.

His thoughts drifted toward home. At this time of night, Becky would be curled up on the couch, blanket over her legs, reading a book or possibly watching her dancing show. She allowed herself half an hour before bed to wind down at the end of the day. Right now she would be comfortable and warm.

How he wished he were with her.

14

Women love a man in a uniform.

At least, Robert had always heard that in the movies. He stood in front of the mirror in his room and adjusted his shirt. By the time he reached work it would be out of place again, but for the moment, he looked good.

Camden Security used a dark gray uniform with a patch over the left breast that looked like a police badge even though it identified him as an unarmed security professional. Robert liked the way he looked in it. For eighteen months he had worn the uniform of a missionary, and now this. Both made him look mature, capable . . . and confident.

Maybe if he looked guard-ish enough, no one would suspect that he didn't know what he was doing. Or how nervous he felt.

Not that it made any sense to be nervous. Security guards mostly just stood around and watched buildings. Any conflict he encountered would be with the forces of boredom. All he needed to do today was stay awake and smile.

A cursory check of the pantry failed to uncover anything that looked particularly tasty. He decided on some un-toasted strawberry Pop Tarts and ate them on the way to his first assignment.

He rolled down the car window and enjoyed the cool morning air as he drove to work. The smell from the newly bloomed citrus trees made him feel a bit heady. This was going to be a beautiful day to start a new job.

Mrs. Landing had told him to head over to Fresh Foods today. At first, he found it strange they would send him to watch over a grocery store. He couldn't remember ever having seen a guard in that kind of setting. Then he thought about his mother being robbed a couple of weeks ago, and it made a lot more sense.

Fresh Foods seemed unusually busy for that time of the morning, not that Robert shopped enough to be an expert. He reported to Miguel Cruz, who introduced him to the employees and gave him a brief tour of the store.

"Our main delivery arrives around ten on Tuesdays and Thursdays," said Miguel. "There are also a few smaller vendors who only deliver when we place an order. You'll need to check the schedule each day to find out if there are additional deliveries and what time they'll arrive."

Miguel pointed to a clip board hanging on the stockroom wall. Robert scanned it and noticed two deliveries were scheduled for the day.

"We want you to patrol the area outside the docks about ten minutes before the shipments arrive and then stay on the dock while the driver and employees unload the trucks."

"Got it," Robert said. "What do I do the rest of the time?"

Miguel scratched his head as he looked around him. "Whatever it is that they normally have you do—I guess."

Great, thought Robert. What did he know about security assignments?

"Our biggest problem," Miguel continued, "has been people being robbed in the parking lot. But we've also had a few really big arguments between customers in the meat department. Standing at the front entrance and greeting people when they come into the store might not be a bad idea. They do that at the bank."

"Why don't I do all three?" Robert watched to see what kind of reaction Miguel had to his suggestion.

"That's going to be a lot of walking for you," said Miguel. "Let's do it that way for now and see how it works."

Miguel returned to the duties of a store manager and Robert started walking.

It took all of ten minutes to stroll around the interior of the store. He stopped at the meat department. His amusement over having to guard meat faded when he saw the number of people waiting at the butcher counter. There were more people in line here than in all of the checkout stands combined.

The biggest part of his job, as Mrs. Landing had explained it to him, was to be a visible reminder for people to mind their manners. This seemed like a good spot for that.

Robert positioned himself near the butcher. During the tour of the store, Miguel had introduced the man as Jerry.

Customers waiting in line cast evil glances in Robert's direction. At least it seemed that way to him. Maybe they were just tired of waiting. In either case, Robert wished they would keep their eyes on the butcher instead.

During his mission, not everyone had been thrilled to see him on their doorstep. But when that happened, he knew that they were reacting to the Church, or religion in general, and not him personally. The same was true here. These people resented the authority and enforcement of the rules that he embodied.

Understanding that made the unhappy stares a little easier to endure.

"Why can't I have three pounds of ground chuck?" asked a large woman with red, curly hair.

"A couple of our shipments have been delayed. We're asking our customers to buy only what they need for the next few days." Jerry sounded as if he was tired of explaining it.

"Okay," said the woman. "You asked me. I still need three pounds of hamburger."

"Please." Jerry rubbed his temple. "I'd be happy to wrap up two pounds of our best ground chuck for you. I can't give you any more than that."

"I thought you said you were *asking* us to limit our buys. My family needs to eat. You can't let us starve." The woman rested her fists on her hips and stared at Jerry.

Jerry stared back at her.

"Fine," the woman relented when the next customer in line began grumbling about having to wait even longer because of her. "Give me two pounds of your lean ground chuck and a pound of regular hamburger."

"That's still three pounds of ground beef. What if you take the two pounds of chuck and a pork roast? I have a nice eight-pound roast that should last two or three meals if you plan it correctly."

The woman said nothing but gave an angry nod of acceptance. She took the meat and stormed off toward the produce section.

Jerry worked his way through a few more customers. They looked over to Robert as they stepped up to place their orders and seemed to be more restrained because of his presence. Even so, something about the situation nagged at the back of Robert's mind.

Five minutes before the first delivery, Robert walked out to the loading dock. The area inside the building looked all right, though he didn't really have anything to compare it to.

Robert opened the back door and stepped outside. It had warmed up since he arrived at work. He scanned the back lot and spied two men sitting against the wall that surrounded the property.

When the men noticed Robert watching them, they stood up and left.

Robert wondered if all this security work had him paranoid. Six months ago he wouldn't have thought twice about seeing a couple of people kicking back like that. Now it made him suspicious.

When the truck arrived, Robert opened the big rolling doors and watched as the store employees unloaded it. He kept an eye out for the two men, but they did not return.

Miguel signed for the shipment. The driver closed the back of the truck and left. Robert helped close the dock doors.

"I noticed that the store is short on beef," Robert said. "Did any come in?"

"Some," Miguel said. "Not enough to fill our order. Beef shipments have been down for the last three months."

"Why don't people just eat more chicken?"

"I wish they would." Miguel looked over the shipment. "It doesn't work that way, though. If people think there's an actual shortage of beef, or any kind of food, they buy more because they worry that it might run out. That makes the situation worse. The supplies are already limited and an increased demand can result in our being completely sold out. And if we run out of a few items because everyone is stocking up, people may think that we are running out of food altogether and panic."

"I get it." Robert stopped him. "People do stupid things when they're worried about starving. Having me in the store will keep everyone calm."

"Let's hope so." Miguel gathered a pair of stock boys and directed them on what items needed to go out to the floor immediately.

Robert still had his mind on the men that had been sitting outside. He made a pass through the store and didn't see any area that looked troublesome. Then he went out the front entrance.

A circuit through the parking lot didn't turn up any sign of the two men, or anyone else that looked suspicious. He made a second pass around the lot and then posted himself at the entrance. From there, if he moved around a little, he could keep an eye on what was happening both inside and outside the store.

About fifteen minutes before the afternoon delivery was scheduled to arrive, he walked around the outside of the store to the back, where the loading dock was located. When he turned the corner, he spotted the two men.

They stood less than ten feet from him.

This was a different position than where he'd seen them earlier in the day. From here, they could see the shipments arrive at the dock without being seen themselves.

Both of the men were older than Robert, but not by much.

They were in pretty decent shape and had a rugged look to them, like construction workers. One was tall and had dark, curly hair. The other had close-cropped blond hair with a bald spot in the back. Both wore jeans and flannel shirts.

The men spun around to face Robert.

His mind raced. His heart raced even faster. These men might be dangerous. If they decided to attack him, he was in serious trouble.

Instead they ran.

Robert ran after them. He didn't mean to. He just did. His body acted on its own accord. They had a good lead, but he was getting closer. Until—

As he rounded the big trash bin, he felt his left foot slide on a patch of gravel. Robert regained enough of his balance to prevent him from slamming into the ground.

That's where he should stay. On the ground. Or better yet, he should go back inside the store and report the incident to Miguel. The training tapes he'd watched at Camden Security explicitly stated that guards should not engage any individuals. Observe and record only.

Robert sprang up and continued chasing the two men.

The men clambered over the top of a block wall that ran along the back end of the property and dropped from sight. By the time Robert pulled himself up on the wall, the men were gone.

As Robert sat atop the wall and tried to catch his breath, he wondered what would've happened if he had caught those men.

15

Becky woke up alone.

For a few seconds, her mind raced for an explanation. Then she remembered the calling. John would be gone for at least six months.

It wasn't as if they'd never been separated before. He'd been away on business and gone to camp with the Scouts. She went for a week every year to visit her parents. And they normally spent a good portion of their time away from one another.

When she knew she would see her sweetheart at the end of the day, or the end of the week, she focused on the tasks that needed her attention and paid little heed to the time apart. But in this situation, Becky felt the weight of the entire six-month absence crush her heart like a giant obsidian stone.

She shook her head to toss aside the unwanted thoughts and then climbed out of bed for her morning prayer. By the time she finished, the dark, lonely thoughts had fled.

This morning's breakfast represented the first one featuring the new "budget menu" that Becky had worked up. The last of the individually packaged oatmeal had run out and she cooked one large batch of oats with the option of raisins and pecan bits to go with it.

"Yuck," Elizabeth said. "What else can I have?"

"If you don't like plain oatmeal, you can have oatmeal deluxe," said Becky, doing her best to sell the change in menu.

"No thanks; I hate oatmeal."

"I suppose you could fix yourself toast and jam, if you want."

"Good idea."

"How about cereal?" asked Cody.

"Oatmeal is cereal," said Becky. "It's hot cereal and it's good for you."

"Noooooo, Mom." Cody shuffled, still sleepy-eyed, over to the pantry. "I want Cap'n Crunch—with crunch berries."

"Sorry, honey. I didn't buy any cold cereal. It costs too much. Besides, it's mostly sugar anyway. I can put raisins and nuts in the oatmeal and I'm sure you'll like it."

"All riiiiight." Cody returned to the table and plopped down with a *humph*.

Sara breezed into the kitchen midway through the meal. She sneered at the oatmeal and then checked the pantry. "No cereal?"

"I didn't get any," Becky replied.

"No Pop Tarts?"

"They're not in the budget anymore," said Becky.

"What about microwaveable pancakes?"

"I'm saving them for tomorrow."

"Fine," Sara said. "I'll just skip breakfast. See you this evening."

"Aren't you coming home after school?" Becky asked.

"Nope. I have plans with Tracey and Tina." Sara swooped up her school bag and left the house before Becky could reply.

The rest of the children finished breakfast and Becky drove them to school. Their old Chevy Tracker sputtered a couple of times along the way but made it back to the house safely.

President Banks had given Becky the task of rounding up whatever furniture and appliances she could find to send out to John and the others at the construction site. Since the call for the Saints to gather had not been officially announced, she needed to avoid explaining the exact nature of the donations.

Her first call went to Trudy Mendenhall.

"Any chance you have furniture around the house you might consider donating to a good cause?" Becky asked.

"I have a couch in the garage that's in pretty good shape, but I plan to sell it. My husband had to take a cut in pay this year. We need the money."

"How about any appliances? An extra toaster or clothes iron?"

"We do have a few items like that, but we plan to sell them too. This is just not a very good time for us to be making donations."

"I understand," Becky said. "Thanks. I hope the situation improves for you."

The ward had over three hundred families and Becky knew about half of them. It took all morning to contact her friends in the ward and the rest of the day to reach out to those she didn't know as well.

For all that effort, she had gotten donations of an old bunk bed, a pair of heavily used toaster ovens, and a fridge that might not work. Just like Trudy's family—just like Becky's family—people had to make do with less. And that meant John and the other volunteers would have to get by with even less than that.

She was about to start calling the names on the list that she didn't know when she noticed that it was time to pick the kids up from school. The Tracker stalled on the way back, but it started up again a couple of minutes later.

At home, the children went into the kitchen to grab a snack and do their homework. Becky took the ward roster and found a spot in the living room where she could make the rest of her calls.

If the active members were reluctant, or unable, to help out, she held little hope that those who hadn't attended church in years would contribute. They might even laugh at her for asking.

Should she even try?

She studied the names on the list. A few of them she remembered from the time when they'd been active. They were good people. The gospel just didn't fit into their lives anymore.

John needed her to do as much as she could with this task.

President Banks expected her to do her best. And maybe the inactives needed to be a part of this.

The first three people she called politely stated they were not interested in any involvement with the Church and hung up. Two apologized for not having anything to give and wished her well in her hunt. Another laughed and hung up.

Then she called Al Bitman.

"You're collecting furniture for people who don't have any?" Al asked in a rough, raspy voice.

"That and any household items that might be useful."

"Yeah, I'd like to help."

"You would?" The question slipped out of her mouth unbidden. Immediately she regretted having said it.

"People everywhere have it tough right now," Al said. "If I weren't a handyman, I don't know that I'd still have a roof over my head. As it is, folks are more willing to pay me to fix what's broken rather than shelling out money they don't have to buy it new."

"That's great. I . . . I mean, it's great that you're willing to help us out. Do you mind if I mark down what you'll be donating?"

"I have an old wooden kitchen set that one of my customers traded me to fix their fridge. It's a little worn, but really solid. I can slap a new finish on it and it should look almost new and hold up nicely."

"Wonderful!" Becky raised her fist in victory. The work crews at the farm probably needed four or five kitchen sets. This was a good start.

"It's kind of funny that you called," Al said.

"How so?"

"Been thinking about God. I don't know that I'm ready to go back to church. However, it seems like a good idea to start talking to Him again. Helping you folks out might ensure that He's willing to listen."

"Being a good neighbor creates a better community for everyone who lives here."

"That too," Al said. "Anyway, if you run across any appliances that aren't working, I can take a look at them, and as long as some-one is willing to pay for the parts they need, I'll be happy to fix them for you."

Becky figured she could make another round of calls for ques-tionable donations. She didn't know if President Banks would pay for a few parts, but it would be worth a try. If nothing else, maybe Al could salvage parts from some of the appliances to get a few of them working.

"Fantastic," she nearly shouted. "I have a refrigerator for you to look at."

"Bring it over Tuesday."

Unfortunately, none of the rest of the calls went that well. As she thought about putting the roster back in the drawer and report-ing her failure to President Banks, Lucas came into the room and dropped himself on the couch.

"What's up, Mom?"

"I was trying to scrounge enough furniture for your father's group so they won't have to sit and sleep on the ground. That and whatever household items we can get to make their stay more comfortable."

"And how's that going?"

"Not very well, I'm afraid. A few of the active families weren't home and I plan to call them again tonight. Even if all of them donate a couple items, we'll still be short of what they need."

"I can help," Lucas said matter-of-factly.

"That's very sweet of you, but I need to make the calls myself."

"Does the stuff have to be donated by ward members?"

Becky stopped scanning the roster and looked at her son. Out of the mouth of babes—or in this case, teens. "What did you have in mind?"

"Jesse and me can call the rest of the guys in our quorums and go around the neighborhood checking to see if any of the neighbors are willing to donate items to a good cause. Then at the end of the week we can borrow President Banks's trailer and collect all of it. That way all that President Banks has to do is drive it over to Dad and they can unload it."

"Do you think the rest of the boys would be willing to do that?"

"No problem," Lucas said. "Our priesthood leaders have been after us to find a service project to work on together. This should make them happy."

A lump caught in Becky's throat.

As a parent, she spent a goodly portion of her time teaching her children to make good choices, noble choices. Then when they did, it surprised her.

"It's like you always say," Lucas said as he stood up and headed for the kitchen. "We have to rely on one another."

16

As his car slowed to a stop, Calvin prepared himself to walk the gauntlet. He adjusted his tie, checked to make sure all the buttons on his jacket were in place, and then checked his hair in the rearview mirror. A valet opened the door and helped Calvin and his "date" out of the dark blue Buick Regal.

Camera flashes blinded him for a moment. He used the pretense of offering his arm to Della to allow his vision to return. Della had dressed in an elegant but reserved black evening dress with a string of pearls. Her auburn hair shined. She looked beautiful.

On the crowded sidewalk, which was blocked by Secret Service agents, someone announced the surprise arrival of the Secretary of State. If the reporter only knew . . . nobody was more surprised by his attendance at tonight's gala than Calvin was himself.

"Wave to the nice people," Della told Calvin.

Calvin did. He even smiled. That didn't help him traverse the twenty feet from the street to inside the building any quicker or easier. He'd rather have been threading his way through a minefield.

His mind was so focused on getting out of the press zone that he nearly missed the two men standing in the crowd. In a solid mass of people, they attracted his attention. They didn't have cameras. They weren't smiling or trying to get the attention of the political well-knowns as they arrived. They were watching the crowd.

One of them reached into a coat pocket and pulled out a pack of cigarettes. The second man stopped him before he could unpack a smoke; the gesture he used had a European quality to it. Even though he had only gotten a quick look at the label, the blue and gold cigarette pack might be a brand popular in Romania and Croatia.

A tug on his sleeve brought Calvin's attention back to Della and the party.

"What do they do?" Della asked.

"I'm not sure. I was just wondering the same thing."

"Calvin." Della took his hand and squeezed it. "If I can pretend to be your date, then the least you can do is pretend to pay attention to me."

"I'm sorry. What did you ask?"

"I asked what this charity does."

"I don't know. Rescues puppies. Hands out books on Renaissance art to inner-city kids. What does it matter? I'm here and smiling. That should be enough."

"If you really want to make an impression on these people, then you need to take an interest in what interests them. Like for instance—this charity. Seriously, Calvin. Get with the program."

"Roscoe told me it was for the Children's Fundamentals Foundation."

"They do good work," said Della. "I should be able to find a couple of points of interest to talk about should the need arise."

Calvin spotted Walter Hoff and his wife near the entrance. The CFF was Leslie Hoff's pet project. Attending this event would help demonstrate Calvin's commitment to working with the members of the government family that were on the other side of the political divide.

In order to affect the events that were ripping the country apart, Calvin needed to stay in his current position. To do that, he needed allies. Keegan Roscoe had been kind enough to arrange for this invitation for Hoff's charity, and Calvin planned to make the most of it.

"Quite a turnout, Walter." Calvin shook hands with Hoff.

"I hadn't realized you were interested in the CFF," said Leslie.

"The children are our future," said Calvin. It sounded cliché. What did an old warhorse like him know about chatting at a fancy party like this?

"Who is this?" Walter gave a nod of his head toward Della. "Did you remarry recently?"

"Della and I are old friends. We were military brats on a lot of the same bases. Then later on I served with her husband."

"A husband." Leslie arched an eyebrow. "Is he here too?"

"No," said Calvin. "Frank passed away three years ago next March."

"I'm sorry." Leslie put a hand over her mouth.

"He fought in both Gulf Wars," Della said. "Served two tours in Afghanistan. Then he retired and was shot during a mini-mart robbery."

"That's terrible." Leslie reached out and laid a hand on Della's arm.

"Well, that is part of the past," Della said. "And tonight is about the children."

"Good for you," said Walter, excusing the two of them so they could greet another arrival and moving quickly away.

Calvin allowed Della to take the lead as they wandered through the gathering. He nodded his head, shook hands, and tried his best to form some sort of witty banter to exchange with people that lived in the same city as he, but not in the same world.

He spotted the Fentons and steered their way. Peter offered a polite smile and introduced Calvin and Della to his acquaintances. They included a senator, a program director for one of Boggs's think tanks, a policy analyst, and a pair of high-end supporters that worked in the entertainment industry. None of them seemed particularly happy to see Calvin, but, then again, none of them offered the icy glares with which he was normally greeted nowadays.

Eventually, he crossed paths with Keegan.

"I see that you took my advice and decided to mingle with us Visigoths." Keegan laughed. "Is this charming woman with you?"

"She's easier on the eyes than I am," said Calvin. "I figured that anyone who got trapped talking to me might appreciate something else to look at."

"Indeed." Keegan shook her hand, giving a slight incline of his head as he did. "I appreciate it already."

"Anyone here you think I should meet?" Calvin asked.

"Of course. Follow me." Keegan scanned the room around him and then pointed toward a group of men and women nearby. "Tonight is an excellent time for reaching across the fence. Charities bring out a wonderful sense of magnanimity. People come to these events with open hearts. The free-flowing booze helps as well."

They spent about half an hour moving and mingling through the crowd. Keegan seemed to know everyone there. If he didn't, he sure knew how to fake it. They stopped when their path brought them next to a refreshment table stacked with a dizzying assortment of upscale crackers piled with expensive cheeses and spreads.

"How are you holding up?" Keegan asked.

"I'm nervous." Calvin smiled at a couple as they passed by.

"Considering you attend so few social functions," Keegan said, "I would expect you to be terrified in a civilized environment such as this."

"That too."

"Then I take it there's something else bothering you." Keegan took two glasses from the table and offered Della one of them. "What is it?"

"Iran."

"I thought it was the Russians that were stirring up trouble."

"They are." Calvin grabbed a glass for himself and took a drink. "My sources tell me they've moved into defensive positions around Iran."

"Your sources?" Keegan looked over at Della with a sly smile. "Is your companion in the military?"

"Della's husband had a long career in the army before he died. A surprising amount of information can be gathered from the military spouse network if you know how to read between the lines."

"I have no doubt you are proficient in doing that," Keegan said.

"Don't get the wrong idea," Della said. "It's not like the spouses can't keep their mouths shut. They do. Calvin just has a knack for noticing what isn't being talked about."

"That isn't surprising," Keegan said. "A man with Calvin's background doesn't make it as far as he has without a significant amount of insight. I knew he was resourceful, but I hadn't truly appreciated the extent of his talents."

"Wait until you know him better," Della said. "I think you'll find that he's full of surprises."

Any chance for Keegan to respond was interrupted by a commotion from outside. The event itself, whatever it might be, couldn't be heard, but a ripple of confusion spread throughout the crowd. Agitation replaced the gentle tones of conversation.

Even as the attendees moved forward to discover the cause of the disturbance, the Secret Service agents mobilized. Their hands went to ears as they listened for instructions on their earbuds. Then they set about turning the crowd away from the front entrance and the windows.

For someone unfamiliar with security protocols, the actions of the agents might be curious, but they wouldn't be alarming. To Calvin, this was the response to a serious threat. The agents did not engage in idle chatter with the civilians; they firmly herded the crowd toward the rooms in the back of the building.

"Della," Calvin said, "would you like to talk to Keegan about the CFF while I answer the call of nature?"

Calvin didn't wait for a response; he moved against the flow of traffic. If this represented a real threat against the patrons assembled here, then more agents were on their way. Any chance to slip by and see what was going on outside would vanish once they reinforced the security team.

He wiggled his way toward a spot where two of the agents had allowed a bigger gap than they could cover. Once he arrived on the fringe of the receding party, he waited until both agents had turned their heads before moving between them, doing his best to look casual as he did it.

Two more agents stood in front of the door; it was closed and most likely locked. Approaching them would get him a personal escort to join the other patrons and the continued notice of the Secret Service until this crisis was over. Instead he headed for a set of windows with the most limited view by the agents.

He looked outside. Down the block a car burned in the street. Police formed a living wall between the CFF event and hundreds of placard-wielding protestors. The protestors had just begun to throw bricks at the police when a hand grasped Calvin's shoulder and spun him around.

"Mr. McCord," said a Secret Service agent, backed up by two others. "You'll need to come with us."

17

The two men didn't return. Robert watched for the rest of the week without catching even a glimpse of them anywhere near the store. He figured they would eventually come back, but he was reassigned to the Healthy Partners call center after his shift on Thursday.

Why transfer him to a different post when he had everything in control? There'd been no more fights between the customers, no more robberies, and no problems on the loading dock. Not that he thought he had turned the situation around in three days. Just having a guard on the premises was probably enough to convince people to behave, or at least take their trouble somewhere else.

Still, he felt a sense of accomplishment and didn't want another assignment.

While he sat next to the phone in the kitchen, he figured he might as well call Sierra and verify their date for the next night. She didn't answer. He left a message and hung up.

As soon as he placed the phone in its charging cradle, it rang.

"Hello, this is Robert."

"What a coincidence; you're just the person I wanted to see." The voice sounded like Bishop Porter.

"When would you like to see me, Bishop?"

"How about my office in an hour?"

A call from the bishop almost always meant he had a church assignment. An hour seemed like short notice. This close to the weekend, Robert expected it would require him to start on it right away.

"Sure," said Robert. "I'll be there."

An hour proved to be plenty of time to grab a sandwich, change into his church clothes, and drive over to the ward building. Then he sat for twenty minutes while the bishop finished with the previous appointment.

Bishop Porter walked out of his office with the Smiths. They talked for another five minutes about the upcoming Easter pageant. The bishop finally bid them farewell and waved Robert into his office.

"How's everything at home?" Bishop Porter asked.

"Fine, I guess." Robert shrugged. "Mom's still a little shook up about being robbed, and we all miss Dad, but otherwise things are good."

"I know it's a tough situation for your family right now. I also know that they can depend on you to help out while your father is gone. However, if you ever feel like you're in over your head, you can give me a call. It's important to remember that we're not alone. All of us are working through a tough time right now and we can help one another."

"Thanks."

"Your mother tells me you found a job," Bishop Porter said.

"I'm working for Camden Security as a guard."

The bishop laughed.

"It's not the best job in the world," Robert started.

The bishop waved off his comment. "I'm sorry. I wasn't laughing at the job; it's just ironic when you consider the reason I asked to see you."

Robert didn't know how to react to that. There wasn't supposed to be an ironic link between the line of work you did to support yourself and the job you did within the Church.

"Robert, I have a calling I would like to extend to you."

"I sort of expected that."

Bishop Porter reached forward to a bowl of cinnamon hard candies that sat on his desk. He offered one to Robert and then grabbed one himself. "Will you be our ward security specialist?"

"You want me to guard the church?" All right, it did strike Robert as a bit funny.

"So to speak." The bishop leaned back in his chair. "There's more to the calling than what you're probably thinking."

"I've never heard of a ward security specialist."

"No surprise there," Bishop Porter said. "It's something new. With the growing levels of violence everywhere, we have to consider the best methods to use to ensure our safety. I'm not expecting you to organize a militia to fight off armed mobs, but we do need to decide what precautions to take to keep the members safe at church and at home."

"Are you sure you have the right person?" Robert asked. "This sounds like a pretty serious responsibility. Maybe someone a little bit older than me or someone who served in the army."

"There's no doubt in my mind that you should serve in this position. Besides, you won't be doing this alone; you'll be working with the security specialists from the other wards and a member of the high council."

"All right," said Robert. "If you're sure you want me, I accept."

"Good man." The bishop opened up a desk drawer and pulled out a calendar. "One of your areas of responsibility will need attention right away—Saturday, in fact. There have been an increased number of protestors at the temple since we started preparing for the Easter pageant. Our stake will be providing security for the pageant this week. We need two men from the ward there each night. Please see if you can arrange for volunteers to go out there."

"I can do that," said Robert.

"You'll be able to do all of the tasks that this calling requires."

Bishop Porter went over the meetings Robert needed to attend during the next month and then gave him a thin white binder with the security procedures suggested by Church headquarters. They shook hands and Robert left.

As he walked to the car, Robert thought about who might be available to provide extra security at the temple next week. Then as he drove, his mind began to make connections that brought on a chill that had nothing to do with the temperature outside.

His father had been given an assignment to lay the foundations for a new farming community. Robert had spent a good portion of his week standing guard in the meat department of the local grocery store. And now the Church thought the situation in the country bad enough to create a security calling.

Crazy events by crazy people happened every day. But that was on the news. It happened to other people. Robert—and the rest of the Mormons—was largely unaffected by the insanity. Go to church, say your prayers, and the crazy people focused on one another.

Except that his mom had been robbed.

And the Church was preparing for trouble.

Robert missed the turn for his street. He decided he wasn't ready to go home and drove toward the Frost Shop.

Part of his mind steered the car toward sweet ice-creamy goodness while the rest of it considered the connection between his new job and his newly appointed church duties. They both involved security. Why?

He couldn't decide which line of thought scared him more: the revelation that the fabric of society had begun to unravel or the fact that his immersion into multiple aspects of security might be part of the Lord's plans for him.

Returning home early from his mission didn't seem to matter anymore. It came down to the simple fact that he was needed here.

***

Healthy Partners served customers all across the United States. That meant that Robert needed to get up two hours earlier than normal for his new assignment. It had taken weeks to get used to sleeping on the same schedule as the rest of his family. Now he needed to change it again.

The assignment bore little resemblance to the work at Fresh Foods. After briefing him on the security procedures that the company used at the call center, they sat him with a senior guard at the main entrance.

Officer Lloyd greeted everyone who entered the building. Except for visitors, he addressed each one of them by name and asked about some aspect of their life. Most of the employees responded with a greeting of their own, but even those who didn't still received a smile and wish for a wonderful day.

Robert sat next to him. And tried to be as smiley as Lloyd.

"Are you ready to take over?" Lloyd asked when a young woman showed up for an appointment with the head of the facility department.

"I . . . guess."

"Not to worry." Lloyd chuckled. "Anyone who belongs here will have a badge and can let themselves through the security gate. The rest will be visitors that need to be escorted to where they're going."

"How will I know where to take them?" Robert started searching through the papers at the guard station, looking for a company directory.

"I'll take care of that when I get back. If you have any visitors show up while I'm gone, have them check in and then take a seat until I return."

Robert took over the responsibility of head greeter. He introduced himself for the first few minutes until he realized that no one cared. When they looked over to the guard station and saw him standing there alone, they walked past him without another glance.

Lloyd returned and resumed his congenial greetings.

That set the pattern for the early part of the day until the morning rush subsided. Then Lloyd sent Robert out on patrol.

"Afraid I can't let you use the guard-mobile," Lloyd said as he pointed to an electric cart sitting just inside the parking garage. "Not until I get a chance to train you on it. Besides, it only takes about fifteen minutes to walk around the entire building."

"And do what?"

"That's it," Lloyd replied with a shrug. "Walk through the parking lot like you're keeping an eye on the cars. If you find anyone smoking next to the building, you should ask them to move over to the smoke station."

"What if I spot something suspicious?" Robert asked.

"Like what?"

"A car being stolen, maybe. Or if I find a person snooping around the building."

"Then you can holler for me on the radio and I'll call the police."

"I think I can probably make it around the building in ten minutes."

"Take your time."

"I'm pretty sure I can walk fast enough."

"Seriously." Lloyd looked Robert in the eye. "Take your time."

Robert attached one of the bulky security radios to his belt and headed out the door. The weather was still pretty cool in the morning, but it had warmed up enough by now for him to appreciate the shaded areas of his route.

A steady trickle of traffic flowed into, through, and out of the parking lot in front of the building. Nothing noteworthy caught Robert's attention as he patrolled there. The east side of Healthy Partners shared a driveway with the neighboring building and had virtually no activity.

Robert turned the corner of the building and narrowly avoided walking into a man leaning against the rear wall. The man, along with two women, held lit cigarettes in their hands. All three of them wore badges that identified them as Healthy Partners employees. They stopped midconversation and stared at Robert.

"Sorry, the smoke station is on the far side of the building," said Robert.

The trio of smokers continued to look at Robert in silence.

"Could you please go over there or put out your cigarettes?" Robert asked.

One of the women drew a couple of quick puffs, then threw the cigarette on the ground and crushed it underfoot. The man took a long drag off his cigarette and then blew a series of smoke rings in the air above his head.

Robert pulled the radio off his belt and keyed the mic.

Nothing happened.

He tried it again. No response. No static. No noise whatsoever.

Robert examined the radio while trying to keep an eye on the two employees that continued to smoke. He fiddled with the knobs and eventually succeeded in turning it on.

The man laughed. "What an idiot."

"Lloyd," Robert called out over the radio.

"All right," said the man with the cigarette. "We're going." He drew another lungful of smoke and then threw the butt at Robert's feet. The three of them turned around and headed toward the front entrance. They mumbled a couple of obscene comments at Robert as they left.

"Did you find someone stealing a car?" Lloyd's voice sounded over the radio.

How did you report a non-incident like this? Did he even want to?

"Radio check," Robert responded after an extended pause.

It seemed like an eternity before Lloyd spoke again. Robert pictured him sitting at the guard station, laughing about the situation with a couple of visitors.

"Your radio checks okay," said Lloyd.

Robert clicked the radio back on his belt, gave a last look at the smokers, and then continued his circuit of the perimeter. He went along the back of the building and turned the corner, scanning the smoke station from a distance. Then he took a route that allowed him to walk next to the parking garage. He had nearly reached the front of the building again when he heard crying.

He followed the sound into the garage and found a young woman standing between two vans, talking on a cell phone.

"Can I help you?" Robert asked.

The woman jumped away from him in surprise. For a moment she looked at him, her mouth hanging open, an angry voice issuing from the speaker of her phone. Then her face hardened into a mask of rage.

"Why don't you mind your own business?" she screamed. "Working security doesn't give you the right to harass me. I'm allowed to make personal phone calls on my break."

"I'm sorry. I thought you might be in trouble."

"You're the one in trouble." The woman jabbed a finger in Robert's direction. "As soon as I get back to my desk, I'm going to report you."

Robert backed away, holding up his hands in silent apology.

"That's right. Get out of here!" she shouted after him.

By the time Robert reached the garage exit, the woman had returned to her phone conversation and had resumed crying.

What was wrong with these people? Robert knew that security guards were often laughed at and called rent-a-cops, but they still represented the company and were authorized to enforce the rules and regulations sent down by the management. Was it a lack of respect for Robert, or guards in general, or did this reflect a declining level of civility in the population as a whole?

He thought about mentioning the incident to Lloyd. Then he thought better of it and decided that unless Lloyd brought it up first, it didn't really need to be talked about.

Robert returned to the guard station and found Officer Milton, the building's head of security, waiting for him.

"Robert," Officer Milton said. "Can you come with me, please?"

There hadn't been enough time for the woman in the garage to register a complaint. At least, Robert didn't think so. Maybe the smokers had reported him. In either case it seemed like an unduly fast response.

Officer Milton waited until they were alone in the hallway before he spoke.

"I'm afraid this isn't going to be fun."

Robert's heart caught in his throat. Was he going to be fired?

"Troy Chavelle is being terminated today," Milton continued. "We'll be escorting him out of the building. Considering that he's being let go because of his aggressive behavior at work, I don't expect this to go well."

Robert's heart stopped pounding heavily against his chest. How weird that he should feel relieved to be on his way to walk a disgruntled employee out of the building.

They made their way through the call center floor and stopped briefly at a desk that wasn't occupied. The cubicle held a variety of pictures that bordered on the obscene and involved scantily clad women holding or embracing guns.

Milton scanned the area around the desk and then headed toward the far end of the room where a man faced a pair of women at the water cooler.

The man had one arm draped on top of the cooler, while still leaning forward, inappropriately close to the women. He gestured with the other arm while he talked, the motions fast and jerky.

Although smiling, the women looked trapped.

"Mr. Chavelle," Milton said.

Troy straightened up and turned to face Robert and Officer Milton. The women bolted as soon as his back was turned.

"Something wrong?" Troy glared at the two security officers. He flexed his hands into fists and then opened them again.

"Management has asked that you clean out your desk," Officer Milton stated with an even tone to his voice.

"Am I being fired? Is that what you're saying?"

"They've asked us to escort you off the property," said Milton. "So I'd guess that you're being let go."

"I can't be terminated without cause," Troy growled.

"I don't know the full details about the situation," said Milton.

"Then why are you marching me out of here?" Troy threw his shoulders back as if he were daring the two guards to move him.

"You threatened Leonard Sandusky," said Milton.

"It was a joke. I was kidding around with him."

"Corporate policy doesn't allow for threats of any sort," Milton said. "Serious or not, Leonard felt the threat was real. And this isn't the first complaint we've received about you intimidating the other employees."

"I can't help it if others find me intimidating," Troy stated as he stepped closer to Officer Milton. "That's just how incompetent people react to anyone who operates at a higher level."

"The complaints are specific that you voiced threats against them. That isn't allowed. Please walk over to your desk and clear it out."

Troy stared into Officer Milton's eyes.

Milton didn't flinch. He didn't move. He just returned the stare.

After what seemed like minutes, Troy shifted his attention to Robert.

"I suppose you think you can make me leave."

The sudden shift in the discussion threw Robert mentally off balance. He had an upset bully in his face daring him to make a move. Robert didn't know how to fight. Beyond that, he didn't know how his employers expected him to act in this situation.

"It seems to me," Robert said, taking a hard swallow. "That as long as you voluntarily go along with us, you could appeal the company's decision to terminate you."

"What if I don't?" Troy asked.

"Then we have to involve the police, it may result in criminal charges against you, and there will be no chance that they will listen to you about why they're making a mistake."

Troy remained tense as he appeared to be thinking it over. Eventually he stepped back and nodded at Robert. Directing a fierce sneer at Officer Milton, he walked toward his cubicle.

They proceeded with the employee ejection without it devolving into a fight. That didn't mean Troy went peacefully. With raging force, he shoved his personal belongings into the cardboard box that had been provided him, uttering an endless tirade about the soulless nature of corporate America and the thieving practices of the health care industry.

A couple of times Troy stopped to pontificate on the degenerate nature of government. Robert worried that these were the precursors to a psychotic rage that would be vented on the two security guards. Instead, Troy made his point and then slammed another of his personal items into the box.

When all of Troy's possessions were packed, they guided him out of the building. Along the way, Troy announced to everyone they passed that he had been unfairly released and not to trust the managers.

Officer Milton prompted Troy to use the side exit next to the parking garage. Then Milton followed, several paces behind him.

Once outside, Troy headed straight for a black Suburban that had been parked in one of the manager's parking spots. Troy placed the box of personal items in the back section of the Suburban and closed the hatch. Then he turned and pointed at Robert.

"Don't think I'm going to forget the part you played in all of this."

With one last glare at Officer Milton, he got into his vehicle and burned rubber out of the parking lot.

When the Suburban had disappeared from view, Milton nodded at Robert. "You handled that nicely. I may have to use you on all of the terminations."

Great. That didn't strike Robert as an effective method of thanking him for a job well done. Placing him on permanent duty of marching people out the door after they got fired seemed more like a demotion.

Robert returned to the front guard desk. He spent the rest of the day either watching employees enter and exit the building and Lloyd guiding visitors to their appointments inside the building, or patrolling the parking lot. Both tasks gave him plenty of time to wonder if Troy would actually follow through with his threat.

As the end of his shift approached, Robert's thoughts drifted to Sierra and their date that night. Part of his mind nagged at him that he shouldn't be dating a nonmember, and he wondered what his parents would say when they found out. But then he though how strange it was to be so attracted to a girl he barely knew.

He didn't believe in love at first sight, although he felt that there were marriages that had been preordained in heaven. Any union with that sort of divine destiny would have to be with someone who had already joined the Church. It must be a matter of him being overly desperate to reenter the dating scene. And Sierra being an attractive and witty girl.

Before he knew it, the end of the shift arrived.

Robert rushed home and changed out of his uniform and into something appropriate for his date. He skipped taking a shower because he was already late. Then he drove across town to the address she had given him.

His hands shook. In fact, his whole body shook with nerves as he sat in the car, too nervous to get out.

Taking a deep breath, he closed his eyes and told himself that this wasn't any scarier than tracting on his mission. At least she wouldn't slam the door in his face and tell him to go away. She already agreed to go out with him. All he needed to do was knock on the door and be prepared to enjoy a well-deserved date.

He summoned up his courage and got out of the car. Forcing his feet to move him forward, he walked up to the door of her apartment, rang the doorbell, and waited.

After a couple of minutes, he rang the doorbell again. And waited.

His effort was rewarded with the sound of turning locks and the rattle of the doorknob as Sierra opened the door.

She wore a thick terry cloth bathrobe over flannel pajamas. Her nose and eyes were red and she held a tissue in her hand.

"I'm sorry, Robert," she said, her voice congested. "Can we reschedule our date?"

It took a moment for all of it to sink in. Bathrobe. Tissues. The very obvious request to reschedule the date. That all meant he wouldn't be seeing Sierra tonight.

Robert offered a weak, "Sure."

Then Sierra shut the door.

As he walked away from the apartment, Robert wondered how a week that started off so good could end so badly. What could possibly happen next?

18

’m leaving.” Jeff King stood in front of John, a rolled-up sleeping
bag in one hand and his personal pack in the other.

"Would you like to talk about it?" John asked.

"There's nothing to talk about." Jeff set his gear down and
folded his arms. "This isn't the army or a prison where I'm forced
to stay here. Church callings are voluntary. And I have decided to
un-volunteer."

John raised his hands in surrender to Jeff's argument. "Absolutely. I wouldn't want to try and stop you. All I'm interested in at
the moment is your welfare. If you tell me what's going on, maybe
I can help."

Jeff didn't answer immediately. He looked away from John and
toward the collection of tents that were still the men's homes at
camp. His lips thinned as his jaw clenched.

"Did you know that Curtis and Scott are getting paid to work
here?" Jeff's tone made it more statement than question.

"I don't know the details of everyone's financial situation," John
said, "but I have heard that several of the men here are getting assistance from the Church."

"How is that fair? They asked me to live off my savings while I work here and then they turn around and pay some of the others. Is that how they thank us for our service?" Jeff's eyes locked onto John's, demanding an answer.

"Did you quit your job to come here?"

"No." Jeff broke eye contact. "My department was eliminated. All of us got our walking papers."

"Did the company you worked for offer you a severance?"

"Yes." Jeff put his hands on his hips and stared at the ground.

"Then it sounds like you're doing better than Curtis or any of the other guys I've had a chance to talk to about their situation. The economy has been pretty bad for a long time now. It hasn't improved since we left. My guess is that the men that are getting paid to work here would have been getting some sort of assistance if they were still back home. Did you ever read about how, during the Depression, Franklin Roosevelt put nearly a quarter million men to work on public projects?"

"Yeah, I think I remember something about that."

"I'm pretty sure that's what's happening here."

Jeff kicked at the dirt. His jaw was no longer clenched, but he didn't seem ready to return to camp.

"Was that it?"

"I can't wait until the money from my severance runs out before I start looking for another job. Not only that, but my family needs me back home. Our car was broken into last week and my wife says that squatters moved into the abandoned house at the end of our block. It isn't safe for them anymore. I have to go back."

John wanted to tell him that the Lord would look after all of their families while the men here worked to construct Camp Valiant, just as He had when the pioneers constructed the Salt Lake Temple. A dozen arguments passed through John's mind as he stood there. All of them valid. All of them scripturally sound.

Not that it mattered, because Jeff was right. He could stay or go as he wished. John couldn't stop him. And John didn't want to stop him.

How many times had he had the same thoughts? Each night as he bedded down and waited for sleep, John worried about his family. Part of him wanted to go with Jeff.

"All right." John laid a supportive hand on Jeff's shoulder. "I had planned to drive into Greenville either this afternoon or tomorrow for the weekly mail run. Can you wait until then?"

Jeff nodded. He grabbed his belongings and then, with slumped shoulders, he returned them to his tent. After a brief delay, he exited the tent and headed over to the command center.

John considered joining Jeff in the trailer. A cup of hot chocolate might take the edge off the cold, and it looked as if Jeff really could use a friend right now. Or Jeff might feel hounded by his presence.

A yell sounded from the dorm. Then howls of pain.

John ran to the wooden framework of the dorm. One of the construction crews was putting the roof on it today. He could see men gathered in a circle at one corner of the building.

Scott Adams lay on the ground clutching a leg. The lower portion of it angled in a direction it shouldn't have been able to bend.

"He fell off the roof," Luis said. "I think he must have hit his leg against one of the supports on the way down."

"We better get him to a doctor," John said as he knelt at Scott's side. "Anything hurt besides your leg?"

"I landed on my shoulder." Scott gritted his teeth. "It hurts a lot, but I don't think it's serious."

John tried to gently examine the area that Scott indicated hurt and noticed a bump forming on the side of his head. Concerned that he might have a concussion, John held up three fingers and asked Scott, "How many fingers do I have?"

"You better have ten." Scott winced. "But you're only holding up three."

That seemed like a good sign.

"Do you feel nauseated?" asked John.

"Nope," Scott replied quickly. "Just stupid."

John knew they should put some ice on the bump to limit the swelling, but that was a luxury that the men in Camp Valiant did without. They needed all the space in the single fridge that they had for food. Still, necessity was the mother of invention.

"We need something cold to put on this lump," said John to the group. "And a stretcher."

Wayne Crawford, Luis, and Curtis sped off toward the trailer. They returned moments later with a folding cot and a bag of frozen peas. The peas went on Scott's head and they folded the legs on the cot flat and set it beside him.

The next part wasn't going to be easy, for Scott or the rest of them. They had to straighten his leg and then move him onto the cot. John looked up to see who would be willing to help him. Most of the crew had backed away. Wayne and Luis had remained close by.

John moved himself to a position better suited to straightening Scott's leg. His hands shook and his heart pounded away. He didn't think he could do this.

"Aren't you forgetting something?" asked Scott.

John pulled back, glad for the reprieve. "What?"

"A blessing!"

John knew that. As the leader of this group, it should have been his idea.

Scott asked John to administer the blessing and Luis to assist.

The moment John laid his hands atop Scott's head, a sense of calm enveloped him. He knew that Scott would be all right. In his mind, he saw what needed to be done to prepare the leg for the trip into Greenville.

When he finished with the blessing, he moved in front of Scott. John asked Wayne and Luis to hold on to Scott while he straightened the leg. Then, with the help of a couple more of the men, they lifted Scott while John slid the cot underneath.

Only after John was finished did his hands start to shake again. He hoped he wouldn't be needed for any more medical emergencies.

They loaded Scott into the back of the Suburban. Wayne and Luis climbed into the passenger seats and John retrieved Jeff from the trailer.

"Looks like we're making that trip now," John said. "We may need you to help carry Scott into the doctor's office, but we shouldn't need you after that."

The trip to Greenville was slow. John had to baby the Suburban over the many rocks and ruts that filled the dirt path. Each bump elicited a growl of pain from Scott. What normally amounted to a forty-five minute trip took over two hours.

Greenville was too small to support an emergency clinic, but it was large enough that they didn't have to share their general practitioner with another town. They pulled into the parking lot just as Dr. Whitton locked his office for the day.

"One of our friends broke his leg," John shouted as soon as he jumped out of the Suburban.

"Better let me see," said Dr. Whitton. The older gentleman waddled over to the Suburban and looked inside.

"Why do you have peas on his head?" Dr. Whitton asked.

"Scott banged his head at the same time he broke his leg," said John. "Frozen peas were the only thing we had that was cold."

"You boys been out camping?" Dr. Whitton asked.

"No, sir," Luis said. "We're building a farm east of town."

The doctor stopped his car-side examination of Scott and scowled at them. He had one eye scrunched and his lips moved as if he were talking to himself.

"You part of a cult?" the doctor asked.

"No," Wayne said. "We're Mormons."

The doctor nodded his head. "That's what I thought."

"Will that be a problem?" John asked.

"Not with me," said Dr. Whitton. "It's my job to fix people up, not judge them. Bring him inside, and I'll call my nurse back to assist me."

The doctor unlocked the door to his office, and they carried Scott inside. Then the doctor shooed them all outside and told them to wait.

"I called my brother," said Jeff. "He's going to drive up and get me. I think I'll wait over at the café for him. Unless . . . you need my help with Scott."

"A hot, juicy burger and an ice cold soda sounds pretty good." John shook hands with Jeff. "Good luck at home."

Jeff left. He didn't talk to anyone else. He didn't look back.

John watched him disappear into the café and then joined Wayne and Luis. The three of them walked over to the post office and collected the camp mail. Letters from home, mostly. A couple of the larger packages smelled like cookies. No sign of the care package John was expecting from Becky.

They stowed the mail in the Suburban and decided to treat themselves to a couple of cold drinks at the grocery store. Halfway down the block, a county sheriff car pulled over in front of them. A large man climbed out of the car. He adjusted his holster and walked around the front of the car to where the three of them were standing.

"If you gentlemen would like to hold up there, I want to talk to you."

"Sure. My name is John and this is Luis and Wayne."

"I'm Sheriff McKinney." He stopped several feet short of where the others stood. One hand rested on his holster, which was positioned away from them. McKinney was a tall, sturdy-built man with a touch of gray in his hair. He took his time scanning each of the men.

"What is it that we can help you with, Sheriff?" John asked.

"I prefer to be called Sheriff McKinney. That is the appropriate address for an officer in my position. I find that it reinforces the nature of our relationship."

"Got it," John said. "Sheriff McKinney it is."

"Good." Sheriff McKinney looked down the street in the direction of the doctor's office.

"I've seen that Suburban before. Are you from the compound east of here?"

"I wouldn't call it a compound," John said. "It's more like a farm."

The sheriff looked over the top of his sunglasses at John, like a parent looks at a child who has corrected him. "Just so you know, that area is under my jurisdiction."

"Sheriff McKinney," John said, "have we done something wrong?"

"Not that I know," the sheriff said. "Not yet, anyway. The thing is—people in town are concerned about what you're doing out there. That is a whole lot of land you're putting a fence around. A lot of lumber sent out there too."

"It's going to be a *big* farm," said Wayne.

"Don't make the mistake," said Sheriff McKinney, "of thinking that because this is a small town, the people who live here are stupid. This isn't the first time the Mormons have built a compound so that they could escape the penalties of the law."

"That isn't it at all," John said. "We're very willing to work with local law enforcement and follow the officially established town and county ordinances."

"Well, I like that." The sheriff smiled. "Because then you won't mind if I keep a real close eye on you."

19

A hand grabbed Calvin by the shoulder and dragged him into the still-dim alley. Before he could react, another hand clamped down over his mouth.

"It's me," Kyle Dalton whispered in his ear. "Keep it quiet."

Calvin nodded and the hands released him.

"What's wrong with you?" Calvin hissed at his friend. A few deep breaths and the sledgehammers pounding against his chest started to slow down. "If you wanted to kill me, there are more reliable methods."

"I couldn't take the chance that we'd be seen together." Kyle leaned toward the mouth of the alley and checked the area nearby. Then he grasped Calvin's elbow and pulled him into the early morning shadows.

"You're spooking me, Kyle."

"Good. Then I won't be the only one sleeping with one eye open."

"I'm guessing this isn't about you getting your butt chewed out for talking to someone on the wrong side of the political divide."

"Ohhh," Kyle groaned. "I'd welcome that right now."

"Enough of the drama," Calvin's voice started to rise. "Tell me what's going on."

"The Russians captured the pipeline."

"They invaded Ukraine?"

"Not according to them. They're keeping this pretty quiet, but our agents over there expect the Russians to claim they moved forces in to protect the pipeline from terrorist activities."

"Does Boggs know?" Calvin asked.

"Of course he knows. Anything the CIA knows, he knows."

"Any idea what he's planning to do about it?"

"Nothing." Kyle nearly shouted the response. He glanced toward the mouth of the alley as two men walked past. They continued along without noticing the discussion taking place in the shadows. Kyle exhaled loudly and continued. "I'm not supposed to know. And I'm not supposed to know that Boggs has ordered this to be buttoned up tight. He doesn't want anyone to know."

"Something as big as this can't be swept under a rug. If our guys know it happened, then the Chinese know about it, the Germans know about it, and probably half the intelligence agencies in Europe know about it. What does Boggs hope to gain by sticking his head in the sand?"

"You got me. Maybe one of your FBI buddies can fill you in on Boggs's motives. Except I bet they haven't been told."

"What is that idiot waiting for?" asked Calvin. "This is the opening salvo for another war in Europe. We can't wait for Russia to deliver their ultimatum to the EU before we do something about this."

"Wish I could help you, Cal. The agency will stick me in a *deep hole* if they find out I supplied you with this information. Not only that, but I think the Russian espionage network has been fully ramped up, Washington included."

"Any sleepers in your department?" Calvin asked.

"Maybe. We have a fair number of former Soviet agents that supposedly sold their allegiance to us. I'm not naïve enough to wonder *if* any of them are still loyal to Russia. I just wonder how many."

A car passed by at the end of the alley. Kyle ducked behind a nearby dumpster. When nothing else happened, he turned back to Calvin.

"I don't know if this situation has me imagining things or not, but I thought I caught someone tailing me earlier today."

"Meeting me has put you in danger from Boggs *and* the Russians."

"Not just me. You've been pretty vocal about this whole thing."

"I'll be sure to keep my guard up."

"Sure." Kyle's body seemed to deflate. "I don't think I can feed you any more information. Good luck, Cal."

"Stay safe." Calvin reached out and grasped Kyle by the shoulders, gave a firm squeeze, and then turned and left the alley.

Calvin stopped before he exited onto the sidewalk. He examined the street in both directions and, deciding it was clear, resumed his trek to his office.

He looked over his shoulder a couple of times, inwardly cursing himself for making such amateurish mistakes. He wasn't going to catch someone following him that way. It only tipped off your opponent that you were on to them.

If there even were anyone following him.

He tried to move quickly without seeming to be in a hurry. As much as possible he stayed with the heavier concentrations of pedestrians. This early in the day, traffic was reasonably light. People bustled along the sidewalks with purposeful strides, making it difficult to spot anyone attempting to keep up with him.

When he saw a woman getting out of a cab just ahead of him, he sprinted to it and crawled inside.

"Take me to the White House."

Five minutes later, Calvin got out of the cab and tossed the driver a twenty. He watched the approaching cars for any sign of being followed. No dark sedans. Nobody pulled over suspiciously close to his cab. No indications that anyone in any of the cars paid any attention to him at all.

Calvin headed straight for the Oval Office. The guards took

even longer than normal to process him through the security checkpoints. They were reinforced by a couple of Secret Service stooges who tried their best to discourage him from advancing any further into the building.

Eventually, he stood at the desk of Boggs's secretary.

"How can I help you?" Ms. Wilks said with cool disdain.

"I need to see President Boggs. Today."

Wilks clucked her tongue a couple of times. "The President has a full schedule today. Sometime next week would be better. Do you want me to pencil you in for Tuesday at 10:30?"

"He can't be that busy." Calvin rested his hands on the edge of her desk and leaned forward. "I only need a couple of minutes."

Ms. Wilks gave a disapproving glance at Calvin's hands and then leaned back in her chair and folded her arms. "I will call your office if a time slot becomes available."

Calvin breezed through the same security points that he'd used on the way in. The guards took a cursory look at his badge and waved him past without a word.

Keegan Roscoe walked into the lobby before Calvin had completely exited the building. Their eyes locked.

Calvin turned around and motioned for Keegan to stop.

Keegan hesitated but offered a smile. "Good morning, Calvin."

Calvin moved in closer and spoke in hushed tones. "I need to see the President."

"I should suggest that you talk with Ms. Wilks about that. Certainly she has a much better handle on his schedule than I do."

"That's not going to work. Boggs doesn't want to see me."

"How unfortunate." Keegan didn't sound sympathetic.

"Listen, Keegan. This is important. I don't have time to play political games right now. The welfare of this country is at stake. If the President won't listen to me, maybe he'll listen to you."

"That is entirely possible. What do you want me to talk to him about?"

"The Russians have invaded Ukraine."

Keegan's posture stiffened. The slight smile that had been on his face disappeared, replaced by a tight-lipped expression of warning.

"Mr. McCord, you should leave this alone. It will profit you nothing to pursue this further. I strongly urge you to keep any mention of this rumor to yourself. Now, good day to you."

Keegan strode off without any further indication that Calvin existed.

Calvin stood there and considered his next move. People passed him on either side on their way to conduct business inside the White House. Guards processed them through the security checkpoint with minimal amounts of delay. And two Secret Service agents kept an eye on him.

He briefly considered going to the few people in his political party who were still speaking to him and explaining the whole situation. Then he thought better of it. As much as the two sides had been squabbling over the violent protests and acts of physical sabotage they'd been blaming each other for committing, news of this nature could start a full-blown civil war.

It had to be Boggs.

Calvin sighed in resignation and left the building. He did his best thinking when he walked. But he couldn't work out this problem and watch for a tail at the same time. He stood outside the White House for fifteen minutes, deciding what to do next.

Then his cell phone rang.

"The President," said Ms. Wilks, "has had an unexpected gap in his schedule. He would like to see you right away."

"I can be there in ten minutes."

"Excellent." Her tone still held icy contempt. "I shall let him know."

A third Secret Service agent was at the security point when he reentered the building. His eyes followed Calvin all the way across the lobby.

"If you'll come with me, Mr. McCord," he said curtly. "I'll make sure you get to the President without any further delay."

No one stopped them or even spoke to them as they marched

to the Oval Office. The hairs on Calvin's arms prickled each time they passed a security point unchallenged. It reminded him of a condemned man's walk to the firing squad.

Ms. Wilks didn't even look up when they entered. "You may go right in."

The Secret Service agent went as far as Ms. Wilks's desk and then motioned for Calvin to go on. He turned his back on the Oval Office and assumed the standard "security" stance.

Calvin entered the office.

"Close the door," said Boggs. The President sat behind his desk, his hands clasped together in front of him. His jaw was clenched tightly. He alone occupied the room.

"We need to do something about Russia."

"Since when do I take my orders from you?" Boggs's voice boomed.

"If we don't stop this now, there'll be another war in Europe."

"At least that's what you keep telling everyone. Calvin, your problem is that you're only seeing a small part of the picture. There isn't going to be a war."

"Are you serious? What about the pipeline? What do you think Russia is going to do with that?"

"I expect them to raise crude prices." Boggs held his hands up in a "what else" gesture. "Maybe they'll put the squeeze on Western Europe to side with them on more political issues. Neither of which is worth starting World War III over."

"If that's what you think," Calvin said, "then you have a bunch of incompetents feeding you your information. This isn't a matter of Russia gaining a little leverage over its neighbors. That isn't their style. They'll use that pipeline to choke Europe until it submits."

"It doesn't matter." Boggs slammed his fist on the desk. "We have problems of our own to deal with. Europe will have to take care of itself for once."

"Mr. President—"

"That will be enough!" Boggs shouted over Calvin. "This is no longer your concern. As of right now, you are no longer tasked with getting the Russians to the negotiation table. You can go back to your office and start packing; as soon as I can find the smallest, most insignificant mission imaginable, you'll be on the next flight out of Washington."

"Why not just give me the boot and be done with it?"

"I wish I could, Calvin." Boggs offered a smile that would make a snake oil salesman proud. "For the time being, you're my proof that I'm doing everything in my power to work with my colleagues across the political divide. I'll be sure to talk that point up when I explain your upcoming vital mission to the public."

A hot, angry pulse pounded away in Calvin's ear. His flesh, his breath, burned with searing rage.

"One more thing before you go." Boggs stared hard into Calvin's eyes. "If I find you prying into the Russian situation again, I'll make sure you're prosecuted for treason."

Calvin dared not speak, dared not move, lest he lose control.

Boggs leaned back in his chair and hissed, "Get out."

20

It wasn't that Robert planned to wake up early. His eyes popped open a good forty-five minutes before the alarm, and once they did, he couldn't stop thinking about Sierra and his date with her that night.

He had free access to the bathroom while the family still slept. Without the need to hurry for the next person in line, he attended to the grooming details that got ignored on most days, took a leisurely shower, and shaved. Twice. He even broke out the cologne that his sisters had bought for him three Christmases back and made liberal use of it.

Making an actual breakfast, rather than grabbing some vitamin-fortified sugary food in a box, he used up the last of his extra time.

The entire morning seemed to flow at a slower pace than normal. Most of that may have been due to the reduced employee and visitor traffic for a Friday. Having his thoughts constantly drifting toward Sierra accounted for some of it too. Eventually the day creeped into the afternoon.

No one gave him the evil eye during his roving patrols around the parking lot. No one had to be escorted off the premises. And

Lloyd even let him escort a few visitors to their destinations within the bowels of the Healthy Partners facility.

Then time caught up with him. The last two hours of the work-day crawled along like a dying man in the desert. Robert's neck started to stiffen from the constant craning around to look at the clock that was mounted on the wall behind the guard station.

"You're not anxious to get out of here, are you?" Lloyd laughed.

"A little," said Robert.

"Woo-hoo-ho. Must have a big date tonight."

When Rhonda Stafford asked if he could help carry some boxes out to her car, Robert jumped at the chance to do something that would take his mind off the tauntingly slow clock.

Then Bob Timmons had him check that all the doors on the second floor were secure and none of the vendors had been left behind after the big third-quarter rollout meeting/party. When he finished, it was time to leave.

Robert had always adhered to the Boy Scout motto: Be Pre-pared. To that end, he carried a spare shirt in the car. As soon as his shift ended, he ducked into the bathroom and changed out of his uniform. If time had permitted, he would've gone home and cleaned up before his date. Instead, he hoped Sierra wouldn't notice that his pants were part of his guard uniform.

He climbed into his car, and after a quick calculation of the fast-est route across town, he pulled out into the street and fought the urge to lead-foot it there.

Instead he turned on the radio.

"Don't forget that you heard it from me and you heard it here first. For any of you late arrivals, let me welcome you to a special Friday afternoon edition of the Roderick Dorgan show.

"The truth never sleeps, my friends—at least not while I'm at the helm. Before you go home and park yourself on your favorite comfy spot, please consider taking up the banner of justice this weekend and fighting for the truth.

"As you all know, the zealots in the religious right have banded together

and are planning to fight against the fair treatment legislation that is being discussed in Washington. They want to prevent anyone who thinks or believes differently from them from getting equal rights in this country.

"So that's nothing new. Religion has always been a tool for forcing restrictions on others. I don't even have to tell you about the number of wars and countless murders that these hate-mongers are responsible for in the pursuit of their faith.

"Hey, nothing says love your neighbor like killing them. Am I right?

"Well, it's way past time that something is done about this. We are modern, civilized people. Let's put this primitive, violent, and bigoted thinking behind us. And I am going to ask all of you to forgo a small part of your relaxation time this weekend to elevate the human race.

"Two hours. Is that too much time for you to invest in making this world a better place? It isn't for me.

"I'm asking you to get out of your house and be heard. Find a place where these small-minded zealots gather and speak up. If you're not sure where to go, I suggest speaking out against the worst of them—the Mormons. Go to their temple and tell them that we will not let them run our lives anymore. This is the land of the free and the brave and we will no longer be intimidated by them or their megacorporations. People have a right to—"

Robert changed the station. He didn't understand why his parents kept the radio tuned to it. If he listened to it any longer, it might affect his mood. By the time he found a spot on the dial that played music from the current century, he had arrived at Sierra's place.

He knocked on the door. And waited. He knocked again, and the door opened.

Sierra had on a flowery blouse and a pair of green pastel slacks. She looked like a garden come to life, except more beautiful. Her hair was curled and it framed her face, the strawberry-blonde locks making the green in her eyes stand out.

"Are you planning on just standing there with your mouth open?" Sierra asked with a grin.

"Maybe," Robert said, and then closed his mouth.

Sierra raised her eyebrows and gave a slight nod toward the car.

Robert shook himself out of his trance and backed out of the doorway so she could shut the door. "So much for the suave approach."

"That's all right." She laughed. "I think stunned and speechless is kind of cute."

"Cute is good," Robert said. "With a little work, I might be able to raise that to hunky by the end of the night."

"You think you can rank that high?" Sierra offered a teasing smile to Robert as she slid into the car.

They arrived at Salty Pete's twenty minutes late. Customers waiting for service packed the entryway. Robert escorted Sierra to the front desk.

"I had a reservation," Robert said.

"Your name?" A tall, thin hostess asked.

"Robert Williams."

The hostess ran her finger down the reservation log and then finally moved it up through the list of those that had already been checked off. "Your reservation was for 6:30. We had to give your table to someone else when you didn't show. I can put you on the list if you like."

"How long of a wait?" Robert asked.

"Ninety minutes."

Robert looked over to Sierra, who just smiled at him.

"No thanks," he said and escorted Sierra back out to his car.

"Salty Pete's," Sierra said. "That would've been nice."

He didn't know if Sierra was teasing him or showing her disapproval for his tardiness.

"Do you like barbecue?" Inspiration hit him. Why not take her to one of his favorite places to eat? Dates were meant to let two people get acquainted. She might as well find out early that he had a powerful yen for charred meat slathered with sauce.

"Sure."

They drove to The Slab Factory. Robert tried to sneak a few quick glances her direction to judge her reaction to the date so far.

Whenever he did, her head was turned to look at something along the street.

Sierra's face remained unreadable as they turned into The Slab Factory parking lot. The lot was crowded, but it still had a few open spots left. Robert parked and hurried to open her door, and the two of them walked inside the restaurant.

To claim The Slab Factory had a rustic décor would be to truly understate the fact. It looked like a stockyard, but it smelled like barbecue heaven.

They put their names on the waiting list and were surprised to be called to a table ten minutes later. Robert let Sierra pick her seat and then slid into the opposite side of the booth.

"What do you recommend?" Sierra asked.

"Everything! But since I can't afford that, you might want to try the brisket sandwich with a side of coleslaw and cheesy potatoes."

"You really had to think that one over, didn't you?"

"All right." Robert threw his hands up in mock surrender. "You got me. I love this place. I used to come here all the time when I worked construction."

"I'll trust you on this. You order and I'll try it."

They ordered two brisket sandwiches just the way Robert had suggested. Then the two of them sat and looked at one another.

There had been plenty of small talk to occupy them while they had searched for a place to eat and waited to be seated. With the waitress gone, Robert scanned his brain for a topic the two of them could discuss. Immediately his mind went to the missionary discussions. Habits were a hard thing to break, but he managed to resist asking her if she wanted to hear the Joseph Smith story.

"You used to work construction," Sierra said, breaking the uncomfortable silence between them. "What happened?"

"I served a mission for the LDS Church."

"Ah, you're a Mormon."

"Yes." Robert paused for a moment. "Is that okay?"

"It doesn't bother me, if that's what you're asking. I never dated a Mormon before."

"Well, we're a lot like regular people."

"That's good to know." Sierra giggled. "Tell me about when you were working construction. Did you like it?"

"Not at first. Your muscles ache until you get used to the work. It's hot outside during the summer, which I don't mind as much as the cold. For someone like me, who has a hard time sitting in a chair for hours, it was a pretty good job. What I liked best about it was the feeling that I had really accomplished something. When we finished a house I could stand back and look at it and say that I had helped build a home. A family would be moving in there soon and children would be playing in the yard."

Robert stopped talking. He worried that his mouth had been running on without giving her a chance to talk. When he looked over at Sierra, her eyes sparkled.

"You probably hear that sort of thing a lot where you work," Robert said, giving her an opening into the discussion.

"Not really. The men who work there spend most of their time complaining about how they work too hard and don't get paid enough."

"They should feel lucky they have a job," Robert said without thinking.

"Yeah, they should."

The waitress arrived carrying two of The Slab Factory specials. She brought them refills on their drinks and then hurried off to attend other customers.

Robert raised his hand and held up a finger. "If you're going to have a brisket sandwich, you have to do it right."

"You mean there are instructions for how to eat a barbecue sandwich here?" Sierra's expression said she was waiting for the punch line.

"Not exactly." Robert opened up his sandwich, forked coleslaw in the middle, and poured barbecue sauce on top of it. Then he replaced the top half.

"Coleslaw on the sandwich." Sierra looked skeptical.

"You're just going to have to trust me on this."

Robert watched her take a bite and burst into a wide grin as she nodded her head.

"I told you." He followed suit with a big bite of his own.

Sierra took a couple of bites of the sandwich and then set it down. "Tell me about your mission."

Robert alternated between eating and telling. By the time he reached the part of his story where he had come home, Sierra had long since finished her meal. He felt a little embarrassed at having monopolized the conversation and at the same time a little amazed at how quickly the evening had sped past. His watch showed a quarter till ten.

"I think this was a much better choice than Salty Pete's," Sierra said.

"You liked the sandwich that much?"

"Although the sandwich was good, it's not that. This place reminds me of you. It's not fancy or pretentious. From the outside it doesn't look all that special. But if you give it a chance, you'll find that there's good stuff on the inside."

21

Becky gently nursed her car back home after dropping the children off at school. If she didn't push it too hard, the Tracker could make the trip without stalling.

"Come on, baby," she told the car as she patted the dashboard. "You can do it."

Her eyes were drawn to the warning lights on the dash panel, and she didn't see the two men until they were right in front of her.

She slammed on the breaks.

The Tracker stopped about a yard short of the men. If she hadn't noticed them when she did, they could've been killed or badly injured. Of course, if she watched the road the way she was supposed to, she would've noticed them in plenty of time.

Her heart pounded.

Her mind jumped from thought to thought.

Thank goodness she didn't hit them. Were they all right? Was the car okay? What should she be doing? She needed to get out of the car and talk with them.

Except they didn't seem to want to talk. They were hurrying away from the car, pushing a lawn mower loaded down with tools, leaving behind an outdoor grill.

There was something wrong with this scene.

The men were strangers. If they were doing yard work in the neighborhood, then they should be parked in front of the house and not carrying the tools down the street. And now that she had a chance to study the grill, the mower, and the tools, they looked like the ones John had bought.

She jerked her head toward her house. A portion of the chain-link fence that separated the front yard from the back lay on the ground. The thin metal doors of the toolshed had been caved in and tossed aside.

Thieves!

She reached for her cell phone to call John. Then she stopped. John was half a state away. He couldn't help her. She needed to take care of this herself. And soon. The men had already reached the end of the block.

The police could handle this.

Her hands shook so badly that when she flipped open the phone, it tumbled out of her hand to the floor of the car. She tried to grab it and only succeeded in sliding it under the seat where she couldn't reach it.

Becky rejected the idea of getting out of the car to retrieve the phone or to confront the thieves. Even though the windows were no real barrier to these men if they decided to attack her, she felt safer inside the vehicle. A ton of metal on her side helped to even the odds for her against these two men.

The Tracker. It was the only resource available to her. She turned the key in the ignition and offered a silent prayer that it would start.

It did.

Becky backed up enough to maneuver around her grill that now stood in the middle of the street, and then pulled forward. She steered straight toward the two men. When she got within a few feet of them, she slowed down to match their speed and laid on the horn.

The men's heads whipped back and forth as they scanned the neighborhood. They didn't look happy. One of the men shouted at Becky; the sound of the horn blocked the intended message.

Becky switched from one steady blast from the horn to a series of honks. She didn't want anyone mistaking her distress call for a vehicle malfunction.

The man that had yelled at her, a short and grubby man, dropped most of the equipment in his arms. He held on to a heavy circular saw, raised it above his head like a weapon, and charged Becky.

She threw the Tracker in reverse and slammed down on the gas. The car went about thirty feet before it stalled.

That must have been the angry thief's intent, as he turned around and ran back to his companion. They grabbed up what they could carry in their arms and ran down the street.

Becky pushed on the horn and kept pushing it, too afraid to stop and try to start the car again. Tears streamed down her face. She could hear herself sob.

The men turned a corner and passed from view.

She continued honking the horn. In the back of her mind, she knew that the thieves were gone and that she should stop making all this noise. But she couldn't think of what she should do next.

A rap sounded from the window next to her ear.

Becky jumped. Her heart leaped up to her throat. She looked to her left and spotted a police officer standing by her car. The officer was thin and young, and he had kind eyes. His badge identified him as Officer Swanson.

"Are you okay, ma'am?" the officer asked.

A huge sob burst out of her chest. She nodded and rolled down the window.

"I, they . . . the car . . . I saw . . . honked horn." Becky paused and took a deep breath.

"Can you tell me what happened?" the officer asked patiently.

"A pair of men broke into our toolshed. I honked the horn to scare them off."

The officer nodded. "That seems to have worked. It looks as if they dropped a lot of the items they were carrying. And you were smart to stay in the car. But it probably would have been best if you'd just called us instead."

"Next time I will."

"Let's hope there isn't a next time."

Now it was Becky's turn to nod. Once . . . no, twice . . . was enough.

"What did these men look like and where did they go?"

Becky gave Officer Swanson a description of the two thieves, and he reported it to the precinct on his radio. Additional units were dispatched to the area and Officer Swanson cleared from the channel.

"Why don't you park the car while I start moving your stuff out of the street," the officer said.

The Tracker started up on the first try and Becky pulled over to the curb. She got out of the car and opened the hatch so they could place the discarded tools in back.

"This is crazy," Becky told Officer Swanson as he pushed her grill toward the house. "They stole our tools during daylight hours. Anyone could see them do it. Not that I want people to break into my house at night, but it doesn't make sense."

"The criminals are definitely getting bolder with their activities. You'd almost think they were daring someone to catch them in the act."

"And shouldn't they have a car, or a truck, to carry this stuff away?"

"Not if they're local," said Officer Swanson.

"You mean my neighbors are robbing me?"

"That would be my guess, since they're on foot."

"But this is a good neighborhood," Becky declared. "We don't have robberies around here. We don't have very much crime of any kind around here. Why would the people that live in the neighborhood start doing this?"

"Sorry, that question is above my pay grade."

"What?"

"I don't know." Officer Swanson shrugged. "I just chase the bad guys. It takes someone smarter than me and with a bigger view of the situation to figure out why we're seeing these changes in your neighborhood."

"So it's not a matter of me being paranoid; our neighborhood has changed."

"I've definitely noticed the difference in the last few months. All of the areas I patrol have seen a steady increase in petty crimes."

At least this wasn't a matter of living in a declining section of town. Things were getting worse all over. Becky wasn't sure if that made her feel better—or worse.

A couple of patrol cars slowed to a stop alongside Officer Swanson. He pointed in the direction the thieves had gone. "Two males in their twenties pushing a lawn mower loaded down with tools."

The additional patrol cars sped off in the direction the thieves had gone. They returned before Officer Swanson finished taking Becky's statement.

"No sign of them, Swanson," said the officer driving one of the cruisers.

"Do you mind patrolling the area for awhile?" Officer Swanson asked the driver of the first car. He motioned for the second cruiser to pull over and park.

It took almost half an hour for Becky to check the shed and give Officer Swanson a list of the items she thought were missing. When they finished, both officers went through the house and made sure no unwanted visitors had hidden themselves inside. Then they left.

Her sense of security left with them.

Becky decided to transfer all of the equipment in the shed to the garage. She used the wheelbarrow to shuttle the tools. Each time she returned she noticed the shed's ruined door. It reminded her of an ugly scar on her home.

Until the fence and the shed were repaired, the assault upon her home would not be forgotten or put aside in her thoughts. She wanted John to come back home. He could fix everything.

As nice as it would be to have him back, she needed to find a way to get the fence and the shed repaired on her own. She could probably drive down to the hardware store and ask for instructions on fixing the fence and pick up the needed equipment at the same time. Robert and Lucas could give her a hand.

The cell phone chimed at her. Caller ID showed Kaylie Mendenhall's number. She wondered why a friend of Elizabeth's would be calling.

"Hello."

"Mom!" Elizabeth shouted over loud background noise. She sounded scared.

"What's wrong?" Becky ran toward her car. She sensed she had to get to the school right away.

"Some of the kids have gone crazy." Elizabeth cried as she talked. "Lucas got hurt. They attacked one of his friends, and he tried to stop the fight."

"How badly is he hurt?"

"Not too bad, but I think he's going to need stitches on the side of his head."

Shouts and screams came through the phone. Becky could clearly hear them whenever Elizabeth wasn't talking. It sounded like a full-blown riot in progress.

"Where are you? Where's Lucas? Where's Jesse?"

"A bunch of us are headed toward the south gate. Jesse's helping Lucas walk because he can't see very well. We're all together. Please, Mom, come get us."

"I'm on my way, Sweetie. Make sure you stay together."

"We will."

Becky fired up the Tracker and had already peeled tires backing up before she remembered that she had to take it easy on the car or it would stall. She hadn't even fully stopped before she slammed the gear into drive and pressed on the accelerator.

The Tracker leapt forward. She gunned the gas more than she intended, but it was impossible to take it easy when her children were in danger.

At the intersection of Fifteenth and Plainsview, she slowed to check for oncoming traffic then ran the red light. It was the first time she'd ever purposely broken a traffic law—or any law, for that matter. She held her breath as she crossed and sighed in relief when nobody slammed into the side of the Tracker.

Three more blocks and a right turn on Magellan and she could see the school straight ahead. It looked like a scene out of a science fiction movie, one where aliens have invaded the Earth and everyone is fighting each other to escape.

The front parking lot was jammed with incoming vehicles. Parents had their heads out the windows, shouting for their children, at other children, and at one another. On the school grounds, teens were threatening, fighting, and throwing things at one another.

Becky turned on the road that would take her to the south entrance.

As she turned the corner, she could see that it held more of the same, but there were fewer people and they didn't seem to be fighting.

The Tracker stalled half a block away.

Becky bailed out of the car and ran for the south gate. Her gaze darted back and forth, looking for her children in the crowd. Getting closer, she could see that a knot of teens had formed at the gate and was facing a larger group. Plenty of shouting volleyed back and forth between the two groups. It looked like the situation might be ramping up for another brawl.

Becky briefly spotted the neon-green blouse Elizabeth had been wearing this morning. Then it vanished within the surging mass of bodies at the gate. Becky homed in on that spot.

As she got closer, Becky could see that many of the kids at the gate were LDS. A few parents and teachers were scattered in the group, trying to move the now angry teens beyond the gate. They needed help.

Becky ran up to the gate and grabbed Brady Jones's arm.

He spun around ready to take a swing. "Sister Williams," he stammered.

"You're not helping the situation here," she said. "Step back and let's get everyone on this side of the fence before someone gets really hurt."

Brady nodded his head and moved away from the gate.

Left and right, Becky pulled teens through the gate. Most of them went willingly enough, once they received a firm prod in the right direction. Reuben Walters did not. He threw his right arm out and sent Becky sprawling on the ground. Only then did he look to see who he'd attacked.

He looked mildly ashamed. Not ashamed enough to move away from the gate or to help Becky stand up.

She launched herself from the ground and thrust a finger right at Reuben. "Have you bothered to think about what you are doing?"

Reuben blinked.

"Is this how your seminary teachers have taught you to behave? Is this how your parents raised you to behave? Is this what Jesus would do in this situation?"

Reuben gave her a sheepish look and shrugged.

"I didn't think so." Becky took her finger out of his face and pointed across the street. "Go stand over there and wait. I'll give you a ride home."

When she turned around, Elizabeth pushed her way through the gate and threw herself into Becky's arms. "Oh, Mom, it was horrible. Everything went crazy and then kids started yelling at us because we're Mormon."

Elizabeth went on, but Becky's attention was on the boys.

Jesse came through the gate, pulling Lucas along behind him. Lucas had one hand clutched to the left side of his head, blood leaking out between his fingers. Large crimson stains spotted the front of his shirt.

Becky led the two of them away from the crowd before she pulled Lucas's hand away from his head to look at the wound.

"Hi, Mom," Lucas said.

"How do you feel?" Becky examined the gash on his head. It definitely needed a couple of stitches, but it wasn't too bad.

"My head hurts," Lucas said. "Other than that I'm okay. I tried to stop a fight and someone clocked me with a can of soda."

"What are we going to do?" Elizabeth asked as she watched the mayhem on campus.

"We're going to take Lucas to the doctor's office for stitches, and then tomorrow I'm going to make arrangements for homeschooling."

22

"This doesn't mean I'm going back to church," Kevin said as he continued watching out the car window instead of looking at Robert.

"I hate to be the one to spill the news that the universe isn't centered on you," Robert said with a grin, "but this is all about me needing help with the temple security assignment tonight. Besides, since I started working, I haven't had much chance to hang out with you."

Kevin readjusted his position in the seat and uncrossed his arms. He still didn't look Robert's way, but he turned his head at least part of the way in that direction.

"Aw, come on." Robert leaned over and gave his friend a gentle nudge with his elbow. "This is the perfect chance for you to continue your rant against the recent actions of the Church leadership."

"Those are serious concerns." Kevin turned and faced Robert full-on. "You need to open your eyes and see what's happening around us."

"Absolutely!" Robert offered with mock sincerity. "Eyes open and hands on the wheel. None of this traffic is going to catch me unaware."

"Spoken like a true-blue Mormon." Kevin's tone had lightened.

"They don't call me Mormon Smurf for nothing."

Kevin returned to staring out the window opposite Robert.

"All right," Robert said. "I was just trying to get you to lighten up some. Your whole argument about how the Church should be reaching out to help their neighbors instead of isolating themselves has been locked and loaded in my brain."

"What do you plan to do about it, then?"

"Nothing. There's nothing I *can* do about it."

"The situation in the country will continue to deteriorate as long as people don't care enough to do something about it."

"I care," Robert said, getting serious about the discussion. "At work, at home, at church, I see that people are suffering. Families are struggling to find jobs and pay the bills. I care about all of that. What do you suggest we do to help?"

Kevin rested his elbow on the open window frame and leaned his head against his fist. He looked far less certain of his words than when he lectured Robert about it last week.

"We have to be where the people need help," Kevin said at last.

For the first time, Robert wondered what would happen to the neighborhoods and communities if all the Latter-day Saints left. He had heard it suggested that there could be a literal gathering of the Saints that would separate them from the modern-day Sodoms and Gomorrahs before they were destroyed, but he had never given it serious consideration. Would the cities where they lived become so wicked that Church members had to flee to avoid sharing in the destruction?

Or could that be avoided if the righteous stayed put and worked hard enough?

"You're right," Robert said. "I'm willing to go where people need help."

It surprised Robert that he had said it. It surprised him even more that he meant it.

They pulled up to the back parking lot of the temple and saw that it was full. It took three tries before they found a street with an open spot where they could park.

Robert had on the suit he wore during his mission and Kevin wore slacks, a white shirt, and a tie. They were a jacket short of looking like a pair of missionaries. Too bad Kevin had grown disillusioned with the Church before he served a mission. Maybe things would be different if he'd had the chance to see how the gospel changed people's lives.

Active or not, Kevin had always been a good friend. With all the craziness that Robert had been experiencing in the last few weeks, he was glad for that stability in his life.

The temple grounds were filled with people who had come to watch the Easter pageant. It would be another hour before the evening's performance started and a good number of the seats had already been taken.

In front of the temple, protestors walked along the sidewalk, carrying anti-Mormon signs and chanting. They were too far away for Robert to make out what they were saying.

Up ahead, about a dozen men had gathered near the visitors' center. Robert recognized Steve Smith in the group and headed toward him.

"Good," said one of the men. "It looks like we're all here. I'm Brother Lance, and I want to thank all of you for coming out and helping me with temple security."

Kevin looked at Robert and rolled his eyes.

"For those of you doing this for the first time," Brother Lance said, "please keep in mind that we are here to keep the temple peaceful. That means we want to avoid conflict. You can see where we have the brethren standing now. They are far enough away not to excite the people who have a legal right to protest on the sidewalk.

"Our purpose is to provide a visible deterrent to the protestors. We want to make sure that the group that has gathered to enjoy the Easter pageant can do so safely. To do that, we ask that you stay with your partner, smile, and do nothing unless you spot our guests or the temple being accosted. Please, brothers, keep in mind that you represent the Lord in this matter. Act accordingly."

They had a short prayer and then Robert and Kevin were

assigned to a position in front of the temple. The two men they replaced gave a friendly wave in passing.

Kevin immediately turned around and faced the temple. Robert looked the crowd over. They reminded him of the protestors he'd seen on television who were angry over the President's failure to pull the troops out of Afghanistan, which is to say that they appeared angry and ready for confrontation.

"I hear you're dating now," Kevin said.

Robert nodded his head without looking at his friend.

"I hear she's not LDS."

This time Robert turned to respond. "Not yet."

From the crowd someone yelled, "Mormons worship a different Christ!"

"That's ridiculous," Robert said. "We read the same Bible that they do. That's the same Jesus that they read about. It's the same Jesus that they teach about."

Kevin shrugged.

"Grace not works," a woman yelled. "It's by grace that we are saved. Works are filthy rags. Stop your filthy deeds."

"What about 'Faith without works is dead'?" Robert turned to face the crowd.

"Let it go," Kevin said as he took hold of Robert's arm and turned him toward the temple.

"How can they believe those things?" Robert protested.

Kevin shrugged again.

"Just say no," shouted another woman. "To the cult worship of the Josephites."

"Josephites." Robert turned again and caught sight of an elderly couple trying to move through the line of protestors on the sidewalk. He nudged Kevin and then hustled to help the two temple visitors.

Although the protestors didn't make any physical contact with the couple, they waved their signs in front their faces and leaned in close to call out their protests against Mormons.

Robert stepped up and waved the protesters back.

"Hey, buddy," a tall man said in an angry voice, "this is a public sidewalk. You can't make us move."

"I'm not trying to make you leave. Just as you have a right to be here, so do these folks. Please let them through."

"We're not stopping them," snarled a thin woman with a bitter face. "We're just warning them about you Mormons."

"Fine," Robert said. "How about you do that without harassing them?"

"Don't think you can force us away," said a heavy man, "like you force your women to become baby factories."

"Or kidnap young women and hide them away in your temple," shouted a woman's voice out of the crowd.

"And we know about your midnight orgies," an unseen voice boomed.

"And we know about your sacrificing babies and virgins in the underground dens of your building of evil," came another faceless voice.

The elderly couple passed Robert. He turned to follow them, but the crowd had closed in on him. Just as he wondered how he'd get out of there, a pair of hands grabbed him from behind and pulled him away from the swirling cloud of angry faces.

"Easy, boy," Kevin said as he kept pulling. He didn't stop until both of them were a safe distance from the sidewalk.

Prying his gaze from the mob, he saw the elderly couple nod their thanks. Beyond them, Brother Lance walked with a companion toward Robert. They arrived out of breath.

"Maybe," said Brother Lance, "we can have the two of you watch over the parking lot in back. I'll stay here while you go back there. If you could, please, send the gentlemen that are there now up here to me."

Kevin pulled Robert along.

"Thank you, brothers," Lance called to them. "Thank you for your willingness to serve."

They had walked about halfway to the back when Kevin looked over to Robert.

"Way to go. You nearly got us fired from a volunteer job."

Robert woke up the next morning feeling like a failure. With his father gone, the responsibility for protecting the family fell on him. How could he do that when it was beyond his ability to just stand in front of the temple and not start a riot?

Only a few weeks ago, his sole responsibility had been to share the gospel with the good people of Italy. Nothing really difficult, just a willingness to get up each morning and face a series of rejections from people he didn't know. Now it fell upon him to protect his family, the ward members, and his coworkers.

Nothing had prepared him for the role of a protector. All the instructions he'd received at work and for his calling had amounted to not much more than advising him to stand and smile. How did that keep people safe?

When that elderly couple had been in trouble last night, they needed more than a pair of smiling faces watching them. Robert couldn't stand by and do nothing when people needed help. He had to act.

This revelation bothered him. It was like waking up one morning and looking into the mirror to find you had a whole new face. A face you weren't sure you liked but knew you were stuck with.

Robert had no business pretending that he could protect the people around him. No one in his family was aggressive. He normally avoided conflict. Most important, he didn't have any idea what to do in a crisis situation.

So why was he now immersed in the role of protector?

His mind searched for an explanation while he readied himself for work. He discarded one lame answer after another until he noticed Lloyd standing at the front desk of Healthy Partners.

"Good morning." Lloyd laughed. "For a moment there I thought you were going to walk right by me."

"I'm glad you said something when you did; otherwise, who knows where I'd be by now."

"Must've been a humdinger of a party last night." Lloyd winked.

"I wish." Robert sighed. "I had a security assignment for the Easter pageant."

"You got yourself a second job?"

"Sort of. I don't get paid for it, though."

"Sounds like a lousy job then. Oh well, it's time for me to grab a cup of coffee. Want anything from the break room?"

Robert shook his head as he turned his attention to the group of employees coming through the door. They ignored him, as pretty much most of the employees did.

Employees passed through the reception area. Visitors signed in and were escorted by Lloyd to their designated locations. Robert patrolled the parking lot. All of this before nine forty-five.

Lloyd had just left with the latest visitor when the phone at the guard desk rang.

"Healthy Partners," Robert said into the phone.

"There's nothing healthy about what your company is doing to the people," a man's voice shouted. "You're taking billions of dollars from us for substandard medical care. If the government won't do anything to stop you, then I will."

"I'm sorry you feel that way, Mr. . . ."

"No. No names. You can just list me as a disgruntled ex-employee that got tired of seeing your company profit at the expense of innocent lives. The only thing that you need to know is that I planted a bomb in the building and it's set to go off at noon."

"Did you say—a bomb?"

"Yes. The timer is set for noon. If you don't have everyone evacuated by then, the blood is on your hands." The line clicked dead.

Robert looked around for a big red button to push, like the one they have in the movies that warns everyone they're in danger. He didn't see one.

A pair of men entered the building and headed for the turnstile.

"Stop!" Robert shouted at them.

The men jumped away from Robert, their eyes wide.

"You can't go in the building," Robert said as he vaulted over the counter. "I'm sorry, but you will have to stay here until I can get hold of Lloyd."

The men stood still, their mouths open.

"Stay there." Robert pointed to the floor at their feet.

Again he vaulted over the counter and grabbed the security radio.

"Lloyd. I mean Officer Lloyd. I need you to return to the front guard station—*immediately.*"

The radio crackled. "What is it?"

"I don't think it would be a good idea to talk about it over the radio. Please come back here right away. It's important."

"Don't go all noodles on me. I'm on my way."

By now, the number of employees had increased to around half a dozen. Robert set the phone on top of the counter so he could reach it from the other side and then moved to block the turnstile.

"Lloyd's on his way," Robert stammered. "Please stay where you are until he arrives."

"We're going to be late," said one man as he moved forward.

"Then I suggest you call your office and tell them that I am detaining everyone. You can use the guest phone in the visitors' lounge or a cell phone if you have one."

Robert didn't budge. The man stopped short of running over the top of him and didn't appear to be ready to wrestle Robert out of the way. More people came in the door and added to the cacophony of complaints.

Visions of screaming people trampling one another in their haste to exit the building kept running through his head. That's exactly what he expected to happen if he told these people about the bomb. But how else was he going to prevent them from going into the building?

A woman stepped up to the front of the crowd, arms crossed and a sneer on her face. "You need to get out of the way so all of us can get to work."

"I can't let you do that."

"Let me make this clear for you," she said as she moved in closer. "We are going through the security point. It's just a matter of whether you have a job once I reach my desk."

"I still can't let you past me."

"Everyone, relax," said Lloyd. He shut the security door behind him and motioned the crowd to silence. "Give me a moment to find out what's going on, and then I'll see about getting you on your way."

Lloyd pulled Robert away from the crowd, or as far as he could in a room filled with employees concerned about reporting late to their desks. "What is going on?"

"I received a bomb threat while you were gone."

Lloyds attitude changed; now he looked concerned. "Are you sure? Who was it? What did they say?"

"A man identified himself as an ex-employee and said he planted a bomb in the building. It's set to go off at noon. He didn't give me his name."

Lloyd looked over the crowd and then leaned in and whispered to Robert, "You stay right where you are and don't let anyone inside."

Then he turned around and faced the anxious employees. His hands fidgeted, a miserable attempt at a smile plastered on his face. "I need to check with Officer Milton, but I think that we are about to start a fire drill. Robert was trying to save you the trouble of walking halfway to your desks before you had to turn right around and go back outside."

The crowd looked uneasy at the announcement. Robert wondered if they suspected that something out of the ordinary was taking place. And if they did, how long before they started to panic?

Lloyd called Officer Milton.

Robert overheard him ask to replay the call that had come through the front desk phone and verify the threat. It took several minutes before Lloyd nodded. The ashen expression on his face told Robert that the threat had been confirmed.

Lloyd hung up the phone, but before he could address the employees, the fire alarm went off and all eyes fixed on him. A bit slowly, he pointed to the door. "Um."

Robert stepped up and spoke. "Everyone head over to the assembly spot at the parking garage. No need to panic. You guys do this drill all the time, I suppose."

"Right." Lloyd seemed to have come out of his daze. "Please go out through the door and head over to the assembly point for your department. Check in with your managers and wait there for further instructions."

They left. More employees followed. Within fifteen minutes the managers reported that all of their people had exited the building.

Robert, Lloyd, and Officer Milton conducted a quick inspection of the building to make sure no one had missed the alarm. They met on the far side of the building and exited out the back.

By the time they walked around to the front, police cars had the driveway blocked off and were scooting the employees even farther away from Healthy Partners.

An officer motioned the security team over to stand behind one of the squad cars.

"The bomb unit should be here any minute," explained the officer. "They'll want to question you about the phone call."

Robert stared past the flashing red and blue lights at the vacant building. His knees trembled. He tried to swallow but his throat was too dry. Now that he'd slowed down, he noticed how his heart slammed against his chest.

This must be a dream.

He pinched himself but nothing changed. He willed himself to wake up, but the lights continued to flash. He tried to remember how people went about waking themselves up from dreams and thought of nothing.

Someone had planted a bomb in his workplace. A queasy sensation in his stomach started to grow. That didn't happen in real life. At least not here. The events that were reported in the news happened in Washington and New York. Government buildings and military bases were targeted for terrorist attacks—not medical call centers.

His life had just taken a step into the realm reserved for suspense novels and news stories.

23

John noticed two middle-aged women watching him as he pulled into the gas station at the edge of Greenville. The way they both faced him, inclined toward one another, it made it obvious they were talking about him. They didn't look happy, and when they noticed John had spotted them, they didn't bother to turn away.

He filled up the tank and went inside to grab a treat. How strange that getting a candy bar and a soda from the gas station had become something he looked forward to during his trips into town. It reminded him of taking trips with his father out to his grandparents' farm. What a thrill it had been then to stop anywhere and pick up something sweet.

It took almost five minutes to make his selections. When you lived mostly on beans, eggs, and Ramen, all the offerings in the snack aisle tempted you. Finally, he decided on a root beer and a king-size Crunch bar and placed them on the counter next to the cash register.

The cashier, a paunchy man with an unkempt mustache, wrinkled his nose at John. Then he stepped away from the counter as if he were afraid of catching a virus.

"That's it," said John when the cashier failed to ring up his purchase. "That's all I'm getting this trip."

The cashier glanced around the otherwise empty store and then stepped back up to the register. His fingers stabbed at the cash register buttons. John handed the man a five, and the cashier made change and then slammed the money down on the counter.

John pocketed the money and left.

His second stop, and the main reason for being in town today, was the hardware store. The trailer had blown a fuse and they had used their only spare. If another one blew, they would be without electricity for their kitchen.

A brawny man with a thick neck stood behind the counter. He wore a blue shirt with the store logo and a patch that said, "My name is Merle."

John pulled the blown fuse out of his shirt pocket and showed it to Merle. "I need a couple of replacement fuses."

"Not here," Merle said. He folded his arms and leaned back.

"It seems odd that you'd be out of fuses," said John. "They're just the standard twenty-amp variety."

"I didn't mean we don't have them," Merle snarled. "I meant that you can't buy them here."

It took a moment for the implication of the man's words to sink in. "You're refusing to sell them to me?"

"That's right," Merle said. "We don't want you in our town. We don't want you anywhere near our town."

"We haven't done anything illegal," John said.

"I don't care. I want you out of my store." Merle unfolded his arms and leaned on the counter, his face a scarce foot away from John's.

"Yeah," said a gangly man standing in the paint aisle. "Why don't you cultists find another place to practice your strange rituals?"

"Our beliefs and methods of worship are similar to your own," John said.

"Except that you force young girls into your harems," said an older woman as she walked out from behind the broom stand.

156

"Then you pick a place out in the country so that no one can keep an eye on you."

"We don't have extra wives," John said. "You're confusing us with another group. The people you're talking about believe differently than we do."

"You're all Mormons," said Merle. "They worship Joseph Smith, just like you do. You can go ahead and claim that you're different, but we know better."

Another pair of store patrons came forward from the back of the store. They all surrounded John, edging closer to him with each new accusation.

John cleared his throat. "We believe that people should have the privilege of worshiping in the manner they choose, and in return we hope they will grant us the same courtesy. That's one of our Articles of Faith, which describe our beliefs. We want to be good neighbors."

"That sounds good when you spin it like that," said the thin man from the paint aisle. "Cults want to be left alone because they're breaking the law. We're not going to let this turn into another Waco."

"Or a home base for survivalist nut jobs," said Merle.

The situation reminded John of being stuck in quicksand; any comment he made sucked him further into the current argument. Nobody benefited from this exchange.

"If you don't want me to shop here," John shouted so he could be heard above the continuing barrage of criticism, "then I won't. I'll leave, and the rest of you can return to your shopping."

John squeezed his way past the blockade of townsfolk, trying to smile without seeming smug or condescending. He had nearly reached the exit when the door opened. Sheriff McKinney gave a brief glance at the patrons in the store and then fixed his stare on John.

"Step outside," McKinney said in a low, commanding voice.

Merle and his customers moved toward the door, but the sheriff motioned with an upheld hand for them to stay put.

"Appears that we have a bit of trouble here," he said.

"All I did was ask for a couple twenty-amp fuses."

"Doesn't matter." Sheriff McKinney bent closer to John's face. "Next time something like this happens, I'm going to arrest you for disturbing the peace."

"I haven't broken any laws," John said.

"The people here don't want you around. You know that. So the way I see it, whenever you come into town, you're asking for trouble. And I won't have it. Take your business someplace else."

"That's discrimination," John said. "You can't legally do that to us."

"Then write the governor." Sheriff McKinney straightened up and thumbed toward the Suburban. "Get moving—or I'll run you in right now."

John climbed into the Suburban. He drove over to the post office and picked up Wayne and Curtis, whom he'd dropped off earlier, and then stopped long enough at Doctor Whitton's to collect Scott.

Sheriff McKinney leaned up against his car and watched them until they headed down the road out of town.

John called for a camp meeting after dinner. The dorm had a roof as well as interior and exterior walls by now, so they were protected from the wind and some of the cold night air. They met in what would be the common room when the building was finished. It was the only location inside the dorm that held all twenty-three men comfortably.

Since their return, Curtis had complained about the way the postal worker had treated him and Wayne. It didn't take a rocket scientist to figure out that tonight's meeting had something to do with that.

The incident in town might be a peek at what they could expect in the months ahead. John's thoughts took him back to the stories he'd read about the persecution of the early Saints in Missouri and

Illinois. This situation certainly bore a strong resemblance to those events.

Had they come full circle? Was this just the beginning of another round of blind, unreasoning prejudice? Or could they avoid the mistakes of the past? A fair amount of pride had contributed to the problems Church members encountered when they'd tried to establish communities in the eastern half of the country. If John and the others continued to be good neighbors, would that change the outcome of this conflict?

Technically, they had another ten minutes before the meeting started. John weighed the merits of structure and standing on formality with the need for adaptability and flexibility. Without much to do in camp, everyone was already here and talking about the trip to town. Holding to a schedule in this instance meant ten more minutes of wild speculation that didn't help their situation at all. Adaptability won—John started the meeting.

Other than Tom Gordon, none of the men had brought hymnals. That meant they sang whatever songs the majority of them had memorized. It wasn't a large selection. John had gained a greater appreciation for the people in charge of hymn selection. At a time like this, a good song about forgiveness, or brotherly love, or staying the course would make his efforts to address everyone easier.

He settled on attempting "Let Us Oft Speak Kind Words."

Tom acted as chorister for the song. He was the only one who didn't mumble his way through the song. But John was happy with the result. He felt that it had set the tone of the meeting.

"Brethren," John said, "I suspect that you have probably heard that we had a bit of a problem in town today."

A volley of comments confirmed his statement.

"I am sad to report," said John, "that there's more to it than what happened to Curtis. Sheriff McKinney has requested that we get our supplies from another town from now on."

"They can't do that," Curtis shouted. "We have the right to be there."

A couple of the men agreed with him.

"Yes," said John. "Yes, we do. Constitutionally we're protected from this sort of reaction to our efforts here. But that may not be the direction we want to go with this. For one, turning this into a legal battle will distract us from our work on Camp Valiant. I'd hate for that to be all it took for the adversary to prevent us from doing what God directed us to do."

Curtis fidgeted in his seat. He seemed uncomfortable with the conversation so far.

"We also need to consider," John continued, "that in winning a battle you can lose the war. Forcing the people in Greenville to do business with us will not get them to accept us. I think it'd be better if we strive to be good neighbors and win their hearts."

"How are we supposed to do that when they won't even let us into town?" Curtis demanded.

"I don't know," John said. "If all of us put an effort into finding a solution, I think an answer will reveal itself. Until then, I think we should travel to Springfield for anything we need."

"What about our mail?" asked Wayne.

"We'll continue to have it delivered in Greenville," John said. "I don't think Sheriff McKinney will interfere with that. I'll take another one of you with me and we can plan to be there right as the post office opens. In and out—no problem."

Curtis didn't look convinced. Neither did several of the other men.

"And I'll notify Church headquarters about the situation," John said. "Maybe they can advise us of what they'd like us to do. Hopefully we're the only ones having this problem."

"I doubt it," Curtis said.

John spent a few minutes going over the daily list of snags the work crews had encountered. It felt good to deal with matters that could be resolved with some extra parts and a little elbow grease. Then he closed the meeting with another hymn and a prayer.

Bill and Luis came up afterward and pulled him aside.

"We may have another problem," said Bill.

That is exactly what John didn't need right now. He had his

hands full keeping the project on schedule and putting out the proverbial fires.

"A couple of the guys in my group are complaining about the living conditions here," Bill said.

"Same here," Luis said.

"None of us are comfortable with the accommodations," John said. "In a couple of weeks, that will change. They finished drilling the well yesterday, and as soon as all the plumbing is done in the dorm, we can start taking showers again. No more sponge baths."

"Ahh," Luis crooned. "I like the sound of that."

"I don't think some of them will last a couple of weeks," Bill said. "Besides, that isn't the only thing bothering them. Don Archer has been questioning whether any of this is really necessary."

"Curtis too," Luis added.

"Until the sky starts falling," said Bill, "some people aren't going to believe that anything needs to be done. This is a difficult time and place for all of us. Not everyone is going to have the faith to see it through."

John had noticed the signs of unease growing each day. He heard scraps of conversations between the men as they worked. Some were worn down from the hardships associated with such primitive living conditions while others worried about how their families were going to get through the economic trials they faced back home. And recently many of them had begun to fear that the situation would turn violent.

How was he going to guide anyone through a personal crisis of faith when he himself wondered whether he should pack it in and go home to his family?

"Part of this is our fault," John told the other two. "We have approached this as an extended service project. It isn't. The men serving here need more than direction on the work they do; they need us to watch over their spiritual needs as well. I'll see about getting some more hymnals up here, and starting tomorrow, we have seminary before we begin work."

"Seminary." Bill arched his eyebrows.

"We can call it institute if you think that sounds better. The important thing is that we introduce some sort of uplifting activity for them each day."

"Good," Luis said. "I never had the chance to attend institute."

The three of them agreed to take turns conducting the morning meeting, starting with John. When they stepped outside, they heard a commotion in the direction of the front gate. A flickering light illuminated the area.

John ran and joined the rest of the camp. A human effigy burned outside the gate. Next to it someone had staked a sign that read:

MORMONS GO HOME.

24

Getting through the security checkpoint took twice as long as normal. Ever since the CFF riot, the White House guards made the whole experience as troublesome as possible. The Secret Service agents had been even worse.

Calvin trudged into his office and asked Gwen for his messages.

"There are none." Gwen fidgeted in her seat and did a poor job of pretending to be busy.

"What about all the calls I asked you to place yesterday afternoon?"

Gwen stared at her hands. "I did. And their executive assistants promised to pass along the messages."

"Why do I get the feeling that there's more to this?"

"It's a brush-off." Gwen finally looked up at Calvin. "I can tell from the tone in their voices that your calls aren't going to be returned. Not only that, but I'm getting the cold shoulder from everyone."

"I'm sorry they're taking it out on you."

Gwen shrugged.

The fallout from Calvin's current disfavor was affecting Gwen too. He hoped that it wouldn't permanently damage her ability to find work in Washington. His career was screaming toward a fiery end. What could he do to prevent the same result from happening to her?

"Dial Barbara Warner," Calvin said. "I'll talk to them myself."

Gwen punched the numbers and the phone rang.

"Barbara Warner's office," said a pleasant voice on the other end of the line. "How can I help you?"

"This is Calvin McCord. I need to speak with Ms. Warner."

"I'm sorry, Mr. McCord. That won't be possible. Ms. Warner is out of the office right now, and I don't expect her back for the rest of the day."

"You're sure she's won't be in at all?"

"Oh, absolutely. I have her calendar right in front of me."

"If she happens to check in, can you have her call me?" Calvin asked.

"Will do," said the perky voice. "Thanks for calling, Mr. McCord."

Calvin hung up the phone.

"What are you going to do?" Gwen asked.

"I think I'll stop in and see Barbara."

"She's out of the office."

"So they say. I think I'll take a look for myself."

Calvin sat down at his desk and checked his emails. Nothing in his in-box was from the upper echelon of political figures. Gwen was right; he was being ignored.

He had to pass through a security checkpoint to reach Barbara Warner's office. Again, they took their time checking him before they let him through.

Barbara's assistant looked up as Calvin walked into the office. Wide-eyed, her mouth hung open for a moment. Then she seemed to regain her composure.

"Mr. McCord. As I told you over the phone, Ms. Walker isn't in today. Is there something else I can help you with?"

"I happened to be in the neighborhood and thought I would check to see if she just happened to drop by—unexpectedly."

Calvin heard a voice coming from Barbara's office.

The assistant's quick glance was evidence that she heard it too.

"Maybe you could knock on her door and make sure she didn't walk in while you were away from your desk."

"I'm positive she isn't in," said the assistant.

Barbara opened her office door and stuck her head out. "Tara, get me those files on the emergency security bill that's going to be voted on next week."

"That's strange," said Calvin. "It looks like she's in."

Barbara scowled at Calvin. "What do you want?"

"I need to talk to you. As few of our party as are in office, we need to work together."

"Oh." Barbara threw her hands up in the air. "Now you remember that."

"Shall we continue to argue where everyone can hear us," Calvin said, "or can we go into your office and talk?"

Barbara snarled, but she opened the door and motioned for Calvin to enter.

The office looked like a tornado had hit it. Folders were strewn all over the desk and on the chairs next to the desk. A stack of take-out food sat next to a wastebasket overflowing with coffee cups.

"We needed you to work with us," Barbara barked as soon as the door closed. "Instead nobody has heard a peep from you until now. Things not going well with Boggs?"

"Things have never gone well between me and Boggs."

"That's not how it looks from my perspective. You're still in his cabinet. You're still part of the planning meetings. You even attend the parties they throw for their friends. In case you haven't noticed, they've decided to start playing rough."

"You mean the Anarchists?" Calvin asked.

"We have a different name for them," Barbara spat. "We call them Boggs's Thugs."

"I don't think they are getting their orders from Boggs."

"Why am I not surprised to hear you say that?" Barbara offered a mirthless chuckle. "What is it you hope to accomplish by coming in here and defending Boggs to me? Are you getting a laugh out of shoving this in my face?"

"I'm trying to prevent a war!" Calvin shouted.

"Between who?"

"Between ourselves. Look at you. Look at them. How much longer before you see them as the enemy and start to act accordingly? The Russians are behind all of this. I need you to sit down with Boggs and work out some sort of plan that will get us focused on the real problem."

"Listen to yourself." Barbara put her hands to her temples as if to contain an explosive headache. "The Russians. Couldn't you make up a story a little more believable than that? Communism is fading off the face of the earth. In another thirty years it'll be gone. It's insane to think that the Russians are plotting against us."

"I have evidence," Calvin said. "They may have troops inside Iran."

"Get out," Barbara shouted. "Get out!"

A pair of Secret Service agents were waiting for Calvin when he exited the room. They escorted him back to his own office, breezing through the security checkpoint and asking him to confine himself to the events scheduled on his calendar.

Half an hour later, Calvin took a break from clearing out the trivial tasks that had accumulated and headed for the bathroom. He noticed that security guards had been posted at the end of the hall by the elevators.

Somebody was making it clear that they didn't want Calvin to bother them. The problem was he didn't know if that was a message from his party, Boggs's party, or both.

He continued to work away at the mountain of boring, repetitive tasks that were part of his normal duties. At lunchtime he had Gwen order sandwiches from Sammy's Deli and worked while he ate.

At two o'clock Boggs had scheduled a cabinet meeting, which was to include Barbara Warner and several of the other high-power members of Calvin's party. Perhaps with both sides meeting together, he could get them to finally listen to him.

Calvin made sure to leave early enough to get through the beefed-up security measures. The guards at the end of the hall watched Calvin but didn't try to stop him. It would have been interesting if they had.

When he arrived at the meeting, the scene before him reminded him of his days on the battlefield; chaos ruled as people shouted at one another, pointed fingers at members of the opposing party, and got into each other's faces. Harry Lipinski had someone cornered that Calvin couldn't see, but he could hear the accusations of party betrayal that were being leveled at them.

An entire detail of Secret Service agents, backed by security guards, was strewn amid the cabinet members and their guests. The security personnel hadn't adopted their usual stoic poses, which allowed them to appear intimidating while they watched the area in front of them for problems. Instead, their gazes scanned back and forth in an attempt to watch everyone at once.

Calvin spotted Keegan Roscoe in the hall. He looked like he was acting as peacemaker between Marion Salazar and Harry Lipinski. As Calvin negotiated a path between the feuding politicians, Keegan looked up and saw him. Keegan made a brief comment to the two men he was speaking to and then headed into the conference room.

By the time Calvin squeezed, dodged, and bumped his way into the room, Keegan had taken a seat and was surrounded by members of his own party. They probably wanted the same thing he did: support from the influential senator in the upcoming battle royale. In his case, Calvin needed the man's level head more than he needed the political weight he wielded.

Secret Service agents entered the room and started ushering people to their seats. The commotion settled to an almost reasonable level. When everyone was seated, Boggs walked into the room, bracketed by even more agents.

"Will the room come to order!" shouted Agent Jones, the lead member of the President's security detail. "The meeting will begin as soon as everyone calms down."

Boggs stood. The confident smile he wore like a suit was missing today. His body language was defensive and stiff.

"We are in the midst of a crisis." Boggs paused until the room was entirely silent. "The rules of political decorum have been cast aside. If we, the country's leaders, have lost the veneer of civilization, then what hope is there for all of us?"

For once, Calvin found himself agreeing with Boggs.

"Kudos to Richard Donnelli for writing a great speech," Harry Lipinski inserted during Boggs's dramatic pause. "It would have a lot more impact if you could tell us when you'll be reining in the Anarchists."

Shouts broke out from all points in the room.

"Mr. President," Calvin called out, hoping to get Boggs's attention.

The President motioned for everyone to stop their arguing and let him speak. Eventually they did.

"My party does not condone the actions of the Political Anarchists," Boggs said. "They are damaging to our cause and an embarrassment to this country. We have not sanctioned them to act in our behalf."

"Then when are you going to stop them?" Barbara Warner asked.

"No connection has been established between them and our party," Marion Salazar said. "They operate independent of us and against our wishes."

"Mr. President." Calvin raised his hand as he shouted for attention.

Boggs gave no indication of having heard or seen Calvin.

"A task force has been formed with the goal of finding those responsible for these acts of terror and bringing them to justice," Boggs said.

"The purpose of the task force is to find out who is responsible for the bombing in Houston and the attempted bombing in Charleston," Lipinski said. "What about the acts of extreme vandalism they're responsible for? What do you plan to do about the protest in Miami, where the Anarchists broke all the windows at the convention hall right after Barbara spoke there?"

"Or about the apparent campaign here in DC that targets the cars belonging to members of our party?" said Edwin Stack. "Dozens of cars have been stolen, and within the last two weeks, they've started setting them on fire."

"It could be anyone!" Ken Farr bellowed.

"No." Barbara spoke without shouting. "Each of the arson incidents had the Anarchist symbol spray painted next to the vehicle. It was clearly their work and they are just as clearly targeting us."

"Mr. President." Calvin stood this time as he called for Boggs's attention.

"Agent Jones," Boggs said, "have Mr. McCord forcibly removed from the room if he interrupts this proceeding again."

Jones nodded. Calvin couldn't be sure, but it looked like he smiled.

The rest of the room continued as if Calvin hadn't said a word.

"I can't stand the hypocrisy any longer," Dennis de la Pena shouted as he stood up. "They want to sit there and accuse us of orchestrating attacks on them while ignoring how their constituents stormed the CFF charity last week. I was there and it was the first time in my tenure as a public servant that I feared for my life."

Harry stood up so fast that his chair skittered along the floor. "You can't be serious. I spoke with several congressmen who attended the charity event, and they said the protest was over by the time anyone knew about it."

"You weren't even there." Dennis shoved his chair back so hard that it bounced off the wall.

"It's about time that you got a taste of what's been happening to us." Edwin jabbed a finger in Ken Farr's direction.

"If you think—" Martin Posey shouted at Barbara Warner, only to be drowned out by Marion Salazar's booming voice.

"How dare you suggest that I'm covering up the results of the investigation." Marion moved away from his seat and headed toward Harry.

The Secret Service moved into the argument, placing themselves between opponents. Already a few of the participants had adopted intimidating poses. Harry had even poked Marion Salazar in the chest. Calvin was convinced that if the agents hadn't stepped in when they did, the next riot would have been here.

A good portion of the attendees left of their own volition. Agents escorted the rest out as quickly as their limited numbers allowed. Keegan was one of those who left voluntarily and Calvin hurried to catch him.

"Keegan," Calvin called out three hallways later. "Please, wait."

"I'm sorry," Keegan said when he turned around. "I can't help you."

"We're on the verge of another Civil War."

"I know." Keegan drew a deep breath. "The fabric of the country's leadership is unraveling. I am doing all that I can to prevent it. I suspect that you are too. But I can't continue to work with you and hope to be effective."

"We'd be stronger together," Calvin protested.

"No, we wouldn't. In the end, my career would be brought down along with yours. You're much too clever for your own good, I'm afraid."

Keegan laid a hand on his shoulder. "Good-bye, Calvin."

25

Not even the building anticipation of a second date with Sierra could help Robert's frame of mind. He continued to dwell on the bomb threat, more scared now than when it had happened. During the event he'd been focused on what needed to be done. Now his mind worked through scenarios of what could have happened.

The police hadn't found any explosives at the call center, but at the same time the bomb squad was occupied there, a man brought a shotgun to the Healthy Partners corporate office across town and killed eight people.

It just as easily could have been the other way around.

The police suspected Troy Chavelle. Robert suspected they were right. He had personally helped escort Troy out of the call center when the man had been fired. Troy had issues.

So far, Troy had evaded the police and remained at large. That probably explained why Camden Security had called Robert last night and given him a new assignment. Downtown. Far from the call center location.

He reported to Raúl Dominquez at the Parthenon Plaza building. It was one of the smaller buildings in the area and contained mostly law offices and mortgage companies.

Raúl stood in the front foyer. He wore a uniform that identified him as building security; a name tag was prominently displayed on the front of his shirt. Another guard stood next to him wearing a uniform like Robert's.

"You must be Robert," Raúl said and shook his hand. "You'll be working with Aiden today keeping an eye on the lobby here."

Robert reached over and shook hands with his fellow guard.

"If you have any questions, ask Aiden. And if Aiden has any questions, he can give me a call over the radio." Raúl pointed to a handheld mobile unit hanging from Aiden's hip.

"That seems simple enough," Robert said.

Raúl gave a worried look in the direction of the glass front doors and then walked toward the back of the building.

"All right, what do we do?" Robert asked.

"We stand here and call the police if any trouble breaks out. Not exactly here. You can stand pretty much anywhere in this front area."

"Call the police."

"We're unarmed guards." Aiden sounded perturbed. "If a fight breaks out, we lock the doors and call the police. Oh, and make sure that none of the employees or guests go outside until the police clear everything up."

Robert noticed that Aiden seemed nervous. His fellow guard kept glancing toward the door.

"Is there something wrong?" Robert asked. "I mean, do you expect trouble today?"

Aiden nodded. "We received a call this morning from the police that there might be a political protest in the area."

That made sense to Robert. Posting a couple of guards in plain sight would hopefully deter anyone who had wandered off from the main crowd from doing something stupid. It occurred to him that this would be a one or possibly two-day job. Then he could be back at Healthy Partners or wait for a more permanent assignment.

Robert moved to a spot about six feet from the door and watched the activity outside. Aiden positioned himself behind the customer service kiosk at the far end of the room.

The morning started out quietly. People walked along the sidewalks in typical business-hurry mode. Employees of the building entered the door, and Robert gave them a friendly greeting. A pair of foot patrol officers walked by, peering through the door as they passed.

Around eleven o'clock, all of that changed. The amount of suit-wearing foot traffic dropped to nothing. Then the streets began to fill with men in T-shirts and jeans carrying signs that said, "Not this time" and "Buildings don't fight back."

"What's this about?" Robert asked Aiden.

"I heard that the Political Anarchists group planned to protest at the rally being held here today." Aiden had moved lower in the chair so that he could just barely look out over the top of the kiosk.

"Isn't that a contradiction of terms? The Anarchists clearly support one of the political parties; political parties are government and anarchists are against government."

"Hey, man, don't ask me. I just work here."

Robert looked back outside. He noticed a few signs decrying the evils of the political party the Anarchists supported. He guessed that these were not the anarchists Aiden was talking about.

Angry men marched along the street, heading farther downtown. They looked like they were not only ready for trouble—they wanted it.

A few businessmen and businesswomen made their way through the stream of protestors to enter the building. Robert greeted them with a smile as they came through the door. The number of visitors dwindled as more protestors arrived. Before long, no one passed in front of the building.

If Robert stood at the door, he could see a crowd assembled in the area next to the Civic Plaza. They waved their signs, and even from two blocks away he could hear them shouting.

Just before noon, the noises from the Civic Plaza changed. Shouting and chanting gave way to screams and breaking glass.

Robert opened the door to get a better look at what was happening and the full clamor hit him. Lesser bangs and thuds joined the louder sounds of battle as objects slammed against buildings or were wielded as weapons.

A swirling mass of bodies moved slowly toward Robert. Those who still had signs in their hands swung them as weapons. Men in black ski masks tried to fend off the much larger force of protestors that Robert had seen earlier. In the few moments he'd been watching, the riot moved close enough that he could make out the groans of pain from the injured.

"They're fighting!" Robert shouted to Aiden.

"Lock the door!" Aiden shouted back.

Robert quickly checked himself for keys before remembering that he didn't have any for this building. He turned and sprinted for the kiosk where Aiden frantically tried to dial the phone.

"Give me the keys!" Robert shouted.

Aiden pulled the keys from his belt and fumbled the phone. He tried to catch the receiver but ended up dropping both the keys and the phone to the floor.

Robert snatched up the keys and raced for the door. He slid to a stop, nearly slamming into the glass.

His fingers nervously manipulated the keys on the ring. He tried the first one. It didn't fit.

Looking up, he spotted four men about ten feet from the door. Three of them were advancing on the fourth. They held the broken remains of protest signs in their hands, swinging them like clubs. Their victim already sported a couple of gashes on his face and was bleeding.

Without thinking, Robert stepped outside.

"Hey," he shouted at the men, his hands held up, motioning for them to stop.

The three armed men looked at Robert.

"Stay out of this," one of them sneered.

From behind him, Robert could hear Aiden shouting for him to lock the door and then excitedly calling for Raúl over the security radio.

"I can't let you do this." Robert tried to sound calm. He tried not to sound scared.

"Go back inside," said another of the men.

The wounded man scuttled backward in an attempt to escape his attackers. He hadn't moved more than a couple of feet before the three men closed in on him.

Robert grabbed the arm of one of the attackers, preventing him from swinging his makeshift club. He'd nearly wrestled the stick out of the man's hand when something collided with the side of his head.

His vision darkened and bright pinpoints of light swam in front of his eyes. Another blow caught him across the back. He dropped to one knee, pulling the stick down with him.

Fists hammered his face, head, and shoulders.

Robert covered himself as best he could, but they came at him from the front and the side. When he tried to get away, he fell backward.

He lashed out with his feet and connected with something. As soon as he did, he rolled to his feet and tried to stand.

A heavy blow smashed past his upraised arms and slammed against his skull. Darkness closed in once again. He felt hands grabbing at him from behind and then—nothing.

26

A siren announced the sheriff's arrival at the gate.
John barely heard it over the angry shouts of the townsfolk and his own work crews. He spotted Sheriff McKinney pushing his way to the center of the mob.

"Break it up," McKinney shouted above everyone else. The noise diminished, although it didn't stop altogether.

"These people are trespassing." Curtis shoved his way to where John and Sheriff McKinney stood. "Do something."

McKinney's jaw tightened as he glared at Curtis. He waited a moment, almost daring Curtis to say something else, and then turned to John. "People have a right to assemble. They have a right to orderly protest."

"That's fine, Sheriff," said John, "as long as they assemble in a public area and not on private property. Our land extends all the way to those markers down the way." John pointed to the stakes that marked their western boundary, even though they were too far down the dirt path to see.

The sheriff split his attention between John and Curtis, giving the latter warning glances each time Curtis moved or gestured. A couple of the townspeople closed the small gap between them and Scott, who, despite having a broken leg, wasn't backing down. Sheriff McKinney placed a restraining hand on the two townsfolk and directed Scott to go stand inside the gated portion of the property.

"That may be," said McKinney, "but it isn't posted. If you don't want these people marching outside your gates, then I suggest you put up a couple 'No Trespassing' signs to let them know. Until you've done that, I don't plan to stop them from letting their concerns be known."

"You are the law enforcement for this area," John protested. "I'm reporting to you that these people are on private property and officially request that you move them away from here."

"Get a sign." Sheriff McKinney stepped between another brewing fight and gave Wayne a none-too-gentle prod toward the gate. "If any of my people breach the fenced area of your property, I'll take care of it. Otherwise, I suggest that you get inside. It'll be safer that way."

John didn't know the law well enough to determine if the sheriff was correct or just supporting the mob mentality of the people of Greenville. Now wasn't the time to press the matter. Sheriff McKinney appeared willing to prevent the townspeople from entering Camp Valiant itself, and that provided a safe haven for John and the rest of the Saints.

"All right," said John. "We'll go inside."

John turned to coax the work crews back into the camp just as one of the townsfolk pushed Paul Young. Paul wasn't big by any means, but he had worked construction all his life and all five feet seven inches of him were solid. He also had a construction worker attitude to go with it. Paul pushed right back.

The Greenville citizen flew back and slammed into a pair of his fellow protestors. All three staggered back a step. From off to Paul's side, a townsperson wearing a red and brown flannel shirt launched a punch that glanced off his shoulder.

Paul caught the attacker by the arm and tweaked it so as to force the man to the ground. The man who originally pushed Paul barreled into him, knocking him free from the downed townsperson. A pair of Greenville teens rushed Paul as well.

Wayne moved in to help his outnumbered friend.

A foursome of townspeople, including a woman, moved to intercept Wayne. They flailed at his arms in an attempt to grab them, but Wayne thrashed about wildly, not allowing them a good hold.

From somewhere within the portion of the crowd that had not yet joined the growing brawl, a rock flew through the air and struck Wayne above the right eye.

Wayne dropped to the ground and didn't move.

Those few Camp Valiant workers that still remained inside the fence climbed or vaulted over it. A couple of them had picked up makeshift clubs along the way.

A gunshot rang out.

The violence halted as everyone looked around for the shooter.

Another shot drew everyone's attention to Sheriff McKinney, who had his pistol aimed high in the air.

"This fight will stop NOW!" McKinney shouted. He scanned the crowd, staring down anyone who didn't immediately back away from the conflict.

When the crowd had untangled itself from one another, he moved over to where Wayne lay on the ground, bleeding.

"This man is going to need medical attention," the sheriff said.

"I suppose you're going to expect us to drive all the way to Springfield to find a doctor," John said.

"Don't push it," McKinney told John as he continued to examine Wayne. "I don't think this is life threatening, but he is definitely going to need stitches."

The sheriff motioned John to come look after Wayne. Once John moved to Wayne's side, McKinney stood up and faced the Greenville mob. He holstered his gun and then stood to his full, imposing height. The commotion died down to a few whispered comments.

"That'll be it for the day," the sheriff announced loudly.

"We can protest if we want!" someone shouted from the back of the Greenville mob.

"This isn't protesting," said the sheriff. "It's rioting. As far as I know, these people haven't broken the law—yet. A couple of you have crossed the line. I want everyone to turn around and go home."

A few of the people shuffled uneasily on their feet. None turned to leave.

"Right now!" Sheriff McKinney's tone made it clear that he meant it.

The people of Greenville dispersed in small groups, continuing to look back at Camp Valiant and the people inside as they walked away.

"Get your friend loaded up," said Sheriff McKinney. "I'll escort you to Dr. Whitton's office. You can stay there until the doctor has him patched up. Then I want you out of town. No mail runs this week either."

John glanced up at McKinney. Maybe it was too much to expect the sheriff to arrest someone in the Greenville mob for assaulting Wayne, but he overstepped his authority by denying them access to the mail. If members of Camp Valiant wanted legal and fair treatment, they weren't going to get it anywhere around here.

Tom Gordon and Rick Siptroth applied a quick wrap around Wayne's head to slow the bleeding and then carefully carried him to the Suburban. Tom and Rick worked the same crew as Wayne and were anxious to accompany him to the doctor.

They followed the sheriff into town. Bill Winters had used the Bobcat to scrape a semblance of a road over the last week so the trip wasn't as bumpy as it had been.

"They kept on talking about Waco," Tom said.

"And the Unabomber," said Rick.

"How bad does the wound look?" John asked.

"It's going to leave an ugly scar on his forehead," said Tom.

"Then I guess no one will notice," Wayne mumbled.

John gave a silent sigh of relief. He was glad that Wayne could joke about the situation. An injury like that could have had serious consequences. They'd been lucky today.

Who knew what would happen next time.

John followed the sheriff into the doctor's parking lot and stopped right in front of the door. He helped Tom and Rick carry Wayne inside although Wayne insisted that he could walk on his own.

They placed Wayne on an examination table and were ushered out of the room. John took a seat that gave him a view of the Suburban and watched over it. Tom paced the length of the waiting room floor. Rick found a copy of the Bible on a table and started to read.

The doctor reappeared nearly two hours later—without Wayne.

"All done," Dr. Whitton announced. "Took some fancy stitch-work, but he'll be fine. I'm going to keep him overnight to make sure there aren't any complications or delayed signs of more serious brain trauma. You can come back in the morning and pick him up."

"He's going to stay here?" John asked.

"That's what I said. I have a room fixed up here where I can keep an eye on him. I'll check him every couple of hours to make sure his vitals are where they should be. I don't expect any problems."

"Thank you," said John. "It really—"

"I said he could stay," interrupted Dr. Whitton. "Not you. The office is closed. Come back tomorrow."

The doctor marched them out the door and then locked it.

Outside, Sheriff McKinney leaned against his patrol car, talking to two men in suits. They stood beside a dark sedan that was parked next to the Suburban. McKinney looked uncharacteristically pleased. He pointed John out to the men and grinned.

The men in suits picked up an envelope from the hood of the sedan and advanced toward John.

"I'm Agent Mathis, and this is Agent Kane," said the man, handing John the envelope. "We're with Homeland Security, and this is a cease and desist order. You and the members of your group will stop all construction until an investigation of your activities can be completed."

27

Boggs had finally gotten the better of him, and why wouldn't he? Nelson Osborn Boggs was the President of the United States and arguably the most powerful person on the earth. Calvin had no chance going up against him in a political duel.

That didn't make it any easier for him to accept that the world was headed for another bloody global war. Knowing that he had done his best to keep Russia from getting the upper hand on the United States in the upcoming conflict only served to remind him that his best wasn't enough. He had failed to protect the country and the people he loved.

He grabbed a handful of rolled-up socks out of his chest of drawers and fitted them into the remaining open spots inside his suitcase. Then he slogged over to the closet and looked over the selection of suits again, wondering if it mattered which of them he took for his junket to Vanuatu in the South Pacific.

Boggs certainly had made good on his threat. If a more distant, less-crucial diplomatic assignment existed, Calvin didn't know about it. In Vanuatu, he would be isolated and politically impotent. And he had no doubt that once he finished there, Boggs would find an equally meaningless assignment for him.

He was still rummaging through his closet without actually seeing the clothes when the phone rang.

"Are you bringing a date to the big presidential gala tonight?" asked Mike Costa. "Or will the two of us be batching it?"

"No, you go. I'm being exiled tomorrow and need to finish my packing."

"I've seen the way you dress." Mike chortled. "A blind monkey could pack your bags in five minutes and you'd be better off. Besides, if they really are shipping you out of here, we need to drink a couple of beers and talk about old times. Like when we met those girls in Panama."

Calvin stopped rummaging through his underwear drawer. The two of them had been in Panama, but they hadn't managed to run into one another while they were there. Mike had a flawless memory for details. Which meant he wanted to arrange a meeting with Calvin without tipping off anyone who might have tapped the phone line.

"A couple of drinks sounds good," said Calvin. "After all, it's not as if I'm the one that's going to be flying the plane."

"Good. See you there."

One thing Boggs knew how to do was throw a party. Or at least his wife did. Bright lights. Loud, fast music. And people dressed in sixty-four-thousand-dollar smiles and outfits that cost more money than the average American made in a month.

Calvin had selected his best, most stylish suit: a black-striped, two-button navy affair with a peak lapel and a charcoal-striped dress shirt. Compared to the rest of the guests, he looked like he'd grabbed his clothing off the rack at Sears. Not that he had anything against the suits at Sears—he owned several—but it set him apart from the Washington crowd.

He didn't know the men at the check-in point, but they appeared to know him. After a few whispered exchanges they let him pass, but they mouthed something into their cuff mics as he moved on.

Calvin meandered through the glittering rooms filled with the VIPs of Boggs's political party and the media darlings that adored them. All stops had been pulled out to make this event a success. Under different circumstances he might have enjoyed it.

When he failed to find Mike at the bar or the snack line, Calvin wandered toward the back section of the building. The area near the kitchen would have a volume of traffic for the serving staff and thus fewer persons of importance around it. That would make it the most logical spot to meet.

Calvin made it all the way to the point where the party ended and the servitor realm began without finding Mike. He turned around and headed toward the front of the building, intending to make the whole circuit again if need be.

He was glancing back toward the kitchen access points, scanning one more time for Mike, when it struck him that something was amiss.

Calvin stopped and studied the room again.

Everything looked normal. His instincts screamed that something was wrong, but he couldn't identify the threat that existed in the scene before him.

"I might've guessed that I'd find you next to the kitchen," said Mike Costa.

Calvin spun around and found his friend standing next to him.

"This is the direction they take when they toss out unwanted guests," Calvin replied as he continued to search the room for the cause of his alarm. "I expected them to bring you along this way eventually."

"Enough of the friendly trash talk." Mike lowered his voice, his tone serious now. "I have solid information that the Russians have been responsible—"

"That's it," Calvin interrupted. "The Russians. They're here."

Calvin frantically searched the faces of the waiters in the room. The missing detail had snapped into place. He remembered seeing one of the waiters before. That man and two others had been present prior to the riot at Boggs's last fund-raising event.

"An Eastern European agent is posing as one of the wait staff," Calvin told Mike. "Help me find him."

The man was no longer in the room. That meant he had passed by while Calvin had been talking to Mike. The problem was that there were two directions he could have gone. Calvin gave a quick description of the man to Mike and they separated.

He jogged into the next room.

The fast motion alerted the Secret Service agent stationed at the door.

Calvin changed direction and headed straight for the agent. "The President is in danger. Get on the radio and get him out of here."

The agent held still, his hand hidden under his suit jacket, undoubtedly grasping his government-issued firearm.

"For Pete's sake," Calvin shouted at the agent. "Look at me. I'm Secretary of State Calvin McCord. Use your wrist mic and have the President's security detail move him out of this building."

A dawning light glowed in the agent's eyes. He started yelling into his cuff and ran to follow Calvin until he collided with one of the waiters and they both went down into a tangled mess.

Calvin pushed on. He doubted that the spy would waste his time in this room. All of the juiciest targets would be farther along.

Sure enough, Calvin spotted the man just exiting the room. He was pushing a serving cart and didn't bother to look back at the commotion Calvin had caused.

Calvin burst into a run. He tried his best to weave his way around the guests but sent several of them crashing to the ground and another one into a waiter carrying a tray full of drinks.

The spy glanced back and spotted Calvin making straight for him. He responded by pushing the cart forward at a run.

"Stop that man!" Calvin yelled and pointed at the spy.

That was a mistake. His shouts brought curious guests his way to find out what all the excitement was about. They filled the space between Calvin and the spy.

Calvin pushed his way through the thickening crowd. He elbowed, shoved, and ran over anyone who had the ill fortune to be in front of him. He bulled his way through the unsuspecting guests until he came across an unmanned cart.

The spy must have given up on the mission and was making an effort to escape.

But which way?

Calvin had put on a few extra pounds since his military days and he used them to good effect to move the milling guests aside. He jostled his way to a table and climbed up on one of the surrounding chairs.

It took a few moments, but he spotted the spy hastily threading his way through the crowd, toward the kitchen. Calvin also noticed Mike pressing his way between the guests.

Calvin cupped his hands and shouted to Mike. "Evacuate these people. Move them out of here now."

Then he jumped down from the chair and set after the spy, slashing his arm violently to the left and right to motion people out of the way.

They moved aside.

Calvin gained ground on the fleeing spy, who still attempted to move through the building without attracting attention to himself. By the time the spy reached the service way leading to the kitchen, Calvin had closed the gap to a couple dozen meters.

The spy broke into a run once he cleared the kitchen door.

Calvin followed. The distance between them widened with every step. He couldn't keep up this pace for long. Too many years politicking had left him old, slow, and short-winded.

Then a dishwasher stepped around a corner and Calvin slammed into him. Both men fell to the ground. Calvin scrambled to get back on his feet, but the slippery floor prevented it.

The Secret Service agent who had stopped him earlier helped Calvin to stand.

"Call ahead," Calvin ordered the agent. "We can't let that man escape. Block all the exits. Don't let any of the serving staff leave the building. And get more agents over here to help find this guy."

Calvin pushed off from a nearby wall and slid along the floor until his shoes finally got traction and he burst into a run.

He followed the trail of turned heads and downed servers. Just ahead, shots rang out. One. Two. A moment filled with shouting and then a triple tap of ballistic death.

Calvin burst through the doors leading to the next room and found the spy standing next to the fallen body of a Secret Service agent, the agent's still-smoking gun in his hand.

The spy snapped the gun in Calvin's direction and fired.

Calvin felt a tugging on his suit. The flare of the pistol momentarily blinded him. He pushed his legs forward, let his body drop, and slid into the spy feet first.

The spy landed on top of Calvin and slammed an elbow into Calvin's ribs with a cracking sound that sent a spike of pain shooting through his body.

Calvin grasped the pistol in both hands, fighting to keep it pointed away from him, a fight he was losing.

Then the world shook.

Lights flickered off. A wave of force rippled through the floor. The walls and the ceiling shuddered, showering the area with flecks of white and chunks of gray. Then a thunderous boom hit them.

A second explosion followed the first.

The concussion of the blast slammed the spy into a support column.

Calvin pushed himself to his knees. His ribs screamed in agony and blackness tugged at him.

Not in my house! Calvin's mind shouted. *I won't let a little pain stop me from bringing this guy down.*

Calvin screamed as he stood fully. Then he tottered over to the spy.

The spy raised his head and shook it, his eyes a bit dazed as he looked around. He spotted Calvin and crawled to where the pistol had dropped during the explosion. His hand clasped on the pistol grip just as . . .

Calvin dumped all his weight on top of the spy. Like the grand-daddy of all "hop on pop" games, he jumped into the air and crashed down on top of his enemy.

The spy screamed.

Calvin screamed.

Then the cavalry arrived. The Secret Service agent who had accosted him earlier ran into the room.

"Are you all right, sir?"

Calvin opened his mouth to scream at the agent, but his ribs said no. Instead, he just nodded his head.

"Do you remember who I am?" Calvin hissed between clenched teeth.

"Yes, sir," the agent shot back. "You're Calvin McCord, the Secretary of State."

"This is the man responsible for setting off the bomb." Calvin brought a fist down against the back of the man's head to emphasize who he was talking about. "Call in another agent and take this spy into custody."

The agent nodded his head and continued to stare.

"Now!" Calvin shouted. His ribs shouted back.

The agent raised his hand to his mouth and spoke into his cuff mic. "Priority one request for backup at Service Corridor DD-14. This is Agent Dixon making a priority one request for backup."

Calvin adjusted his weight so that he was sitting on the spy's back instead of being sprawled partially across him.

The spy lay there groaning—and wheezing.

As much as it must hurt to have Calvin positioned where he was, it had to hurt worse to try and struggle out from underneath him. Calvin tried to take solace in that knowledge with every stabbing breath he took.

A pair of Secret Service agents arrived. They looked to Agent Dixon and then to the Secretary of State, apparently not sure who they should be speaking to.

"Slap some restraints on this piece of garbage so I can get off him," Calvin told the two new arrivals. "He's the terrorist responsible for the bomb."

"Both bombs? Or just one of them?" asked a blond-haired agent.

"There were two bombs?" Calvin asked. Without a chase in progress, he now remembered the second blast.

Calvin held up a hand and Agent Dixon helped him to a standing position.

The other two agents assumed responsibility of the spy. One knelt in the center of his back, while the second yanked his arms behind him and tightened a strap around his wrists.

"Is the President all right?"

"Yes, sir," said Agent Dixon. "His security detail moved him to a safe room as soon as you told us about the threat. They were just coming back for the rest of the cabinet members when the second bomb went off. Things are pretty confused up there right now, so we don't know much more than that."

Calvin limped through the service area. The farther inward he moved, the more dust thickened the air. By the time he reached the service access doors, he could smell burning wood and plastic. It finally registered that the fire alarm was blaring away.

The room where the first bomb had exploded still sported a couple of small fires. Walls had been blown outward, the roof sagged to the point of collapse, and nothing remained of the bright, festive decorations that had adorned the rooms.

So far, Calvin hadn't come across any bodies. Maybe Mike had been able to clear everyone out before the bomb exploded. He prayed that he had.

The damage in the room itself was too severe for Calvin to enter. He picked a route that would circle around the blasted area and looked for anyone that might need help.

Several bodies lay broken in an adjacent hall.

Mike Costa was one of them.

Calvin sprinted over to his friend, ignoring the pain that lashed at him with every step. He kneeled next to him and gingerly turned him over. Blood flowed from a wound on the left side of his scalp and several other points on his arms and torso. A large wood fragment had wedged itself in his chest, which made a sucking noise every time he breathed.

Mike opened his eyes a slit. "We did it." He coughed. "Those Russian spies can limp back home with their tails between their legs. Don't mess with the US."

Calvin could tell that Mike meant it as a shout, but it came out a whisper.

"Yeah," Calvin managed. His struggle to hold back his tears prevented him from saying any more. Instead he just nodded.

"I have something for you." Mike unclenched his hand. It held a flash drive.

Calvin clasped his hand around the memory stick—and his friend's hand.

"Nail Boggs to the wall."

Mike's chest stopped moving. His eyes continued to stare at Calvin.

"Count on it."

28

Sharp pain lanced Robert's side whenever he laughed.

"I'm sorry," said Sierra. "Maybe we should talk about something more serious."

That definitely wasn't what he needed. Ever since he'd come home from the hospital, his family and friends had admonished him for taking such a horrible risk. Even Kevin had disapproved. Robert wanted to enjoy this moment. He wanted to enjoy Sierra's visit to his makeshift bed that the family had set up in the living room.

"Like what?"

Sierra shifted in her chair. "Do you plan to go back to work as a security guard?"

There it was. Now his potential girlfriend had joined the choir of protests.

"It might not be up to me," Robert said. "They placed me on temporary leave."

"What do you think that means?"

"That they don't want to fire me until my ribs have mended. And maybe they should; they keep telling me to observe and report."

"Sounds reasonable to me," said Sierra.

Robert sighed, which brought on another stabbing pain from his broken ribs. "The funny thing is I don't think I can do that. I can't sit back and just watch people when they need help."

"I don't see anything funny about that."

"Not the helping part," Robert said. Did he really want to get into this? Diving deep into his problems was probably the best way of scaring Sierra away. He'd rather keep things light and put up with the physical pain that resulted from an unavoidable laugh.

"Then what?" Sierra looked at him expectantly.

"Me. Fighting. Or at least trying to stop one person from beating on another. That isn't like me at all. I don't like violence. And as we can all see, I'm not very good at it."

Sierra reached over and grabbed his hand. "It takes courage to stand up for someone else's rights." She gave his hand a squeeze and let go. "Especially," she said with the barest hint of a smirk, "when you seem so very lacking in aggressive skills."

Robert laughed, then grunted in pain.

"I'm sorry." Sierra held her hands to her mouth. "I shouldn't try to be funny."

"No." Robert shook his head. "You should. It's just what I need right now."

"Really?" Sierra arched an eyebrow. "And all this time I thought this is what would do the trick."

She leaned forward and kissed Robert.

Two days on the couch was all Robert could stand. When his mother failed to reappear after dropping his siblings off for homeschooling with the Ramsdens, he decided to get up. Despite the doctor's orders, his mother's orders, or the pain involved, he planned to get busy doing something besides sitting and watching television.

His ribs screamed in protest as he rolled his legs over the side of the couch. He sucked shallow breaths between his teeth until the level of pain returned to the usual dull throbbing. Then he closed his eyes and willed himself to stand up.

Even keeping his body as straight as he could, the pain lashed at him as he rose. For one panic-inducing moment he lost his balance and nearly toppled forward. It hurt to stand, but it would've hurt a lot more if he'd pitched forward on top of the magazine table that sat next to the couch.

He considered walking into his room and changing clothes. Then his brain started working again and he realized that he had no chance of pulling off the shirt he currently wore, much less of putting on a new one. If he wanted to find out what had happened to his mother, he'd have to do so in the shorts and T-shirt that served as his pajamas.

The first couple of steps sent him wobbling. But he soon improved, and by the time he reached the front door, he had worked out a pace that minimized the stress to his injuries. He turned the doorknob and then took a backward step, pulling the door along with him.

His mother stood in front of her car. The hood was up and she had her hands on her hips as she stared at the engine. She looked up as he approached.

"What are you doing out of bed?" She rushed to his side and took his arm.

"I came to see what happened to you."

"That's sweet of you, but you shouldn't be up and moving around."

"My ribs feel better."

"Feeling better and actually being better are two different things. Let me help you back to bed." She gently pulled on Robert's arm. "Are you feeling hungry? I can fix you some breakfast and then turn on the television."

Robert tried to pull his arm away from his mother. He stopped as a sharp stabbing in his side let him know they weren't ready to cooperate.

His mother stopped too. "Oh, Robert." She used the "poor baby" voice. "I know you want to help me. What I need is someone to fix the car, and in your condition I don't think you'll be able to maneuver around to do that. Maybe we can figure a way for you to help out around the house *and* still stay in bed."

"Sure. I can add my weight to the couch and prevent it from floating away."

"No need to be sarcastic, Robert," his mother said sternly. "I think that if the two of us put our heads together, we can find a way to keep you productive and not thinking about your injuries. We'll do that over breakfast."

"What about the kids? How did they get to homeschool today?"

"Camile Ramsden happened to drive by and gave them a ride."

Robert ambled into the house with his mother hovering nearby, arms ready to catch him if he started to fall. They made it inside and to the kitchen table without incident.

As short a trip as it had been, walking out the front door and then to the kitchen had worn Robert out. He legs shook and threatened to buckle. His mother was right; he couldn't help anyone in this condition. At least, not in any of the ways he knew how.

What a time for all of this to happen. His family needed his help more than ever and he could barely walk himself to the bathroom.

"How about an omelet?" his mother asked.

"With real eggs?"

"No. Powdered eggs from our year's supply."

"Those are nasty tasting."

"They're not so bad as an omelet." His mother opened the ten-pound can of powdered eggs and scooped out enough for their breakfast. "The cheese and onions really flavor it up."

"They still have a weird texture." Robert grimaced.

"You can get used to them—if you put your mind to it. We don't always get what we want. Nor should we. For the time being, this is what we have."

Robert waited for the "people are starving in Africa" speech as his mother mixed the eggs, but she was silent. No speech. No singing while she cooked. Not even a hummed hymn.

A small part of his mind told him that he should be grateful for what he had.

Then a much louder portion of his brain argued that poverty, broken ribs, and an early release from his mission were not joyful events. Life was tough right then, and, other than his budding relationship with Sierra, he'd received his share of bad news recently.

He fought against the anger that accompanied his thoughts. Getting upset over the disappointments and hardships he'd suffered hadn't helped matters any. There was no reason to think that would change. Maybe it was time to stop focusing on what he wanted to happen and start worrying about what needed to be done.

Right away, his mood improved. He knew that he had the answer to his prayers.

"If you dislike the powdered eggs that much," his mother said, "I can make something else for you."

"That's okay. An omelet will be fine. I'm not going to be picky about my eggs when children are starving in Africa."

Becky slowly turned around and watched Robert's face. "Is that more sarcasm?"

"No. That's just me deciding to act like an adult."

His mother finished making breakfast and they ate. She made a few attempts at a conversation, but Robert could tell her mind was elsewhere, most likely on getting the car fixed.

Robert contributed little to the table talk himself. He needed to rethink his situation and come up with a new plan. The rest of the morning he thought it over.

Maybe this was the Lord's way of getting his attention. Stuck in the house, weak, sore, and definitely humbled, he decided to listen to what God wanted him to do.

He was still listening when his mother got the news about the car.

"The engine needs to be replaced." She sighed. "That's going to short us about two months on rent and utility payments. Your father and I didn't budget any major repairs like that into the plan."

A solution sprang into Robert's mind. "I can pay for it out of my savings."

"What about college?" his mother asked. "You set that money aside to become an engineer. That's your money."

"We're a family. All of us are in this together."

"I don't know, Robert." His mother folded her arms and fidgeted with the hem of her shirtsleeve.

Robert forced himself up from the couch, limped over to his mother, and placed his arms around her. "If the two of us can find a way for me to be helpful while sitting on the couch, then I think Heavenly Father and I can figure out another way for me to become an engineer."

29

Only three stations came in clearly on John's old radio. One broadcast a wide range of music styles, another dealt in news-talk, and the last was in Spanish. That didn't leave much in the way of variety. Even though John had packed the radio so everyone would have music to listen to while they worked, he found it tuned to the news-talk station most of the time.

Missing family, friends, and home was a given. John had expected that. The occasional call home helped—some. But what surprised him were all of the other things that added to the group's sense of isolation.

How could he live with nearly two dozen other men and feel so alone?

A few of the men were missing spring baseball training. A couple talked about all of the movie releases that they were going to have to catch up on when they got back home. And some had campouts or other family traditions that they were sacrificing for this assignment. But everyone felt a growing gap between them and the rest of the world.

Listening to the news bites kept them informed about what was happening beyond the wire fences they had built. It also let them know how removed they were from everything else they cared about. The news itself didn't help matters any. Riots. Increased terrorist activity. Nations lining up for war. The world seemed to be falling apart.

Even though John understood that it was the news industry's job to sell terror to their audiences to keep them tuned in, he couldn't force himself to change the dial. He found himself repulsed by what he heard, yet riveted to every word at the same time.

For the last two days, news coverage had increased about an approaching storm front. It picked up intensity as it moved farther inland. The west coast had been hit by it already and a couple of the towns at the storm's center had taken heavy damage. Just before lunch, the weatherman announced that the storm should hit the Greenville area by nightfall.

Alarm bells sounded inside John's head when he heard the news.

He could see the storm clouds on the horizon. They didn't look particularly dark or foreboding. It would be hours before they arrived. And if it was going to rain, this would be a good time for it.

The feds still had them shut down. John kept the fence crews busy staging the supplies along the designated fence lines so that when they resumed work they could move along at a pretty good clip. The construction crews had been cleaning up the area and providing the minor amounts of maintenance that the finished structures needed.

A storm passing through meant they would spend their time inside the crudely finished dorm and looking for a way to keep themselves entertained. Not exactly the worst of scenarios.

As he sat and ate with the others, a nagging sensation kept sending his gaze toward the approaching storm. By the time the fence crew readied themselves to head back out and stage the last of the supplies, John decided to change the orders of the day.

"Can I get everyone's attention for a moment?" John shouted. He raised his arms and motioned for them to gather around him. "I think this storm might hit us hard. So I'd like to spend the rest of the day getting ready for it. Let's get all the gear inside the warehouse. It might be cold in there, but it should keep everything reasonably dry. That includes any of the lighter supplies that could be blown away and anything that might be damaged by the water."

"Do you think it will be bad enough that we need to board up the windows?" Jeff asked.

John rejected the idea. This area just didn't get any storms bad enough to justify that kind of precaution. He was surprised to hear himself say, "Yes."

"If you're going to do that," Scott said, "we might as well brace up the unfinished buildings."

"All right," John said. "Why don't you grab a few of the guys and supervise it?"

Scott gave a thumbs-up, grabbed his crutches, and hobbled off with Paul and Tom in the direction of the half-completed workshop.

They should've had plenty of time to finish preparations, but the storm raced in quicker than John, or the weathermen, had expected. As soon as the first strong gale blasted its way through Camp Valiant, John got on the two-way radio and called the fence crew back.

Rain started falling before they returned. Then the storm hit, in all its fury, just as everyone filed into the dorm.

The door blew open a few minutes later. They hadn't bothered installing a dead bolt and now the door and the frame were shaking too much for the regular doorknob assembly to keep it in place.

John pushed the door shut while Wayne and Jeff slid one of the donated couches against it to hold it in place.

Thunder crashed. The sound vibrated the windows in their panes.

Wind howled outside. Frigid streams of air managed to find their way through the cracks and unsealed seams of the building.

"I guess this is as good a way as any to find out what kind of job we did weather-proofing this place." Bill wore a nervous smile.

"This certainly qualifies as a field test," said John.

That elicited a few chuckles.

Even though they'd finished the building several weeks ago, everyone gathered in the dorm's community room and found a spot to ride out the storm. Possibly, John thought, because the only heat in the building came from a pair of space heaters located there. But a more compelling reason could be the sense of security that came from being surrounded by the men of sterling character that shared in this undertaking.

The storm worsened.

Timber creaked. Rain pounded against the roof like stones.

Something crashed. Something big.

Cracking. Snapping. Tearing.

Everyone scrambled to their feet and ran to the windows. Which didn't help since they'd been boarded up. The sound had come from the direction of the workshop.

"I'm willing to go outside and see what happened," said Paul.

"No one's going outside," John said. "This is the safest place for us to be. We can find out what happened when the storm is over—which will be the same time we can actually do something about it."

"What do we do until then?" Luis asked.

"Well"—John clapped his hands together—"since the storm is howling at us, I say we howl right back at it."

Most of the men looked at John as if he'd lost his mind.

"Hymns!" he shouted, not sure why he felt calm. "We don't have enough books for everyone, but I think we can pick a couple that everyone knows. Any suggestions?"

Someone called out, "'I Am a Child of God.'"

The brethren laughed.

"That's a wonderful hymn," John said. "I think we can handle a song a little more robust than that."

Bill raised his arm. "'The Lord Is My Light.'"

Again, mighty thunder shook the dorm.

John passed out the handful of hymnals they had and got in position to lead the music. If you could call it that. He planned to wave his hand about and hoped that the brethren knew enough of the words to make this work.

He brought his hand down and they sang.

The Lord is my light; then why should I fear?

By day and by night his presence is near.

John felt a change in the room. The storm still raged outside, but there was peace and calm inside. He was so focused on that thought that he nearly missed the chorus.

He is my joy and my song.
By day and by night He leads, he leads me along.

Whatever they might find outside when the storm lifted, John knew that they could deal with it.

The worst of the storm passed through the area before morning. A steady rain pattered against the roof. An occasional gust of wind pushed against the building. All in all, these were pale shadows of nature's fury that had been demonstrated just hours earlier.

John pushed the couch aside and opened the door leading out of the dorm. He stepped into the pool of icy water that had formed at the base of the door and gazed around the compound.

Part of the roof had come off the warehouse. A couple of two-by-fours stuck through a window and the sheet of plywood they had put up to protect it. However, it was still mostly intact.

The dorm as well as the trailer appeared to have come out of the ordeal with only minor damage. Unfortunately, the same could not be said for the half-completed workshop. The portions that still remained lay in a jumbled pile of shattered studs and beams. Most of the stacks of building supplies were scattered—or gone. He could easily imagine the fate of all the fence materials that had been left out in the open.

John estimated it would take two or three days to clean up the mess and then another week to rebuild the portion of the workshop they'd lost. In just one night they had suffered a horrible setback.

Still, it could've been much worse. The work could be redone. The supplies could be replaced. And their lives had been preserved.

He wondered how Greenville had fared.

30

Becky hurled the hammer to the ground and clutched her left thumb with the other hand, counting to ten in order to avoid uttering any words she would later regret. An examination of the throbbing digit showed a cracked nail and some discoloration of the knuckle, but it didn't appear to be broken.

Unreasonable anger flared within her—first at John for being away from home, then at Robert for getting injured in a fight, and finally at herself for thinking she could replace a couple of broken fence slats between fixing the children breakfast and starting the day's homeschooling lessons.

She rocked back from a kneeling position and plopped down on her butt. It took several deep breaths to keep a scream of frustration submerged deep within her. Intellectually, she understood that something as minor as a bruised thumb shouldn't bother her.

But it did.

Robert had offered to do the repairs, and she had firmly reminded him that his ribs wouldn't mend if he didn't keep still. For a moment she reconsidered the offer. It would take Robert less than five minutes to complete the fence repairs.

Becky pictured him swinging the hammer and grimacing in

pain with every stroke. In her mind, she could hear him trying to downplay the discomfort he felt.

No. She could do this.

Becky rolled over on her hands and knees, crawled to where the hammer had landed, and retrieved it. She'd tapped nails into wood before; there was no reason she couldn't do this now. That wasn't even the real issue here. This was a matter of the stress associated with the family's recent trials building up to the point where a tiny incident threatened to overwhelm her.

Now all she had to do was ignore her feelings and get busy.

Easier said than done!

"Mom!" Cody hollered from the back porch. "Are we skipping school today?"

Becky took a deep breath and sighed. "Get your books ready. I'll be right in."

A few nails and fifteen minutes later, she had the replacement slats attached to the fence. They wobbled a bit in the brisk wind, but they were in place. And she had accomplished it without damaging any more of her fingers.

The children, all except for Sara, were clustered around the television.

"This is boring," Cody said as he twirled around on an office chair that had been moved into the family room.

"Sorry, Code-man." Robert raised the remote and turned up the volume. "This is important. You can watch *Belching Bubble Battles* later."

"What are you guys watching?" Becky asked.

"A major storm hit the area where Dad's working." Robert glanced up at her with a deer-in-the-headlights look. "I just wanted to see if . . . Dad's okay."

All thoughts of mended fences, bruised thumbs, and homeschool lessons fled her mind. Becky whipped her head toward the television. She located Greenville on the map. Or rather the location of the closest town big enough for the news services to care about. Unless the storm changed direction, Camp Valiant was about to get slammed.

"On second thought," said Robert, "I haven't seen any good bubble belching in a while. Maybe we should watch that."

Becky transfixed Robert with a stare that pinned him in place.

BAM!

The sound thundered through the house, causing Becky and the kids to jump.

BAM!

The front screen door slammed shut again. A strong wind played with it, tugging it one way and then slapping it the other.

Radio stations had mentioned the turbulent front approaching the city, but Becky had scarcely given it a thought. If she waited until after homeschool, it would be too late to prepare for the storm.

Her eyes drifted back to the television. A weatherman stood outside, the storm raging all around him, and rattled off a list of statistics that added up to this being the worst storm the region had ever faced.

And John was sitting in the middle of the danger path in an overgrown toolshed.

"Does that mean school's been canceled because of the weather?" Jesse asked.

Becky mentally scrambled for an answer. It burst out on its own. "Storm drill."

The children's heads all swiveled from the television to her. Their faces clearly expressed the question none of them asked: "What are you talking about?"

"A storm drill. You had fire drills all the time at the public school. This is the same thing. We are going practice getting the house all buttoned up for a storm."

"That's our school lesson for the day?" Elizabeth asked.

"Yes."

"How exactly do you plan on grading it?" Lucas asked.

"Pass/fail," Becky said. "You participate, you pass."

"You don't, you fail," said Robert.

"I guess I should've seen that one coming," Lucas said.

Becky clapped her hands together and started issuing tasks to the children. She sent Lucas outside to secure the shutters. They were mostly decorative, but they should provide at least some protection for the windows.

She assigned Jesse to help her tarp the garden. Elizabeth pulled out the hurricane lanterns, placed one in each of the rooms downstairs, and pulled out a box of stick matches from their camping supplies. Cody gathered up all the flashlights in the house and made sure the batteries worked. Reluctantly, Becky asked Robert to check on the generator unit they had in the garage. If the power went out, she wanted to keep the refrigerator and freezer running.

It wasn't until after Robert reported that the generator was ready to go and they had enough gas to last three days that she thought about the butane tanks for the outdoor grill. Keeping the food from spoiling wouldn't do them much good if they didn't have a way to cook it.

She dashed out to the shed and checked their butane supply. Of the three tanks they had, two were empty and the third was full or near to it. That should be enough to last almost a week if she was careful.

Becky looked over to where they kept the grill and noticed it was gone. For a moment her heart pounded away double-time before she remembered she had moved it into the garage after the attempted theft.

For some reason, storing the grill inside the garage during the storm struck her as a good idea. Now that she thought about it, she remembered seeing it there earlier this morning.

A strong gust of wind buffeted the shed. Becky took a quick look around and failed to spot anything from their emergency prep manual that needed to go inside. She closed the shed door and headed toward the house.

Along the way, she ran through the storm drill assignments once again to make sure she hadn't forgotten anything.

Sara!

Becky sprinted into the kitchen and snatched up her purse. She rummaged through it until she found her cell phone and called Sara.

The call went to voice mail and Becky called again.

"Yes." Sara sounded impatient.

"It's getting ready to storm."

"I noticed. No big. I brought my heavy coat."

"This is supposed to be a really big storm. I want you to come home."

"Mom! I have plans tonight."

"Not tonight." Becky packed as much firmness into the statement as she could. "I think it would be best if all of us were together at the house."

"That's ridiculous, Mom. Our house isn't any better protected from a storm than any of the other houses in town. Besides, I'll have my cell phone with me and if anything happens I can call you."

"Please, Sara." Despite the words she used, this was no plea—it was a declaration that Becky had reached her limit on this issue.

"All right. I'll come home."

The connection terminated.

After thirty long minutes, Sara walked in the front door and the heavens commenced to pummel the city with rain. A moment later, thunder shook the house and the power went out. Even though it was only midafternoon, the dark clouds blocked out enough of the sunlight to make it necessary for them to light the lanterns.

"Aw, man." Cody threw in an ample amount of body language to accompany his statement. "The television isn't working. What are we going to do now?"

"I don't know about you," Sara said as she held her cell phone above her head, "but I'm going to my room to watch a movie on my laptop."

"Can I watch it with you?" asked Cody.

"No." Sara walked out of the room, using the illumination from her cell phone to navigate the dark hallway.

"We could play a board game," Lucas said.

"Board games are lame," said Jesse.

"I don't like board games," Cody said.

"Then how about we get out our scriptures and read them?" Becky offered.

"Board games it is," Jesse said.

"I pick Monopoly." Cody raced toward the game closet. "Dibs on the battleship."

Becky moved to the living room window and peered through a gap in the shutters. The rain prevented her from seeing anything beyond her front yard. Even the street lay hidden behind the curtain of water.

"Don't worry, Mom." Robert had walked up behind her. "Dad will be okay. He's where he's supposed to be and doing what he's supposed to be doing. The Lord is looking after him."

Becky looked at Robert and nodded. A twinge of guilt passed through her. At the moment, she was less concerned about John's welfare and more scared that she had to face this ordeal without him.

Lightning flashed and thunder cracked almost simultaneously.

A yelp escaped from Becky as she jumped. She cupped her hands over her ears too late to protect them from the bone-jarring explosion of sound.

"Mommy!" Cody hollered. He ran to Becky and wrapped his arms around her waist. "That was loud."

"It's just noise, Sweetie." Becky ran a hand through the wavy, blond hair on Cody's head and wished she could talk herself into not being afraid of the thunder.

"Is anyone else having trouble with their cell phones?" Sara asked as she walked back into the room and stood next to Becky.

Lucas reached into his pocket and pulled out a phone. "No network. That last lighting bolt must have struck the cell tower."

Becky walked into the kitchen and retrieved her phone from the counter. It failed to make a connection when she opened it. Then she picked up the receiver for the landline. No dial tone. She nearly tripped over Cody when she turned around. Sara stood just beyond him with her arms crossed and an expectant look on her face.

"Looks like all the phones are down," Becky announced.

"I guess I'll play games with the family then," Sara said. She sounded less than enthused.

Everyone gathered in the dining room. Jesse had brought out a pile of board games and set them on the kitchen counter. He opened the Monopoly box and set the board on the dinner table.

Becky had a chance to observe all of the children as they readied themselves to play. Cody still hovered at her elbow. Elizabeth sat at one of the tables and chewed on a fingernail. She noticed that each of the children exhibited some form of nervous behavior. Becky had never realized how much John's presence in the home had brought stability and a sense of security to the family.

A sound like a freight train passing by roared to life, louder than even the heavy gusts of wind they'd been hearing. Becky turned her head toward the living room. The panes of glass were flexing violently. Should she move her family to a safer spot in the house? But where would that be?

A horrible sound that was a mix of breaking and tearing came from outside. It might have been out back; she couldn't be sure.

Crash.

Something collided with the front of the house. Glass flew across the living room along with bits of the shutter. Then rain poured in through the remains of the ruined window section.

Elizabeth and Sara screamed.

Cody cried.

Becky stood and stared. Her heart pounded fast and hard against her chest.

Robert rushed forward and examined the area beyond the window. "There's a wagon on the ground. It's pretty bent up. That must be what took out the window."

"Be careful, Robert!" Becky shouted over the roaring wind. "Who knows what else might fly through that window."

"Yeah." Robert pulled back from the window. "Good point. I better get this covered before anyone gets hurt."

"That's not what I meant. Just get away from the window. We can move to another room."

"All the furniture will get ruined." Robert moved away from the window.

"We can get new furniture."

"There are a couple pieces of plywood in the garage from whatever project Dad was working on before he left. I can have one of them hammered to the front of the house in less than a minute."

Becky rushed over and grabbed Robert's arm. "You can't go outside in that storm."

"Someone has to," Robert said. "And I'm the oldest."

"No. You're hurt."

"Listen." Robert held a hand to his ear. "The wind has slowed down. Lucas can go with me. I'll hold the plywood in place and he can hammer in the nails. If we go now, we can get that hole covered before the wind picks back up."

Her mind screamed no. She couldn't allow her children to place themselves in harm's way. But a tiny voice inside her said this was what needed to be done.

She gave him a single quick nod.

Robert motioned for Lucas and the two of them raced into the garage. They came out moments later with a half sheet of plywood, a hammer, and some nails.

When they opened the front door, it slammed against the wall, the doorknob punching through the drywall there. Robert staggered back a step as he fought to hold on to the plywood and advance against the wind. Lucas put a shoulder into Robert's back and pushed the two of them out the door.

Rain and debris blitzed through the open door. Becky closed it and waited for her boys to return. Every moment stretched on in agonizing dread. She thought she heard the pounding of a hammer against the wall and prayed it was Lucas working to secure the window and not parts of the neighbors' houses slamming into her home or either of her sons.

Lucas came through the door first. The wind pushed him to the middle of the living room before he could stop.

Robert struggled against the relentless gale. One careful step at a time until his foot slipped out from under him. He went down hard.

Lucas and Jesse fought against the wind to reach the door and close it.

Becky ran to Robert's side.

He had his arms crossed in front of him, his face a twisted mask of pain. The storm had completely soaked him in frigid rain. He shivered violently.

"Lucas, Jesse," Becky commanded. "Help me move Robert."

"No," Robert attempted to holler. It came out as a weak whisper. "Moving me . . . will cause it . . . to hurt . . . more. Let me . . . lie here . . . awhile . . ."

Sara brought a comforter and placed it over Robert.

Becky kneeled next to Robert and worried.

The fury of the storm increased once more, hurling pieces of the city against their home. Despite the many thuds and whumps, nothing more broke through.

After a while Robert stopped shivering. He held a hand out and let Lucas slowly pull him to his feet, his face locked in a grimace the entire time. Then, once he was standing, he shuffled into the kitchen and sat at the table.

"Monopoly?" Cody asked.

"I was thinking we could do a little scripture reading," Robert replied.

Becky noticed that this time none of the children rejected the idea. They placed lamps so as to best illuminate the kitchen for reading. Everyone sat at the table. Robert offered to start off and read the portion of 1 Nephi where they crossed the ocean and encountered a terrible storm.

They took turns reading until dinnertime. By then, the worst of the storm had abated, though the rain still drummed away at the roof and windows like ten thousand mice with tiny little hammers.

Without electricity and not wanting to burn the house down by using the grill in the garage, Becky prepared the fallback menu of sandwiches and chips. She inwardly groaned about offering the children a dinner without vegetables.

They didn't seem to mind at all.

In the dim lamplight, without television, video games, or phones, the children tired quickly. They went to bed without being told. When eight o'clock rolled around, only Becky remained awake. Robert had tried to stay awake, but she had insisted that he take one of the pain pills the doctor had prescribed, and he had passed out within minutes.

Since the furniture in the living room had been soaked, she trudged into the family room and sank into the over-stuffed couch. She leaned her head back and made a mental list of what needed to be done in the morning: pick up the broken glass in the living room, use the shop-vac to suck up the water from the carpet—

Becky opened her eyes. When she moved her head, her neck screamed in protest. No doubt it would remind her all day about the dangers of falling asleep on the couch.

The lamps had gone out. Dim gray light came through the windows. When she peered outside, overcast skies greeted her. At least it wasn't raining at the moment.

A stiff back and sore legs joined the chorus of misery that her neck had started. She limped to the back door and went outside.

The shed was gone.

Only a few of the yard tools that they stored inside it were littered across the backyard.

How was the family going to clean up this mess without tools?

She waded through the icy puddles that filled her lawn. The coldness of the water brought her out of the hazy half-sleep of morning. Now alert, she noticed in quick succession the damaged areas of the home.

A fair amount of tiles were missing from the roof. Several of the shutters had been torn off the portions of the house she could see, and the slats she had replaced yesterday in the fence were gone.

Well, they were probably with the rest of the fence. Wherever it might be.

She forgot about the sting of the cold water around her feet. A burning rage seared her thoughts. Or it might be the black fumes of despair threatening to choke her; she couldn't be sure which. They battled within her: shout, cry, strike out, give up.

This couldn't be happening. All the money and work and sacrifice that went into buying the house and maintaining it. Then a stupid storm came through and ruined it.

Emotions pummeled her.

"Why me?" pity cried.

"Why not tear the Cromptons' house apart?" anger railed. "They deserve it."

"Why bother?" despair mumbled.

A calm voice inside told Becky that this could have been so much worse. One of the children could have been badly hurt. One of them could have died. The house could have been blown completely away.

Becky turned her face to the sky. "I work hard to help others. I say my prayers and read my scriptures daily. I fulfill all of my callings to the best of my ability. Shouldn't that be worth catching a break once in a while?"

A light drizzle began to fall.

Becky lowered her head. "I don't know if I can do this anymore."

"Mom."

The voice called her back to the present, to reality. Something warm streaked down her cheeks. Becky kept her back to the voice in order to hide her face.

"Mom," Elizabeth said. "Are you okay?"

"I—don't—know."

31

About an hour into the recovery efforts, a thought crept into John's head.

He had a fair idea that it might not be popular with the others. Even now they were working hard to gather up the storm-tossed building materials and make any repairs that needed to be done right away.

The broken warehouse window had been replaced already. He had a team on the roof making good progress with that. Any of the minor damage that the dorm had sustained could wait until later. But the notion floating around in his head needed to be acted upon without delay.

John continued throwing debris in the garbage pile while he thought it through again. This was the sort of thing he needed to be sure about.

Finally he called out for everyone to gather. The fence crews were still helping with the cleanup around the camp. That meant he wouldn't have time to chicken out while they were driving in from the fence line.

"What's up?" Bill said. "More hymns?"

"From what they've been saying on the radio this morning,"

John said, "we were pretty lucky. Most of the towns in this area have suffered major damage."

"Back home too," Tom said.

"Yep." John nodded. "Back home too."

His concern for Becky and the kids flared anew. For a second he regretted accepting this assignment and coming all the way out here to sweat and suffer only to have their work destroyed. But he hoped someone back home was looking after them; he knew that this was the right course of action for them.

"We've left our families in good hands," John said. "They're in the midst of family, friends, neighbors, and the community of Saints that will help them out. In fact, if we were back there right now, what do you think we'd be doing?"

"Fixing my fence," Luis said. "Or as much of it as I could find."

John laughed along with the others and then looked to the other crew chief for a response.

Bill gave an almost imperceptible groan and looked away.

"Bill," John prompted. "You have something to add."

Bill addressed the crowd, his arms folded. "I'd probably be making calls to see who needed help. If we happened to be in an area that didn't get hit very hard, I imagine I'd be volunteering to help with disaster relief efforts for those towns and neighborhoods that got clobbered."

John checked the reaction of the men. It looked as though most of them had picked up on where this was headed, although none of them made the leap and suggested they do the same thing. That was John's responsibility.

"There's a good chance that parts of Greenville relocated to the next county. Electricity may be down. They could use our help."

"We have problems of our own to worry about," Wayne said.

"The only thing that *has* to be done is the warehouse roof. And we can't all be up there. I suggest that we leave a team to continue working on that. When they finish, they can start on the minor repairs that are needed on the dorm. The rest of us can go into town to help."

"Not me." Wayne pointed to the stitches in his head.

"How do you feel about being part of the roofing team?"

"I can do that."

"Me too," said Paul.

More hands flew up. In fact, most of the hands flew up.

"Come on, guys." John put his hands on his hips. "Eight, at most, is all that can effectively work on that roof at one time. I believe that the rest of us should go into Greenville and help those people."

They lowered their hands. None of them moved forward though.

"Not only did these people attack us," Paul Young said, "they're probably the ones responsible for shutting us down."

"I suspect you're right," said John. "That doesn't change the fact that we're expected to adhere to a higher standard, one that tells us to love our enemies and assist all who are in need."

"To a point," Bill Summers said. "The scriptures are filled with stories about the Lord's chosen people standing up to their enemies: David and Goliath, the Walls of Jericho, and even Sampson. If these are the 'last days,' then we'll eventually be facing off against evil people who wish to do us harm."

John was surprised that Bill had spoken out against helping. Bill struck him as one of the most spiritual men in camp. It seemed out of character for him to want to turn his back on someone in need.

"At some point in the future," John said, "we may very well be engaged in hostilities with those who dislike us and our church. That isn't today, though.

"We're not talking about giving in to a group of soldiers that have laid siege to this camp. These are our neighbors. They are God's children and they are suffering. We have it within our power to ease their burden.

"Please, keep in mind that the town has plenty of youngsters living there who have done nothing to us and are cold and scared and can use our help. Are you going to let them suffer because you're upset with their parents?"

Bill sighed. "No. I guess not."

For a moment it was silent except for the howling wind

"You know," Luis spoke up, "we're not just paving the way for more of our people to follow. We're paving the way for the return of Christ. What good does all of this building do us if we forget that?"

John watched most of the men nod their heads in agreement. He thought they looked a little bit sheepish at the moment and wondered how many times the pioneers had moments like this as they crossed the plains.

"I'm staying here," Wayne said. He fitted his tool belt around his waist and headed toward the warehouse.

Paul followed close behind him.

The rest stayed where they were.

John assigned six more men to remain behind. The rest of them hitched the trailer to the truck, loaded it with hand tools, ropes, and a portable generator. Then they headed down the muddy road to Greenville.

The truck mired in the mud several times along the way. Each time, the men hopped out and pushed until the truck found enough traction to move forward on its own. By the time they reached the paved road headed into Greenville, the men were covered in mud.

They kicked and scraped off as much of the mud as they could and then clambered back into the truck and onto the trailer and drove into town.

Greenville had been ravaged by the storm.

Large sections of missing shingles seemed to be the least of the problems the buildings in town had suffered. Fallen trees had downed power lines in several places and crushed cars and homes in others. The scattered remains of fences, sheds, and other light structures lay broken on yards and in the streets. Windows in homes, businesses, and vehicles had been shattered by flying debris.

The roof that sheltered the pumps at the gas station lay partially on top of the store itself. A wall had collapsed inward. The sheriff was in the process of using orange traffic cones to cordon it off.

John parked the truck on the street a safe distance from the gas station and got out. The rest of the men followed suit.

"Let me go talk to the sheriff by myself first."

"You expecting trouble?" Bill arched his eyebrows.

"I hope not."

The sheriff stopped setting out cones and turned to face John and the others. He unbuttoned the flap on his pistol and left his hand resting on the butt.

"Come to tell us that this is God's wrath for attacking his chosen people?" he called out loudly while John was still a hundred feet away.

"Not at all," John called back, careful to keep his tone loud but calm. "We lost one of our buildings in the storm and the roof off another. I'd say we both took a licking."

"Then why aren't you back there fixing it?"

"We are. A crew is replacing the roof right now." John had moved closed enough that he didn't need to raise his voice to be heard. "I know we're not supposed to be in town, but if we could be of any help to all of you, we'd be happy to lend a hand."

The sheriff gave him a suspicious look, then glanced at the others, who were leaning against the truck.

"You must think that offering to help will change people's minds about you." The sheriff's jaw muscles tightened.

"That'd be great," John said. "We have no desire to be at odds with you. However, it isn't the reason we're here. A part of being who we are is helping those in need, regardless of whether they like us or not."

Sheriff McKinney snapped the flap on his holster closed. "Don't expect this to change the situation any."

"We won't. I promise that we'll head back to our camp as soon as the last tree has been cleared. Or whatever it is you plan to have us do."

"All right." Sheriff McKinney pointed toward the center of town. "Get in your truck and follow me."

The townspeople had made little headway in cleaning up after the storm. John suspected that a pervasive shock still numbed their minds and prevented them from organizing the recovery effort effectively.

Sheriff McKinney led them downtown and stopped.

John organized a crew with rakes, shovels, and a chain saw. He set them to chopping fallen trees and limbs into manageable chunks and then piling them for disposal at a later date. The people gathered in the area watched the crew get out of the truck and ready their tools. They appeared too stunned by the calamity of the situation to frown at the intrusion.

Luis took charge of the chain saw and went after a tree that had fallen and now blocked an adjoining street. He kept the rest of the crew busy hauling the sawed-off limbs away until a couple of the townsfolk joined in.

They gave Luis a surly look when they took the first of the trimmed branches away. Most of the scowls had vanished by the time they returned for another batch of limbs to carry.

"I think they can handle this," John told the sheriff as he nodded his head in the direction of Luis and the men working with him. "We have enough men and tools for two more crews. Where would you like them?"

Sheriff McKinney watched the Saints and the townsfolk working together. He nodded as the two groups began civil exchanges about what needed to be done in the area and how to best go about it. Then he climbed back into his patrol car and led them to the school.

"Power's still out all over town," said the sheriff. "I have Willy, the school's maintenance man, and Bob working on getting an old generator hooked up here. Then we can put anyone who needs a place to stay in the auditorium."

"We have an electrician in the group." John thumbed over his shoulder toward Bill. "He could give them a hand if you like. And I can set our second team to boarding up any broken windows so the auditorium stays warm once they get the power going."

"Better let me go explain the situation to Willy and Bob," said the sheriff. "Both of them were involved in that little tussle out at your camp."

Sheriff McKinney strode over to the two men. He stopped, tucked his thumbs in his belt, and proceeded to discuss the matter.

They reacted pretty much the way John expected. Which is to say they shouted, their faces colored to deep shades of red, and their arms wove angry patterns in the air.

John couldn't hear what the sheriff told them, but they calmed down. Or at least they stopped shouting and waving their arms. Their faces still had the tint of cooked lobsters.

"You might want to rethink this," said Sheriff McKinney. "I convinced Willy to let your man assist him with the generator, and Bob has agreed to supervise the cleanup efforts here at the school. That splits the two of them up so they don't incite one another into starting another fight. It doesn't prevent them from looking for an excuse to get riled up. Make sure your people don't get mouthy."

Until this morning, John wouldn't have doubted Bill's ability to cope with one of the Church's detractors. Not that he had any choice; Bill was the only one at the camp that had experience with electrical systems. John selected Jeff King and two others he knew to be patient and long-suffering, as it were, and advised them to focus on the work and not the disposition of the two townsfolk.

Sheriff McKinney took the rest of them to the hardest-hit residential section and let them decide how best to tackle the problem. The people there numbly accepted the help. They looked up when John and the others approached and silently nodded when asked if they would accept assistance.

John split the rest of the men up into teams of two. Only one chain saw remained. He handed it over to Tom Gordon and his companion and then sent them across the street. A tree had fallen there and crushed a toolshed on the side of the house.

Everyone else had to rely on hand-tools. Of which there were plenty.

John maneuvered the truck to a spot between two houses and then ran out power cords from the generator to each of them. He and his companion laid claim to one of the houses and the final pair of workers took the other.

The house John chose to work on had suffered extensive damage. A huge branch from the tree in the front yard had fallen and collapsed the roof on one end of the house and had caved in a good portion of the wall as well.

An older couple stood beside the wreckage. They switched from looking mournfully at the house to watching John start up the generator and then walk over to them.

"Any particular place you want the tree limbs?" John connected a circular saw to the electrical cord and gave a quick try to verify it had power.

"I hadn't really thought about it," the man said.

"They pick up bulk trash out front," said the woman a moment later.

"That sounds like a good spot for most of it," said John. "Probably wouldn't hurt to stack some of it up as firewood. Once we cut up and relocate the tree limbs, we can look into doing something about your roof and the hole in your wall. If you don't mind me offering a suggestion, you could check around the house or with your neighbors and find something we can use to enclose the area until a permanent solution can be arranged. Plywood and a couple of plastic tarps would probably be best."

The words tumbled out of his mouth without conscious thought. Over the last few weeks, he'd gotten used to "making suggestions" that needed to be followed. Not only that, but the couple didn't seem to be in any shape to take control over their situation.

John scanned the street to see if the sheriff had caught him ordering the townsfolk around.

Sure enough, the sheriff was leaning against his patrol car, watching John. His arms were folded. He didn't appear happy. Then again, he didn't exactly appear upset either. He just slowly shook his head from side to side like a hockey referee waiting for the inevitable brawl.

"I got a couple of tarps in the garage," said the man.

"Then go get 'em." The woman nudged the man. "The sooner the lot of you gets my house covered up, the sooner I can start cleaning it."

The man mumbled something to his wife and then shuffled off toward the garage.

"Be careful when you remove those tree limbs," said the woman. "I don't want you to break anything that ain't already broke. And keep an eye out for my husband. Henry don't seem to understand that he's old. You make sure he doesn't try to lift anything heavy."

"Yes, ma'am." John responded, but Henry's wife had already turned around and headed for the front door.

John set to the task of trimming the branches. He suggested that Henry help him by holding the branches being cut so they didn't fall and cause any more damage. It wasn't strictly necessary, but it kept him from trying to muscle the branches to the growing refuse pile by the street.

John had just sliced through the last of the lesser branches and was thinking about the best way to cut up the main portion of the fallen branch when the radio crackled his name.

John jumped. His focus had been on the task at hand. And this work felt so different from their tasks at the camp that he had forgotten all about the radio and the other teams.

He unclipped the radio from his belt. "This is John."

"We need gas for the chain saw," Luis said.

"Give me a few minutes to get over there. Anything else?"

"I could use another chain saw."

"Sorry, no can do," John said. "How about a couple of handsaws?"

"Aaiiiiiii," wailed Luis. "My arms are aching just at the thought of it."

Another voice laughed over the radio. "We're running short on gasoline too," Bill said. "You can keep the implements of torture, though."

"Right," said John. "See you in a few."

That set the pace for the day.

The crews finished with one storm-smashed location and moved to another, stopping for water or to get supplies from the truck. John worked on disaster relief efforts of his own, but he had to stop whenever the others needed something from the truck or the trailer. Late in the afternoon, he made sure to incorporate a lunch break into his rounds, passing out some of the prepackaged foods they had packed before leaving that morning.

They made steady progress. John was almost finished clearing debris from the third home that day when Sheriff McKinney approached. The headlights from the patrol caught John's attention as they cast shadows on the house wall as he pulled in to park.

"Thought I might let you know that it's dark," said the sheriff.

John stood up and glanced around him. It was dark, all right. Not waning sunlight. Not dusk. It was the black-of-night dark.

"I don't know about you folks," McKinney continued, "but my people are tired. They had a long night and an even longer day. Why don't you give them and yourselves a break and go home."

Now that John noticed how late it was, he felt drained. He lowered the circular saw to the ground and leaned back against the wall of the house.

"Well," John said, "we wouldn't want to keep your people from their dinners. I'll get everyone packing up."

John grabbed for his radio before he remembered that he'd unclipped it earlier and set it down next to his jacket. When he bent over to retrieve it, he just let gravity pull him to the ground. He keyed the radio.

"Why didn't someone tell me it was dark?"

After they all stopped laughing, John told them to wrap it up and he'd be around soon to take everyone back to camp.

Sheriff McKinney stood close by. He fidgeted in spot.

"Is there something you wanted to say?" John asked.

"Yeah." The sheriff looked straight at him. "Can you come back tomorrow?"

32

A knock sounded at the door.

Becky set down the hammer and nails and wiped her brow. Annoyance at the interruption flared up only to be replaced with relief when she realized this would provide her a much-needed break.

"Everyone grab a drink and take a rest," she called out to the children.

When she opened the front door, Ralph and Doris Oldham from the next house over stood there with Mr. Roche, who lived at the end of the block, and a man she recognized from PTA meetings at the grade school.

"Have you heard from John?" Ralph asked.

"He left a message on my cell phone yesterday," said Becky. "They got hit pretty hard, but no one was injured."

"Good." Ralph fidgeted with the hem of the pale green sweater he wore.

Becky forced a smile while she tried to shift her mind from the long list of repairs that still needed to be done on the house to some neighborly chit-chat.

Mr. Roche nudged Ralph with his elbow. "Ask her."

Ralph gripped the bottom of his sweater with both hands and tugged at it. "The thing is," he started. His attention drifted to the area around his feet. "It's been the better part of a week and the power is still out. All the food in the fridge has spoiled. And . . . um . . ."

"We don't have anything to eat," said Mr. Roche.

"Can you share some of your food supplies with us?" Mrs. Oldham asked.

With John out of work, her family needed the year's supply. She could spare enough for a few meals, but would that be enough? And what would happen when the rest of the neighborhood found out? A couple of day's worth of food for ten or twenty households would short her family more than a month of meals. She couldn't do that.

"You don't have any food?" Becky asked.

"Well," Ralph said, shrugging, "we have a box of crackers, a jar full of bouillon cubes, and some cans of cranberry sauce and yams. I guess we could eat them tonight."

"Great," said Mrs. Oldham. "What do we eat tomorrow?"

"What about the grocery store?" Becky scrambled for solutions to the problem. "I was able to get a gallon of milk and a dozen eggs from them just yesterday."

"They shut the doors this morning," said the man from the PTA meetings.

"Just as well," said Mr. Roche. "They were only letting a hand-ful of people in the store at a time. I stood in line for two hours yesterday just so I could pick through what they had left. Even then, the store limited each person to ten items. How are we supposed to feed our families under those circumstances?"

Becky remembered a fight breaking out during her last trip to the store. Is that what it would be like at her front door if she started feeding the entire neighborhood? She knew that once she started handing out food, there would be no way to stop—until they ran out.

"We won't tell anyone else," Ralph said softly.

Thoughts of all the lessons about charity she had heard

throughout the years battled with the instinct to protect her family. Right now, fear shouted the loudest argument.

"Let me see what I can do." Becky stepped back slightly and prepared to shut the door.

The man from the PTA shot forward and blocked the door with his hand.

"When civilized people get hungry enough," the man said in a low, growling voice, "they stop being civilized."

Mr. Roche pulled the man back and Becky slammed the door shut.

Ralph tried talking to her through the door, but her pulse beat so loudly in her ears that she couldn't understand the words.

Becky leaned back against the door and listened for sounds that her neighbors had left. She heard a few muffled exchanges and then nothing. Her breathing slowly returned to normal.

Why did John have to be away at a time like this?

The last few days she had fought off depression and despair in order to push forward with the work that needed to be done around the house. Now the faint trickle of energy she had been drawing from vanished. She couldn't do this alone.

A sense of futility washed over her. Becky closed her eyes to hold back the tide of unbidden tears. They escaped despite her effort. Warm and tickling, they blazed wet trails down her face.

Terrifying images passed through her mind of an angry mob gathered at her doorstep, pounding on the front door and hollering for food. They ended with a makeshift battering ram splintering the door in an explosion of wood.

She didn't have the luxury of giving up.

Becky wiped the tears on the sleeve of her old, worn BYU sweatshirt and allowed herself a small sniffle. She had to find a way to pull herself together. Turning around, she placed her eye to the peephole to make sure the neighbors had left.

Bam-bam-bam.

At the sound, she jumped away from the door. The lock. Becky had failed to lock the door when she shut it.

Bam-bam-bam.

Becky crept forward and quietly turned the lock.

"Sister Williams," came a familiar voice. "This is Brent Higgens."

Peeping through the hole again, she could see the smiling face of the elders quorum president and a couple of the other men in the ward. She unlocked the door and threw it open.

"Brent," she said. "Please come in."

"We were over at the Tices', patching their roof," Brent said as he stepped inside the house. "One of the guys mentioned how it didn't seem the same without John giving us a hand. Then it occurred to me that no one had stopped by to see how all of you are doing."

Becky's lower lip trembled. Tears threatened to return, this time out of relief that she wasn't facing these trials alone. The Lord was with her and, of course, a sizable number of Saints.

"I don't think it has anything to do with the storm," Becky said, "but we had a water pipe break yesterday and could use some help with that."

"Consider it done," Brent said. "Let me grab my tools from the truck and we'll get right on it."

As Brent and the others worked on the broken pipe, Becky hurried to the kitchen to prepare a snack for them. There were a couple of recipes out of the food storage cookbook for no-bake cookies as well as one that jazzed up the powdered fruit-flavored drink mix.

Thirty minutes later, Becky finished the cookies and stacked them on a plate. She loaded the cookies and the punch on a tray and walked it out to the men, singing her favorite hymn and marveling at how much difference a little help could make in a person's life.

"Break time."

Brent set down his tools, grabbed a glass of punch, and downed half of it. "You have ice?"

"We have the fridge running off the generator."

Brent slapped his forehead. "That's right. I remember when John bought the generator. We just ended up canning all of the meat from our freezer on the outdoor grill."

"What about everything else?" Becky asked.

"First we tried packing all of it in ice. We had a couple of extra bags of it in the freezer. When the ice melted, my wife threw a party and invited everyone on the block."

That was it!

The neighbors were hungry and scared and probably felt as isolated as she had. They needed someone to reach out and give them a hand. And a meal.

She could do that. Or rather, the Saints could do that.

Becky set the tray on the ground and hurried to the house. She shouted over her shoulder, "Just leave the plates there. I'll be back for them later—I think."

Fumbling through the ward directory, she found Bishop Porter's number and punched it in on her cell phone. The call went through to voice mail, and she hung up and hit the redial button.

"Hello," Bishop Porter finally answered.

"I want to turn our building into a soup kitchen."

"Sister Williams? Is that you?"

"Yes. Can we do that?"

The bishop chuckled. "You must be psychic. The stake president and I have been talking about who we could get to organize that very thing. You were the first person that came to mind, but with John away and Robert injured, I thought it might be too much to ask."

"An hour ago it would've been." Becky paused to take a breath. "Then I realized that we have a responsibility to the people in our neighborhood, whether or not they belong to the Church. Besides, if we feed them, they're less likely to do anything crazy."

"Are you sure you can handle this?"

"Trust me," said Becky, "I'd be worse off if I didn't. Can we set up some cots and sleeping bags in the cultural hall?"

"If we really need to, I can ask President Banks about it, but for right now the high school is letting anyone who needs a place to stay bunk there. I already have someone working with the principal to get enough blankets for everyone."

"What about toilets? Maybe the city can bring in a couple of port-o-johns until services get restored."

"We're working on it," said Bishop Porter. "You need to leave something for the rest of us to do. If you can organize the kitchen efforts at the building, you will be doing more than enough. The high priests will be in charge of getting food to the building, and you can ask them to scrounge up anything else you'll need."

"When do you expect the food to arrive?"

"Late this afternoon if the high priests can cut someone loose to go pick it up."

"Any idea what it will be so I can plan a menu?"

"I'm not exactly sure yet," said Bishop Porter. "You'd probably be safe if you planned on getting beans as part of the supplies."

"Then I better start making calls for volunteers to help out in the kitchen."

"If you can get ahold of Brent Higgens, he can make the calls to the brethren. A few of them can cook, and the ones that can't might be useful on a serving line. I'll call Robert about arranging for security at the church."

"No need. I'll have him call you. Got to go, Bishop."

Becky disconnected the line and hollered for Robert as she scanned the ward directory for sisters she could call to help in the kitchen. She paused, wondering if she should first make a list of what they needed. Concerns over how this would affect her family and the needed repairs on her home nagged at her briefly, but she pushed them out of her mind. Working together, the family would find a way to get everything done.

As much effort as it would take to run a soup kitchen until the stores fully opened, it sure beat facing the situation alone and without a plan. How horrible it must be for the nonmember families in the area. Feeding them addressed only one of the problems.

She put the directory down, marched across her yard, and knocked on the Oldhams' door. Her stomach twisted in knots as she waited.

The door opened; Doris stood inside. She looked miserable.

"Becky, I . . . I'm sorry," said Doris. "I didn't want to—"

"Good news," Becky interrupted. "Our church is going to feed the entire neighborhood."

Doris stood there with her mouth open, a bewildered look in her eyes.

"Yep," Becky said. "It may not be fancy, but it will be warm and filling. We're hoping to have something ready by tonight. If you want to let Mr. Roche know about it, that'd be fine. I wanted to let you know so you didn't worry about it anymore."

Becky gave Doris a smile and headed back home.

"Wait," Doris called out.

Becky stopped and looked back at Doris.

"Can I help?"

33

Robert walked into the office at Camden Security ready to work. The doctor had cleared him for full activity the day before, and he wasn't about to stay cooped up in the house a minute longer. Besides, the repairs on the house caused by the storm had taken a hefty bite out of his savings and he needed the money.

Mrs. Landing raised an eyebrow when she spotted Robert. She motioned him to follow her, and they walked down the hallway to a small room at the end. It contained a desk with only a lamp and a computer on top of it.

"Has the doctor stated that you can resume work?"

"Yes, ma'am." Robert flashed her a smile.

She opened the top drawer of the desk, pulled out a file folder, and dropped it on the desk. "I'm sorry to have to do this, but we will be terminating your employment with us today."

Mrs. Landing looked up from the folder and met Robert's gaze. Her expression was as sparse as the room.

"You waited until I got well enough to work to fire me?"

"Unfortunately, that is our procedure in a situation like this," said Mrs. Landing.

"Did I do something wrong?"

"You failed to observe and report as you were instructed to do during your initial training." Mrs. Landing set the folder down and clasped her hands in front of her. "That policy is in place to protect our employees as well as our clients. The police receive training on how to deal with hostile encounters; our guards do not. When you engaged those gentlemen in a physical confrontation, you not only left a door unsecured, but you also left our clients' property vulnerable to the rioters, and you left our company open to legal action from any of the men you aggressively attempted to restrain."

"A man was getting beaten by those jerks," Robert objected.

"That is a matter for law enforcement. As soon as you observed the event, you should have reported it to your supervisor and then the police."

Robert sat there, too stunned to respond.

Mrs. Landing pulled a paper out of the folder and slid it across the desk to Robert. "You received your last check while on sick leave. This form indicates that you acknowledge you've been paid in full for any and all hours you have worked for the company."

"Is that it?" Robert took the document and scanned it. Once he verified that the paper had no hidden clauses or tricky wording, he signed it.

"I'm sorry about all of this," Mrs. Landing said as she escorted him out of the office. "All of the client satisfaction reports we received on you were very positive. It's a shame to lose a worker like you. Good luck in your efforts to find another job."

The door to the office closed and Robert found himself alone in the parking lot. Just like that—he was fired and on the street. What had started as a beautiful day had turned into one of life's sobering challenges in less than a handful of minutes.

What he needed to do was head right home and start searching for another job. That would've been the responsible thing to do. It would've been the logical thing to do. But he decided to head over to the church and see how Mom and the neighborhood soup kitchen were doing. He'd still be working security; he just wouldn't be getting paid for it.

Robert stopped at the house long enough to change out of his uniform and grab a quick snack to supplement the skimpy breakfast he'd had earlier. Then he left for the church. He figured the walk would give him time to think about his situation and maybe come up with a solution.

Instead, a silver Charger pulled alongside him about halfway there.

"Need a lift?" Kevin hollered through an open window.

Robert got into the car and they drove down the road.

"Thought you were supposed to be working," Kevin said.

"So did I. They fired me."

"It's about time." Kevin pumped a fist in the air.

"Thanks a lot."

"No. I mean we should go out and celebrate. Considering your state of unemployment, the milk shakes are on me."

"I'll pass," Robert said. "Losing a job is not exactly a cause to party."

"Not what I meant." Kevin wagged a finger at Robert. "I'm suggesting that we salute the good fortune that resulted in freeing you from that job. You have no business working as a guard."

"I suppose I shouldn't be the security coordinator either."

"If you want to spend your evenings in the parking lot while the ladies sit inside the church gossiping and eating cookies, that's up to you. The important thing is that you can't possibly get hurt—or killed—with a calling like that."

"You never know," Robert said. "With all the goodies they bring out to us, we could develop a serious stomachache."

Kevin chuckled. "Whatever."

They pulled up to the church building. Several tables had been set up just outside the kitchen door. His mother had decided they would cook the food inside and then lay it out on the table once it was done. People formed lines at mealtime and were served by volunteers.

The number of people showing up for the free meals had increased every day. Even though lunch, the first meal they offered, was still an hour away, there were at least a dozen people milling around in the parking lot and lounging on the lawn.

Robert noticed that the door to the kitchen had been left open a crack. His guard training shouted that this was a serious security breach. An open door was an invitation for anyone to walk inside. Even though it had been an ongoing practice for as long as he could remember, it bothered him today.

He opened the door and stepped inside.

"Robert?" Becky called out in surprise. "I didn't expect to see you."

"Yeah, that's the same reaction I've been getting all morning. We can talk about it later. I noticed that you have the outside door open."

"I'm expecting another shipment of food anytime now."

"If they don't have keys to the building, they can knock. This isn't safe. And not only that, I thought Lucas was supposed to be monitoring the parking lot. Where is he?"

"That's the other reason I left the door open." Becky talked while she mixed the contents of a big, steel bowl. "I sent him over to the Johnsons' to pick up a recipe for lemon bars. He should be back any minute now."

"Then you definitely should have it closed and locked." Robert walked over to the door and it swung open.

Lucas walked in with a piece of paper in his hand. "Shouldn't you be at work?"

"Shouldn't you be at school?"

"Nope." Lucas smiled. "We're on disaster recess."

"Awesome," Kevin said.

"Please," Robert said as firmly as he could to his mother, "keep the door locked."

"All right, dear."

Robert removed the can of peaches they had propped the door open with and flipped the lock on his way out. He motioned for Lucas to follow him.

"Any problems with the guests?"

"Not really."

Robert scanned the area and spotted a group of four men hanging out at the corner of the building. He nodded his head in their direction. "What about them?"

"This is the first I've seen of them. I don't recognize any of them."

"They look like trouble," said Kevin.

"That's what I'm thinking," Robert said. The weather was reasonably warm, but the men all wore jackets and had their hands tucked in the pockets. One of the men glanced in Robert's direction and then turned around and faced the opposite direction. Watching the men caused the hairs on Robert's arm to stand on end.

A white Chevy truck turned into the parking lot and passed behind the men. It backed into the parking spot immediately in front of Robert and the others. The heavyset Jim Fuchs extricated himself from the truck with some effort.

"It looks like I have some strapping young men to unload these supplies," Jim said. "I was afraid they were going to have me do it by myself."

"Go ahead and take it easy," Robert told Brother Fuchs. "We can take care of this. My mom's in the kitchen if you need to talk to her."

Robert lowered the tailgate of the truck and then walked over and unlocked the kitchen door. Kevin and Lucas each grabbed a box of food and followed him. When they returned, the four men had left the corner of the building and were headed toward the truck.

They reached Jim before Robert could let out a warning.

"Give us the keys to the truck, old man," one of the men growled as he pulled a baseball bat out from beneath his coat.

The other three men moved to surround Jim. Two slapped fists into their palms in a threatening manner while the third produced a large monkey wrench from his coat pocket.

"Lucas!" Robert shouted over his shoulder. "Call the police. Get them here now!"

The thug with the bat swiveled around to face Robert. He shook the end of the weapon in Robert's direction. "Stay back and no one has to get hurt. We just want the food."

Lucas dashed inside the building.

Robert moved to interpose himself between Jim and the thugs. "Please leave. My brother has called the police and they're on their way."

"Out of our way, Mormon," said the man with the bat. "Our families are hungry and we plan to make sure they eat tonight."

"There's no need for violence," Jim announced. He held his hands up, signaling everyone to stop. "If your families are hungry, they can stop by later to have lunch with us."

"Is that when you force us to join your church or starve?" one of the unarmed thugs sneered.

Robert looked over his shoulder at Jim. "You might want to go inside and make sure the women are safe."

Jim nodded and plodded toward the building.

When Robert turned back around, the lead thug was swinging the bat.

Kevin stepped in front of Robert and took a bone-crunching hit to his upraised arm. He fell to the ground.

All four thugs advanced on Robert.

Kevin rolled away and tried to get to his feet. Jim had returned and helped him up and then the two of them backed away from the fight.

When the thug moved forward to attack Kevin again, Robert grabbed the bat before it could be brought down on his friend. His thoughts flashed back to the riot. Those men had been willing to beat anyone who got in their way. They had beaten him into unconsciousness. There was no reasoning with people like this in the heat of the moment.

Something clicked inside Robert.

Still holding the bat aloft, Robert slammed his head forward. The solid portion of his skull connected with the nose and mouth of the thug. Robert heard the crunch of bone; he could feel the man's face breaking. Somewhere in the back of his mind he heard the man scream in pain.

Without thinking and without pause, he brought his knee up and rammed it into the man's side and belly. Repeatedly, he drove his knee upward until the man dropped.

A small, disconnected portion of his mind told Robert that he couldn't fight. He didn't know how. These men outnumbered him. This was a big mistake.

But he wasn't listening to that voice right now.

Robert flipped the bat so he had a good grip on the handle and then he twisted around as he swung, torquing it for maximum force. The blow struck a hefty man across the chest and sent him stumbling backward. That had been the thug with something concealed in his hand.

One of the unarmed thugs aimed a kick at Robert, while the last tried tackling him from the front.

Robert easily sidestepped the kick, but he felt his waist encircled by the fourth man's arms. For a moment Robert teetered, thrown off balance by the attack, but he recovered and braced himself.

Taking both elbows, Robert slammed them into the thug's back. Once. Twice. Three times they struck like pistons and the man dropped to the ground with a huff.

Off to his left, Lucas had returned and defended himself against the previously armed attacker. Whatever weapon he'd been concealing, he no longer had it, and he faced Robert's brother with only his fists now. Blows were being landed on both sides. Despite Lucas's smaller size, neither had established an advantage over the other.

The man who had tried to kick Robert before tried it again. Robert stepped back and let the thug's foot sail past him. Then he moved in and rammed the bat, like a spear, into the man's gut. When the thug doubled over, Robert kneed him in the face and sent him sprawling to the ground.

Robert didn't wait for the man to recover. As the thug stood up, Robert blurred forward, lowered his shoulder, and bodychecked the man into his ally who was fighting with Lucas. Both went down. Robert followed up with a series of blows from the baseball bat. When he finished, neither of the men looked like they had any fight left in them.

The sounds of fighting came from behind him. Kevin and Jim were doing their best to hold back the man who had tried to tackle Robert. The thug had grabbed hold of Jim's hand that held the keys for the truck. Blood flowed from Kevin's nose, one of his eyes was swollen, and he cradled one arm in the other. Jim had a busted lip, but he still had a firm grip on the keys.

Robert ran at the man and drop-kicked him in the back. The man let out a bellow as he fell and then lay on the ground writhing.

That was it. The robbers lay on the ground, unable to act or run away.

Robert wondered if this was anything like what Ammon had experienced. Certainly God had looked over him in the battle with the Lamanite thieves. That was the only thing Robert could think of that would explain his being able to defeat these men.

He dropped the bat.

In the distance, police sirens announced the imminent arrival of the cavalry.

34

"Visitor at the gate," crackled a voice from the radio.

John unclipped the portable unit at his hip. "Be right there."

He stepped out of the trailer and looked the camp over. A pile of broken studs and plywood were the only evidence of the storm. To be fair, though, it was a big pile of mostly unusable building material.

The dorm and the warehouse were completely repaired, but John had held off on replacing any of the damaged workshop structure. They didn't need the feds coming down on them for a violation of the cease and desist order. Nor did they want to give the townspeople a reason to march against them—again. He hoped the visitors were neither.

He walked across the camp to the gate, picking up a few curious tagalongs as he went. Two men in suits stood there waiting. They didn't look like feds or townspeople; they were smiling.

"Can I help you?" John asked as he stopped at the gate.

"Brother Williams," said an older gentleman with gray hair. "The Area President sends you his regards. My name is Phil Carter, and this is Brother Swensen. We've come to see you on Church business."

"Please, come in." John motioned for his men to open the gate and led them back to the construction trailer.

"First," Brother Carter said, "we want to compliment you on a job well done."

Inwardly, John gave a sigh of relief.

"This has not been an easy assignment," Carter continued. "Yet despite the setbacks caused by the weather and your neighbors, you've made good progress on the facility here."

"But . . ." John waited for the other shoe to drop.

Carter and Swensen laughed. "I don't know that I'd phrase it that way. We know that you've reached a stopping point in the project here until the cease and desist order can be resolved. Until then, it doesn't make sense to keep the full crew here doing nothing. What we are proposing is that a team of about six of the brethren be kept on-site until construction can resume and the rest of you go on home and spend time with your families."

"What about the rest?" John asked.

"They will take turns coming up here and keeping an eye on the camp. We think one-week rotations are best and want to continue that until we start building again."

"Great." John clapped his hands and rubbed them together in anticipation. "I'll ask for five volunteers and they can stay behind with me for the first week."

"Actually," Swensen spoke up. "President Drollinger has asked for Brother Summers to assume responsibility for the camp until you return. He would like to speak to you on Friday. That should give you a couple of days with your family before you meet with him."

"And please bring your wife," Carter said.

John considered asking them what this was all about, but he knew that he'd only get that information from President Drollinger when they met. However, with his wife attending, it probably meant another assignment. Oddly, the thought of it left him a bit saddened; he and the rest of the brethren who'd served out here had done a wonderful job. John wanted to see this thing through to the end.

"When are we going to do this?" John asked.

"Today," said Carter. "In addition to your Suburban, we have a couple of high-capacity vehicles that should be here in about an hour. We will leave one of them behind for the people in camp to use, and the other will help you get the rest of the men home. We had them wait until after we talked to you to give you a chance to discuss the matter with the others. You are still the person in charge out here, and we don't want to undermine your authority."

"All right," John said. "I'll talk this over with my counselors, and then we'll break the news to the men."

John called in Bill and Luis. They discussed the matter and decided that Scott, Paul, and Wayne could all benefit from a long break away from camp. That was the easy part. It was tougher to pick five men to stay another week away from their families while the others went home.

When they finally chose the five, John called them into the trailer while Bill and Luis met with the rest in the warehouse. The dust trails of the approaching relief vehicles marred the otherwise blue sky as John shut the door to deliver the news.

They had chosen well. The five men, which included Jeff King, listened to the situation and responded with surprising positivity.

"That means we'll be seeing our families in a week," Jeff said. "That's a lot sooner than I'd expected."

John clapped Jeff on the back and shook hands with all of them. Then he gathered his personal items and stored them in the Suburban.

The others were packed, loaded, and ready within fifteen minutes.

John led the caravan out. All during the bumpy ride on the dirt road, it felt like one of his regular trips into town. It wasn't until he turned onto the blacktop that it really sank in. He was going home.

They passed by the Greenville gas station. The damaged steel canopy that had stood over the pumps had been hauled to the back of the station, allowing vehicles access to the only source of fuel in town. A couple of the windows were still boarded up.

Even though the buildings bore the scars of the storm, functionality had returned to the town. People moved about their business, sometimes having to drive or walk around the debris that still remained.

John had just passed the last intersection in town before the road opened up when he heard a siren behind him. A quick look in the rearview mirror confirmed that it was Sheriff McKinney.

What could he possibly want? They were leaving. That should make him and the rest of the townspeople happy. At least until they found out it wasn't a permanent situation.

John pulled over and rolled down his window.

The gravel on the side of the road crunched under the sheriff's boots as he approached. "Could you step out of the vehicle?"

John turned off the ignition and exited the Suburban.

McKinney motioned with his hand for John to follow and walked off a distance from the vehicles on the side of the road. He turned and faced John when they stopped, his thumbs stuck into either side of his utility belt.

"I think you Mormons need to read the Bible a little more carefully. It's pretty plain what it says in there, and you don't seem to be getting all of it right."

The sheriff paused. He looked over at the vehicles. He looked back at the town. He looked at the ground at his feet.

"The thing is," he continued, "I don't agree with what you folks believe. But . . ."

McKinney lifted his head and looked at John. "You're good neighbors. Not everyone around here has changed their minds about having a bunch of you move in next door to the town, but I have.

"I called the boys over at Homeland Security and retracted my complaint against you people. Hopefully, that will be enough to get them to lift that cease and desist order. I don't know how much good it will do, but it's the least I can do."

The sheriff looked back in the direction of Greenville and squared his shoulders. "And one more thing. I can promise you that there won't be any more problems from my people from now on."

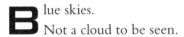 **35**

Blue skies.

Not a cloud to be seen.

Despite what anyone else said to the contrary, there was no such thing as "a good day to die." Or to be buried. A dark storm raged in Calvin's soul; the least the weather could do was meet him halfway.

On a day ideally suited to having a picnic and watching kids play in the park, they were holding Mike Costa's funeral.

The President finished up the speech that was part of the posthumous award ceremony preceding the eulogy, a stirring and long-winded affair that had taken a room full of writers to prepare. Boggs gave the best performance of his political career. He expressed the remorse and thanks of a grateful nation, in front of Mike's coffin, to a select crowd of friends, relatives, and Washington's elite.

Boggs even managed to shed a few tears.

Calvin waited until the President sat down before he walked over beside his old friend and addressed the gathering. Nothing fancy. Nothing prepared. He just started listing all the times Mike had stepped up and did what needed to be done. Most of the time that had meant risking his life to save someone else.

Nearly twenty years of stories took a while to tell. Calvin

didn't rush it. And he didn't bother to embellish any of the accounts. He didn't need to. When it came to heroes, Mike Costa was the real deal.

While Calvin talked, he fidgeted with the flash drive he held in his hand. Getting the drive to him had cost Mike his life. In exchange for a life dedicated to the service of the country, he now had the means to ruin Boggs. It certainly wasn't worth the cost, but Calvin vowed to use it for all it was worth.

He ended the eulogy with a description of the events that transpired the day Mike died. For reasons of national security and the ongoing investigation, the nitty-gritty details had to be left out, but Calvin still gave a good enough accounting of Mike's actions to let his family know that his sacrifice had been noble and freely given.

Calvin walked over and presented himself to the front line of mourners. He offered his personal condolences to Mike's wife, children, and parents. His emotions choked out his words when he tried to say more.

Then he stepped back to his assigned position and watched the rifle party march forward. Seven men from his and Mike's old unit shouldered their arms in preparation for the three-volley salute.

Upon command, all seven men from the 1st Infantry Division fired their rifles.

DUTY

The weapons barked again in unison.

HONOR

A third volley echoed into silence.

COUNTRY

After the funeral, Calvin maneuvered himself into a position where Boggs would be forced to see him. He locked gazes with him and tilted his head to a spot away from the crowd. Calvin did his best to make sure the expression on his face made it clear this was not a request for an audience.

"If you will pardon me," Boggs told his cronies and his security detail. "I would like to have a quiet moment—alone—with Mr. McCord."

The President closed the distance to Calvin and shook his hand. At a distance, the smile on Boggs's face might fool reporters and politicians into thinking the two men shared a cordial moment in honor of the fallen. But up close, the burning fires in the President's eyes were unmistakable.

"Quite the coup, Calvin." Boggs offered a big smile; the tension lines attached to it made it look a little like a feral snarl. "The entire nation is talking about your heroic efforts to save my entire cabinet. There's even talk about nominating you for President during the next election."

"I'm not interested."

Boggs's faux smile faltered for a second. "Then why are we talking?"

"Because we both have jobs to do to keep this country safe, and you choose not to do yours and you won't let me do mine."

"What do you intend to do about it?" Boggs asked.

"First, I'm going to insist that you put me into a position where I can't be touched. Then I'm going to advise you on the deteriorating situation with Russia. And if you're smart, you'll act on what I have to tell you."

"I think you overvalue your current political clout." Boggs flashed a genuine smile. "You may be the heroic flavor of the month, but that will pass. It certainly doesn't grant you the kind of leverage you need to start making demands of me."

"No. It probably doesn't." Calvin held up flash drive, careful that the media couldn't capture the moment on film. "It's the contents of this drive that will convince you to listen to me."

Boggs gave a nervous glance toward the funeral crowd and then at his security detail. With forced calm, he put his hands in his pockets. "Put it away."

Calvin let the small stick of portable memory slide back down into his palm. "This contains evidence that you knew the Russians were behind the recent terrorist activities and did nothing about it. There are also some interesting sound bites of your response to their invasion of the Ukraine."

Boggs's face went taut. "This is not a game you want to play with me."

"It's not a game at all. Too many lives are at stake for me to let you continue putting your political career ahead of the welfare of this country. You either meet my demands or I make sure that everyone knows what you've been up to."

Boggs leaned in close. "You will regret this move."

"Maybe. But you should know that if anything happens to me, I've made arrangements for the contents of this drive to go public."

"How dare you try to blackmail the President of the United States." Boggs's right eye twitched.

"If you don't want everyone to know something's wrong, you better keep your voice down." Calvin gave an almost imperceptible nod toward the group gathered around Mike's coffin. "I don't care if this upsets you. I don't care what you think of me. And I don't care how inconvenient this is for you. You do this by the end of the week, or I follow through with my threat."

The flush on Boggs's face turned reddish-purple. He opened his mouth to speak and then shut it without offering a sound. Then he adjusted his jacket, ran his hands along his hair to wrangle any stray strands, and squared his shoulders. By the time he finished, his face had returned to its normal color.

"Considering your current popularity," Boggs said, "I should have no problem turning your request to my advantage. Then, when the time is right, I'll make you sorry that you messed with me."

The President turned and walked away

Calvin stayed put.

He waited for the rest of the mourners to leave the cemetery. While he waited, he tried to convince himself that his actions were necessary. That the sheer immensity of the stakes involved made blackmailing the President acceptable.

His churning stomach disagreed.

244

Eventually, the last of the mourners had left and Calvin trod over to say good-bye to his friend. He placed his hand on the cool metal of the coffin and patted it.

"Thanks, Mike. You did your part. Don't worry. I'll do mine."

36

obert left the army recruiting station and drove over to Sierra's apartment. He still didn't know how he was going to break the news to her. As hard as it would be to leave his family again, he found himself more concerned about his separation from her.

When he parked the car, he noticed a pair of men carrying boxes to a moving truck. One of them looked familiar. Only after they put the boxes in the truck and headed in his direction did Robert recognize the older man from pictures he'd seen at Sierra's place. That was her dad.

What was he doing here? They lived several states over.

"Mr. Weintraub," Robert said as he approached Sierra's door.

Both men stopped and turned around.

"Can I help you?" Mr. Weintraub asked.

"My name is Robert Williams."

"Do I know you?"

"Dad," said the younger man, "Sierra told you about him. That's her boyfriend."

"She said I was her boyfriend?" Robert brightened at the news.

"You're her boyfriend?" Mr. Weintraub asked. He carefully scrutinized Robert.

"Yeah, I guess so."

"Tough break; she's moving back home," said Mr. Weintraub. "But times are tough. Families need to stick together."

The news struck Robert like a blow. Sierra was hours away from moving out of state and she hadn't even bothered to call him. Maybe things between them weren't going as well as he had thought.

Sierra's brother leaned closer to his father. "She hasn't told him yet."

Mr. Weintraub arched his eyebrows. "Looks like she doesn't have to now."

Just then Sierra appeared at the door. Her eyes moved from Robert to her family and then back. "I called and left a message at your house. I need to talk to you."

"Would that have anything to do with you leaving?"

She lowered her gaze and tilted her head forward like a teen caught sneaking back into the house after hours. Without looking at him, Sierra grasped Robert's hand and led him to the next room.

While Sierra closed the door, Robert looked around. This was her bedroom, and even though it only contained packed boxes, he suddenly felt uncomfortable here.

"I didn't know how to tell you," Sierra said. "I want to stay here with you. I really do. But my family needs me, and I have an opportunity to work an internship back home doing what I've always wanted to do. That probably doesn't make sense to you."

Robert laughed.

Sierra's expression soured. "I expected you to be a little upset that I'm leaving. Besides, what's so funny about wanting to pursue my dreams?"

"Nothing at all." Robert held his hands up defensively. "It's just that I spent the last hour trying to find a way to tell you that I'm going away. You know—the whole 'family needs me, and it's an opportunity to train in the kind of work I've always dreamed about' sort of thing."

Sierra folded her arms and glared at Robert. A snicker escaped and she looked away. And then she laughed.

"Is everything all right in there?" Mr. Weintraub called through the door.

"I'm fine. We're having a possibly life-changing discussion."

"What does that mean?" Mr. Weintraub muttered.

"It means you should mind your own business," Sierra's brother responded.

The Weintraub men exchanged a few words between themselves on the other side of the door. Robert and Sierra moved forward and embraced one another.

"Oh, Robert. What are we going to do?"

Robert hugged her tighter. "How do you feel about long-distance relationships?"

Sierra leaned back and studied Robert's face. "Are you serious?"

He had to think about it for a moment. Not so much to decide if he really meant it—he did—but because he wasn't sure why. The two of them had known each other only a couple of months and had less than a handful of dates together.

And yet a stirring in his breast told him to hold on to this girl.

"Yes," Robert said. "I'm completely serious."

Sierra bounced on her feet a couple of times, and then she kissed him.

Robert forgot about his enlistment, he forgot about her moving, he forgot about the troubled world around them . . . until someone knocked on the door.

"Sierra," Mr. Weintraub called out. "Are you going to come out and help us finish packing?"

"I'm sorry," she said. "He's not going to leave us alone until I'm packed."

Robert slipped his hand into hers. "Let me help."

37

Bed sounded good.

It wasn't even lunchtime and Becky seriously thought about calling it a day. The schedule over the last week had been brutal, but the stores had reopened in full and she didn't need to be taking care of her home, the children, and a neighborhood soup kitchen all at once anymore.

As soon as she summoned enough energy to stand, she would command her feet to march into the bedroom and that would be it for the day.

Her cell phone rang.

Becky crossed her fingers that it wasn't the stake president calling to let her know they had decided to extend the soup kitchen for a few more days. She flipped the phone open and answered it.

"Hello, gorgeous."

John!

"Is everything all right?" Becky asked; a chill passed down her back as she waited for a response.

"Better. I'm on my way home. Should be there within the hour."

Everything changed at that moment. Becky felt better than she had in weeks. She wanted to pump a fist in the air and shout. Her face ached from the stress she placed on the long unused smile muscles. John was coming home!

"Becky?"

When John spoke again, she realized she'd been so busy bouncing up and down that she had forgotten to say something to him. "I have to go."

"That's not exactly the reaction I expected," John said.

"The house is a mess. I'll see you in a little while."

It wasn't until after she disconnected the call that she wondered why John was on his way home. They had another couple of months before they finished Camp Valiant. Had he been released from his calling early?

She decided not to worry about it. If something had been wrong, she would have detected it in his voice. John could tell her about it when he got home. In the meantime, she had a house to clean.

Becky whipped through the rooms like a cleaning tornado, sucking up clothing and sending the children spinning off to contribute to the effort. She bustled from chore to chore, trying to accomplish those that netted the biggest result before moving on to the fine cleaning.

All too soon she heard the sound of a car door outside. It had the heavy thud of their Suburban. "Dad's here!" Becky shouted.

Then she stopped. Every part of her wanted to run and throw herself into John's arms as soon as he opened the door. The logical portion of her brain told her how silly that was. The two of them had been married twenty-two years. She was no flighty, emotional bride. Becky would remain calm and greet her husband in a mature manner.

John grabbed his bag of clothing out of the Suburban and closed the door. The craftsman in him noticed the damage to the house and a missing fence. The father in him only noticed how wonderful their home looked.

Anxious to see his family, he went inside.

Becky ran at him straight across the living room floor, squealing the entire way. She threw herself in his arms, knocking his bag out of his hand, and savaged him with kisses.

He crushed his beautiful wife to him, not wanting to ever let her go.

"You wouldn't believe how crazy it's been here," Becky said as she came up for a breath.

"The people in Greenville were really something," said John.

"I had to homeschool the kids."

"We lost one of the buildings."

"The kids and I fixed up the house."

"I decided to help out the town."

"We ran a soup kitchen for the neighborhood."

"What?"

"I'll tell you later." Becky threw her arms back around his neck and they kissed.

"Get a room," Sara huffed as she passed by.

John leaned in close to Becky's ear and whispered, "There's an idea."

"Joohhhhn." Becky pushed him away—gently—and rolled her eyes. She hid the beginning of a smile by turning around. "Behave."

The phone rang.

Sara disappeared into the kitchen. A moment later she called out, "Dad, it's for you."

"You have got to be kidding," John said. He'd been here five minutes and already someone was calling him. He gave Becky another hug as he passed by her on the way to the kitchen.

"This is John."

"I'm sorry to bother you, Brother Williams. This is Art Spangler, the Area President. Can I stop by to see you and your family tonight?"

The Area President. What could he want?

But as soon as he asked himself that question, John knew. A nervous chill rolled down his back. He must have been released from his position at Camp Valiant in order free him up for a different calling, one that came down from the Area President. Whatever that might be, it scared John more than a little. He was just an average guy. There was no way he should be getting a calling from the Area President.

"Who was that?" Becky asked as she came into the kitchen.

"The Area President."

"What did he want?"

John hung up the phone. "We'll find that out tonight."

The doorbell rang at precisely six o'clock.

John and Becky had the family all gathered in the living room with instructions to stay seated and act reverently. The two of them had dressed in their church clothes and went together to answer the door.

A thin, elderly man with a small crop of white hair stood on the doorstep. He had on a navy-blue suit with a silver-striped tie. President Spangler offered a warm smile that put the couple at ease.

They motioned President Spangler inside the house and guided him to the big overstuffed recliner in the living room.

He first went to each of the children and shook their hands. After he finished introducing himself to the family, he sat down.

"I understand that all of you have been through quite a lot recently."

"Boy, I'd say," Cody said.

"These are difficult times," President Spangler continued. "And as is so often the case, the Lord's chosen people are asked to step up and be an example. We may not always know why Heavenly Father has asked us to do the things He requires, but we do know that they are important."

"Sounds like another calling for Dad," Lucas said.

"I wouldn't refer to this as another calling," President Spangler said. "This will be the first time I have ever extended a request like this. When you hear it, I think you'll understand that we—as a people, as a nation, as a world—are about to enter into a new dispensation. The Second Coming of the Savior is near at hand, and all of us are going to be asked to take a bold step forward in preparation for that event."

John tried to swallow, but his mouth had gone dry. Becky clutched a hand to her throat and leaned in closer to her husband. The children looked to their parents.

"What I have come to ask tonight is twofold." President Spangler leaned forward in the chair and alternated his attention between Becky and John. "The first part is a request for your entire family. As a part of our efforts to gather the Saints, we are requesting that your family sell this home and purchase one of the many foreclosed properties that are in the area immediately around the temple."

"Those homes are so much smaller than ours," Becky said.

"We've lived in this house all of our lives," said Elizabeth.

"I don't want to move away from my friends," Cody said.

President Spangler sat there and listened to the comments from the family; his smile never faltered. He looked sympathetic to the anguish his request caused.

"That's a pretty big request," John said. "Do we have to give you an answer right now, or can we think about it awhile?"

"Of course," President Spangler said. "This is not a matter to be taken lightly."

"I know my answer," Robert spoke up. "Even though I don't own the house and I don't make the decisions for the family, I think we should do this."

"Why?" Sara challenged. She folded her arms and squared her shoulders.

"Because," Robert said, "I think we can all see that things have changed. It seems like every night on the news they announce a terrorist act, or a political protest that went nuclear or another disaster. Conditions in the country are horrible. Conditions everywhere are horrible. Mom had to pull the rest of you out of school because it's too dangerous there. How bad does it have to be before we realize that these are the end times?"

President Spangler nodded but said nothing.

"Robert's right," John said. "At the camp, we had a great deal of opposition from the people in the nearby town. Eventually, we were shut down by the government. And we haven't done anything illegal or wrong. The government is about to fall apart and it looks like we could very well go to war with Russia. These are unusual times and that means we need to consider doing things that were unthinkable before."

"We'd be really close to the temple," Becky said. "That would make me feel safer."

"Fine," Sara said, throwing her arms in the air. "What do I care anyway? I only have a couple months before I leave to college, and we aren't even going to the school here."

Sara slumped in her seat and pouted. The rest of the children mumbled an unenthused consent.

"I guess that settles it," John said. "We will sell the house and move into the temple neighborhood. At least we can be assured of having some great neighbors."

"Are you sure you wouldn't like a little more time to think it over?" President Spangler asked.

John looked over to Becky and she squeezed his hand in response.

"No," John said. "We accept and will start the process on Monday."

"Since we have settled that matter," President Spangler said, "I suppose I should move on to the next one. Brother Williams, I am here to extend another calling to you. If you should accept, the stake president will officially release you from the one you are now serving in at the appropriate time."

"Okay," John said. "What's the calling?"

"We would like you to serve as the director of defense for the Camp Valiant region as soon as they have finished construction. As part of that calling, your family will be among the first to move out there when the official call to gather is extended to the general Church membership."

"Then this isn't the end of the problems we're seeing all around us?" Becky asked.

"I'm afraid not." President Spangler's voice was soft and solemn.

"I don't suppose there's a Church manual for that calling." John chuckled.

"There will be once you finish writing it," said President Spangler.

John let out the breath he'd unintentionally been holding. Becky clung to him.

"I accept," John said.

"Good," President Spangler said. "In the following months, keep in mind Romans 8:30, which says, 'Moreover whom he did predestinate, them he also called: and whom he called, them he also justified: and whom he justified, them he also glorified.'

"All of us will face adversity in the coming years," President Spangler continued. "Stay close to the Lord, and He will watch over you."

President Spangler offered a prayer, and then John and Becky accompanied him to the door. He shared a bit of small talk with the family, but their minds were on the big changes they now faced.

After President Spangler left, John gathered the family together in the center of the living room. He hugged each one of them. Then he hugged them again.

"We can choose to be scared of what lies ahead of us. It will be different, it will be difficult, and it might even be a little bit dangerous. Or we can trust in the Lord and look at this as an amazing adventure that will be among the stories that will be handed down from generation to generation that tell of the events our family encountered during the Second Coming.

"Which will it be?"

38

Y ou're going to miss the swearing-in ceremony," Gwen said, poking her head into Calvin's office. "I'm pretty sure those reports will have the same information on them when you return."

Calvin pulled his attention from the folder in front of him and checked his watch. It was almost seven. He had wanted to squeeze in a few more minutes of work before he left for the official ceremony to replace the Vice President.

"How come you're still here?" he asked.

Gwen arched an eyebrow. "Let's just call it a case of ensuring job security. I'm starting to like it here, and if you don't go and remind everyone how much you've done over the last month, I may have to start updating my resume."

Calvin laughed. It surprised him that he still could.

He took one last glance at the figures on the document in front of him before scooping them up and putting them away. Calvin grabbed his suit jacket, checked to make sure everything was in place and relatively wrinkle-free, and headed toward the West Front of the Capitol.

The halls on the way were filled with stragglers. Unlike Calvin, they appeared to be in no hurry to arrive on time. He wove his way through them like an old cowpoke moving through a herd.

Kyle Dalton appeared alongside him as he pulled into line to be cleared through the last security checkpoint.

"You're really cutting it close," said Kyle. "The ceremony starts in ten minutes."

"I'm not interested in spending any more time with the President than I have to."

Kyle burst out in laughter and slapped Calvin on the back. "You're a funny, funny man. If you decide to change careers, I think you've got a shot at doing stand-up comedy."

"You mean there's a difference between that and what I'm doing now?"

"Hey." Kyle did a quick scan of the hall and leaned in closer to Calvin. "Good call on the Russians, by the way. It looks like Moscow is preparing troops for deployment in Iran."

"Is there a plan in place to move some of our troops into a strategic position to keep an eye on them?"

"Of course," Kyle said. "What'd you expect after that 'we stand for liberty' speech the President gave early this week? And, based on your suggestion, a good portion of the army is being retooled to help with disaster relief issues in Europe. That puts them in a position to react if we need to, but not really be seen as a threat."

"That was what I had in mind."

"As the British would say, 'A bloody brilliant move.'"

The two of them walked onto the West Front lawn. Boggs was moseying toward the podium and making a spectacle of stopping to greet each of the select groups of politicians—from both parties— that had been invited to sit on the platform.

Kyle stopped. The trio of Ken Farr, Dennis De La Palma, and Marion Salazar were clustered together just ahead. "This is where I get off. You're on your own with the three horsemen of the apocalypse."

"Thanks," Calvin said.

"What are friends for?" Kyle flashed him a smile and blended in with the crowd.

Calvin strode past Ken, Dennis, and Marion on his way to the front of the proceedings. He surveyed the crowd. Most of the attendees were in their seats, waiting for the ceremony to begin. They spoke in hushed tones. Many still wore the black stripe of mourning for Evan Phillips.

Keegan Roscoe intercepted him just before he reached the stand. "I hope that you won't be terribly offended if I congratulate you on your success, even if it is a tad bit early."

"Not at all." Calvin shook his hand. "Surprised?"

"Less than most. I always had a feeling that you were going to shake things up."

"Pegged me as a troublemaker from the beginning. Smart man."

"Some might think that, but I prefer to see you as a man who isn't afraid to stand up for what he believes is right. You'll do fine."

Calvin excused himself as the President made his final approach to the podium. People who were still standing took their seats and silence blanketed the audience.

"Three days ago," the President said in somber tones, "we put the former Vice President, Evan Phillips, to rest. The nation lost a great leader and I lost great friend. Today, we are here to swear in his replacement."

Boggs paused. He gripped the edges of the podium with his hands and took a deep breath. Then he put on an Oscar-winning show of forcing a smile to his face.

"Often, like a phoenix, opportunity rises from the ashes of disaster. Of late, our country has been divided against itself. Both of our political parties have been too focused on our differences and have failed to appreciate our similarities. Republican and Democrat. Conservative and liberal. We all have something worthwhile to contribute.

"The heinous attack on our nation is a wake-up call. We can no longer afford to fight one another. We must unite to face our common enemy. That is why I have taken the unprecedented step of asking a member of the opposing political party to be the new Vice President. And who better to serve in that role than the man who personally uncovered the plot to assassinate the top members of our government and who risked his own life to capture the terrorist agent responsible for the attack?

"I ask all of you to express your thanks to Mr. Calvin McCord."

The audience applauded.

If he were an actor, or an athlete, or even a real politician, he supposed the applause would give him a drug-free high, but the reality of it was that to him it was only so much noise. He didn't want the limelight, the praise, or the opportunity to be a footnote in the nation's history. He definitely didn't want the position of Vice President. Then again, this had nothing to do with what he wanted. Becoming VP was the only way he could protect the United States. This was an act of a patriot.

Someone prodded Calvin. The country was waiting on him.

Calvin climbed the steps to the platform and crossed over to the podium. He looked out over the assemblage. Calvin had attended a great many functions over the years and, as a result, could identify them by the mood of the crowd. This one had all the earmarks of a funeral.

39

Over the loudspeaker, a woman announced the final boarding call for the flight that would take Robert to Fort Leonard Wood, Missouri, to start his basic training. His mother and Elizabeth started crying—again.

"Looks like it's time to go," John said.

Robert hugged each member of his family, holding the embrace a little longer than he normally did. Then he stepped back and studied their faces as though afraid of forgetting what they looked like if he didn't.

All of them wore concerned expressions. He knew they thought he was making an incredible mistake.

"Are you sure about this?" John asked.

"I am." Robert looked him in the eye. "This is what the Lord wants me to do. I know that and hope you will have faith enough in me to accept it."

"No worries about that." John placed his hand on Robert's shoulder. "You've always tried to do what is right. If you say the Lord has told you to do this, then I believe you."

Robert wished he felt as confident about the decision as his father seemed to be. The news reported that Russia had taken an aggressive stance in the Ukraine and in the Middle East. The world was poised for war, and here he had joined the Army.

The path he was on was certainly not one he would have chosen for himself. By joining the Army Corps of Engineers, he put himself in harm's way. But it also created an opportunity for him to build things and help people. It even set up an opportunity to go to school and become an engineer. Most important, he felt it would take him to where he was needed most.

He just hoped he'd be coming back.

Kevin stepped up, his right arm in a cast, and gave a nod.

"What?" Robert asked. "No slick comment from you?"

"Not today," Kevin said, his tone somber. "You've traded your suitcase for a duffle bag and I can't even shake your hand good-bye."

"Now I know the world is coming to an end." Robert smiled because he didn't know what else to say. Then he leaned in toward Kevin. "I think things are going to get worse. Stay close to the Church and look in on my family, will you?"

Kevin gave him an uncharacteristic hug and then backed up to where the others stood.

A flight attendant motioned for Robert to board.

He picked up his bag and headed for the plane. Turning, he waved to his loved ones, and then marched along the ramp that led to a new chapter in his life.

DISCUSSION QUESTIONS

1. Would you be willing to share your year's supply with your neighbors? Would you be willing to share your year's supply if that might be the only food available to your family during the next year? If so, how much of it would you be willing to share?

2. Could you bring yourself to help the same people who had previously attacked you, or possibly robbed you?

3. What would it take to get you to fight? What would it take for you to be willing to stand up to a mob of people who opposed your beliefs and your way of life? Could you and would you physically fight back?

4. How would you react to society falling apart all around you?

5. Are you willing to endure the terrible days before the Savior's return in order to experience the great events surrounding His arrival?

6. Are you willing to give up your home and treasures if the Prophet asks it?

7. What concerns you the most about the terrible days leading up to the Second Coming?

8. What cheers you the most about His return?

9. How do you react in a situation where not everyone can be helped? How do you decide who you will help?

10. How can the hardships of the Second Coming bring you closer to the Lord?

ABOUT THE AUTHOR

RANDY LINDSAY is a native of Arizona. From an early age, his mind traveled in new and unusual directions. His preoccupation with "what if" eventually led him to write speculative fiction. According to his wife, everything is a story to Randy. And it is. Although this is his first novel, Randy has been published in a variety of science-fiction and fantasy magazines. He lives in Mesa with his wife and five of his nine children. If you want to find out more, you can check him out at RandyLindsay.net.